ELECTRICITY: A HAUNTED VOICES ROMANCE

CLAIRE GEM

❀ Created with Vellum

WELCOME TO THE WORLD OF HAUNTED VOICES ROMANCE!

I am so pleased you have chosen to join Mercedes and Daniel on their journey—through a haunted mental asylum, and through the treacherous landscape of the heart.

If you are new to Haunted Voices romances, this is book 5. But don't worry—each title is completely standalone, and the books can be read in any order. What ties the series together? An intensely romantic love story set in a haunted location.

Please visit my website, www.clairegem.com, to learn about the other books in the series. Also, if you sign up for my newsletter, you will be the first to know about sales, promotions, and NEW RELEASES!

You can also find me on Goodreads, Facebook, and Twitter. Reach out and get in touch! I love to hear from my readers with all their feedback, good and bad.

Also, PLEASE consider leaving me an honest review on Amazon and Goodreads. Reviews are like blood transfusions for authors, and I'm always anemic! Only you, my readers, can help :)

PREFACE

In the 1960s, a government policy called "deinstitutionalization" caused the closing of hundreds of state-run "insane asylums." The movement left thousands of the mentally ill essentially homeless. Such a state-run asylum in Massachusetts closed its doors in 1973. This facility's cemetery holds the last remains of 1041 people who died while under treatment there. With no one to claim their bodies, they were interred on a three-acre plot, their graves marked by nothing more than a concrete pillar with a number engraved on top. Extensive research by this author has not uncovered the list of names corresponding to these numbers, a list several resources claim, "exists in various archives."
I dedicate this book to them: those who lived tortured lives, died alone, and were buried,
NAMELESS.

Note: The name of the facility and the town in which it operated has been changed to protect present ownership of the property. All persons and incidents in this book are entirely fictitious.

CHAPTER 1

June, 2008

The sagging doorframe wore its own painful grimace. Mold and lichen crept over the paint-flecked wood, adorning it like odd-colored fur. The entry's stone steps were cracked and crumbling and in some places, the green coating had gone black.

Mercedes Donohue climbed out of the van and stared up at the massive, three-story structure. It must have been stately-looking at one time, she thought, regally clothed in red brick. Sitting atop a small rise on the campus, its location afforded a wide view of the grounds, as well as the other buildings, some old and some new. Already a few of the Tech school's students were pulling into the paved parking lot across the street.

Still, Mercy felt a ripple of eeriness pass through her. It could have been the pitiful expression of the front door. Or perhaps the grid of iron bars that secured every window in the place. Even the pretty, woodland setting couldn't temper the building's ominous tone.

She made her way to the back of the van where her new boss,

Conner Graham, was struggling with a set of blueprints in the early morning breeze.

"What did you say they were going to use this building for?" she asked, rubbing her arms.

Was the chill coming from the cool air, or from the inside out?

Conner glanced up. "Student center, they said. We'll be running about as many power hookups as I've ever seen in one place." He turned his head to spew a stream of brown tobacco juice into the weeds lining the driveway. "But first, we've got the bigger job of ripping out everything that's already there."

"But that's not the interesting question."

Daniel Gallagher, the fourth member of the team, rounded the rear of the van flanked by Conner's younger brother, Jacob. He shot Mercy a meaningful look with his sandy eyebrows raised. "The real question is, what was its original use?"

The question hung unanswered as Jacob studied the blueprints his brother held. "What about asbestos? Lead? These prints say the place was built almost two hundred years ago. Surely it's loaded—"

"What do you think I am, an imbecile?" Conner barked. "I did my homework before I even bid on this job. The place closed in 1973, and a couple years later a drug company fancied they'd turn it into their research facility. Tore out all the toxic stuff, then went belly up. That's when the Technical Institute came in and bought the whole campus."

Mercy glanced from Conner to Daniel to Jacob, but none of them explained further. She swallowed. "So, what was it? Before it closed in '73?" she asked.

Conner glared at her, then closed his eyes and nodded. "That's right, I forgot. You're not from the area."

"Well, I am. Or I was. But we moved to Atlanta when I was fifteen. My parents never brought me around this end of town," Mercy corrected.

Conner continued. "All these buildings, the grounds." He swept an arm wide. "All of this. Twelve-hundred acres, in all. It was once the home of the Corby State Hospital."

Weren't most state hospitals for mental patients back then?

Shaking off the thought, Mercy busied herself with her tool belt. She checked each leather slot: wire snips, claw-end hammer, pliers, a pouch containing various lengths of zip ties, chalk, and rolls of black tape. Would she have everything she needed to dismantle the electrical apparatus? Up until two months ago, she'd been a thousand miles away, working on a team doing just the opposite—installing wiring in brand-new track homes north of Atlanta.

This was going to be a whole new ball game for her. A new location, a new team, a different kind of work than what she'd been used to. It was what she needed. What both she and Reagan needed. A new start far away from the nightmare their lives had become.

Mercy followed the men as they mounted the steps and struggled with the front door. Expecting them, security had opened the padlock, but it seemed the door hadn't turned on its hinges in decades. Conner managed to yank it open a crack, but it took both his strength and that of his brother to heave it all the way open with a screech of rusty hinges and damp wood.

The pungent tang of mildew and stale air hit Mercy as she followed Conner and Jacob over the threshold. Daniel came up beside her, standing just a tad inside her personal space. So close she could smell him, the clean scent of soap and fabric softener. Mercy shifted uncomfortably and looked up into hazel eyes sparked with humor.

He leaned down and spoke in a hushed tone. "No lead or asbestos to worry about. Just need to dodge the pissed-off spirits." He winked and clucked his tongue.

Mercy sucked in a breath and held his gaze. "I don't believe in them, so I guess that won't be a problem, then, will it?"

"Whoo whee!" Jacob said, and his voice echoed off bare plaster walls. "This place sure is creepy enough."

The ceiling hovered two stories high above them. Tall windows formed the rear wall, with a patch of lush woods visible beyond. Pale yellow sunlight glinted off dewy green leaves.

The glass wall gave an illusion of openness, but an illusion was all. The panes allowed light to pass through but nothing else. Each tall, rectangular frame wore ominously heavy armor—thick slabs of glass block sandwiched between steel mesh on the inside and heavy black-iron braces bolted fast on the outside.

Jacob took three long strides and kicked at the edge of a peeling floor tile. "Looks like these vinyl replacements didn't hold up any better than the asbestos ones."

Conner stooped to pick at the edge of the vinyl. "The place has been locked up since about 1975. No heat in here, windows closed up tight. I'm not surprised the extreme temperatures and humidity took their toll. There's been nothing in here since."

"Nothing except a wayward pigeon or two," Daniel said, pointing to a sprawled skeleton lying on a bed of feathers at the base of the windows.

A shiver racked Mercy's shoulders. She knew she couldn't react—absolutely could not recoil. She needed to be one of the guys, just like she'd been doing for the past twenty years. Clearing her throat, she turned to her new boss. "Where do we start, Conner?"

"Right here. Power's shut off at the main. First thing is to strip out what's here. Let's get to it."

Daniel and Jacob carried in the heavy fiberglass ladders, though they didn't need them to disassemble the rusted old outlet boxes hanging intermittently along the chipped plaster walls. Conner helped Mercy set a ladder next to the central panel box, since it was a little too high for her to reach. She waited for him to make a wisecrack about the fact and was grateful when he didn't.

Mercy adjusted her tool belt and climbed to the third step, shoving her work boots tight against the sides of the frame. Donning heavy deerskin gloves, she used her tester to make sure the feed line and first few fuses were dead. Then she got to work with her pliers and dykes, pulling wires away from their attachments under ancient screws in the panel.

She had gotten to the very last wire when the lightning struck.

At least that's what it felt like. A burst of blue light momentarily blinded her, and a deafening crack pierced her brain. The force of the jolt blew her backwards and set her ears ringing.

The next few seconds slowed surreally. Dizzy and confused, Mercy, ladder and all, careened away from the wall in silent, slow motion. As if in a dream. No pain, no fear.

Then she landed, flat on her back on the floor, the impact rattling her jaw. Pain shot through her as the ladder bounced off her chest once, and then settled heavy on top, pinning her to the dust-laden tile.

"DAMN it!" Mercy's oath blew out with the last of the air in her lungs.

"What the holy hell?" Conner was standing over her in seconds, yanking the ladder off with one hand. The other two men raced over, and Daniel dropped to one knee to hold Mercy down by one shoulder.

"Don't try to move till you're sure nothing's broken," he muttered.

"I thought you said we were off at the main, Bro! Holy hell!" Jacob was wild-eyed, shoving Conner with one of his gloved hands. "You tryin' to get us all killed?"

Mercy felt as though a horse had just trotted over her ribcage, squashing one breast under each hoof. The back of her head throbbed even though her safety helmet had protected her from a possible concussion. Her breath was coming in short, shallow bursts. "Let me up, Daniel. I'm okay," she barked through clenched teeth, wrenching her shoulder from under his grip and sitting up.

She could not, however, feel her left hand. She stared down at the blackened fingers of her glove. Were there still operable digits under the leather? Or just charred stumps?

As though he'd read her mind, Daniel locked a strong hand around her wrist. His eyes flashed to hers once before he said, "I'm going to see what's going on under here." Slowly, he pressed on each finger of the glove. "Hurt?" he asked.

Mercy shook her head. "No. They're numb. Or gone. I can't feel them at all."

Daniel sucked in a breath and said, "Not unusual to be numb for a while." His eyes slid toward hers again, and she hoped he couldn't see her fear. His gaze was steady, intense. "I'm gonna cut the glove off. Stop me if it hurts, okay?"

Mercy watched, holding her breath as Daniel wielded a pair of snips from his belt and began clipping away at the wristband of her glove. He worked methodically, gently, cradling her hand on his knee the whole time. Once he'd opened the entire back of the glove, he turned her hand over and did the same on the palm side.

He took a deep breath as he slid the cutting tool back into his belt, then raised his eyes to hers. "You ready?"

Mercy swallowed and nodded. Daniel grabbed the edges of the leather and gently worked the covering free.

She let out a whoosh of relief when she looked down on five fingers, only slightly reddened, complete with intact fingernails. They were still numb but began to tingle as she flexed her knuckles.

"Good gloves you got there," Daniel mumbled. He flashed her a narrow gaze. "Forgot to use your tester first, huh?"

Mercy snatched her hand away, fury flaring in her chest. "I used the damned tester on the main feed, and on the first three fuses, like I always do. How the hell was I supposed to know there was more than one source to the freaking panel?"

As she scrambled to her feet, Mercy saw Conner pacing near the doorway, screaming profanities into his cell phone. Jacob was staring at him with his fists clenched at his sides. When Conner finally ended the call, his brother took a step closer and threw back his elbows. For a moment, Mercy was sure a punch would follow.

But Jacob just hissed, "Well? Whose screw-up was this?"

Yup, they were brothers alright. Mercy couldn't imagine Conner taking that from either her or Daniel.

Conner shot a searing glance at him before he turned to face her and Daniel. "They're telling me it's dead—no juice coming in from the main. Something isn't right here. There's got to be more than one trunk line."

The boss shoved his phone back into the case clipped to his belt and reached down for the ladder, struggling a bit now with both hands. Mercy knew how heavy the damn things were, but she'd also seen him yank the same ladder off her with one hand just minutes ago. Adrenalin is amazing, she thought. Turns a man into a super-being in a heartbeat.

Conner slammed the ladder up against the wall with such force that chips of plaster rained down on the tiles. Climbing up one step, he pulled a tester out of his belt, touching it to the last fuse in the panel. The light inside the handle glowed bright and red like a giant Christmas bulb.

"Holy shit. It's live, alright." He spat the words and glanced back over his shoulder at her. "Could have got you killed, Mercy May."

It was then Mercy saw a ridge on the wall beside the box. It had been plastered over, then painted, so it was hard to make it out as anything but an irregularity in the old wall. Conner stepped down off the ladder and, with gloved fingers, traced the ridge around the corner and through an archway just to the right of the panel box. She and Daniel followed him into a short hallway that led off to what must have once been a kitchen area.

Mercy nearly plowed into his back when he stopped suddenly. He was studying a place where the ridge disappeared, seemingly right into the wall. She could just make out the narrow, rectangular panel about the size of a pantry door. The edges had been painted shut, making it nearly invisible. A tiny doorknob was equally disguised, tucked into the corner and coated with the same puke-green paint.

Mercy watched as Conner fumbled with the knob with his gloved hand but couldn't get a grip. Cursing, he snatched off his glove, grabbed it and yanked. The door didn't budge. He growled, a sound Mercy had not heard him make before.

So, big brother has a temper too, she thought, watching as Conner pulled a screwdriver out of his tool belt and scored the edges with a vengeance. He laid one hand over the other and lifted one boot to brace himself against the jamb. His furiously angry tugs sent flakes scattering from the paint-sealed edges. With one last grunt, he staggered back as the door wrenched open.

Mercy stumbled back a step as well, bumping into Daniel, who laid both his hands on her shoulders to steady her. She shook herself free and snapped, "Would you get off me?"

The open door revealed not a pantry closet but a dark hole. A small rectangle yawned open into blackness, and a blast of damp, moldy air spewed out. Conner snatched a flashlight off his belt and snapped it on, illuminating a narrow stairwell with concrete steps that led off into the darkness below.

"Guess we found us a secret passage," he muttered as he spewed a stream of brown tobacco juice onto the curling tiles under his feet. His light beam flashed on grooved metal conduit. It was unpainted here, tarnished and rusted in places. The conduit snaked down the wall beside the steps.

"There's our alternate power source."

Jacob stepped around Mercy to peer over Conner's shoulder. "Is that the basement access?"

"Nope. Basement door's on the west end. This here's nothing that shows up on my set of blueprints," Conner muttered. He ducked and turned sideways to squeeze through an opening barely wide enough to admit his bulky torso. Mercy watched wide-eyed as he stomped down the steps, aided only by the beam of light that seemed puny under the weight of musty black air. Mercy's skin prickled.

Conner had all but disappeared into the abyss when a quiet click sounded and the area below them flooded with light. A bare bulb, caged in cobweb-laced metal, hung from the ceiling just above his head. He looked one way, and then the other, whistling through his teeth. "Now I wonder where the hell this little highway leads to?"

Jacob pushed through the opening in front of Mercy and followed his brother. She glanced back over her shoulder at Daniel.

"You go ahead," he said, a slow grin sparking a glint in his hazel eyes. He was testing her again, daring her. Mercy narrowed her eyes, but he continued quickly, "It'll take me a minute to fold myself up small enough to get through that keyhole." Then he shrugged and grinned, looking more innocent than she was sure he was.

Yup, testing her. Mercy hesitated only a second, thinking, *I can't back down now.*

She crept down the steps, shivering as the chill of underground air crawled over her. Just as she reached the bottom step, something tickled her cheek and she swatted frantically before realizing it was just a fragment of spider web waving from the rafter. The sound of Daniel's snort behind her made her bristle. She shot him a contemptuous glare.

The passageway was low ceilinged, forcing Daniel to stoop, and so narrow a man could almost span the width with outstretched arms. Rough fieldstone walls, joined by random patches of mortar, rose from a cracked concrete floor. The hall disappeared off at right angles to the steps in both directions. Conner strode boldly down one way, then the other, pulling the tattered, hanging cords to bring yellowed bulbs to life, one at a time. Some were dead, but those that still fired bathed the space in an eerie, amber light.

Mercy studied the bench lining the outside wall. Heavy planks formed a shelf about two feet above the ground. Every ten feet or so, a pair of round iron rings hung from the wall, mortared between the fieldstones.

"I've read about places like this," Daniel mumbled. "This was their holding area."

"What do you mean? Like in a prison?" Even to her own ears, Mercy's voice sounded squeaky and unsteady.

Daniel tipped his head, pulling his fingers through his short, tawny beard. His gaze glanced off hers. "Guess you could call it that. Back then they didn't ever know what they were getting into when a new patient came in."

Conner turned and shot a look at Mercy that made her skin crawl. "It was a nut-house, darlin'. When the cuckoos got too rowdy, they brought them down here and chained them up." He shook his head and spat another stream from his chew onto the floor. "Poor, pathetic bastards."

DANIEL KNEW when the team took on the massive job of rewiring the largest of the brick buildings on the old state hospital grounds, they'd need help to meet the deadline. He'd been working with Progressive Electrical for nearly five years, and the three of them could tackle just about anything. They always beat the expectations of any homeowner or contractor. But this project was a whole different deal.

The Corby Technical Institute had already transformed four of the other old mental wards into classrooms, lecture halls, and administrative offices—all already in use by students and faculty. But none of those buildings came close to Gravely Hall, either in size or reputation. In addition to encompassing a whopping forty thousand square feet under roof, the Gravely had, up until the mental hospital closed, housed the craziest of the crazies.

It was the only building equipped with steel bars on the windows. He'd come through with Conner to help do an evaluation before they bid on the job. What he'd seen made him nauseous.

Peepholes in the patient room doors, not more than two inches in diameter, were reinforced with chicken wire. But the creepiest part was the basement, full of old-fashioned, porcelain tubs—each still wearing heavy, leather covers with a hole at one end. For their heads, he thought grimly.

After that tour, Daniel sat down at his computer and did a little research. It was a hobby of his anyway, researching old buildings. It was his dream, if only one fit for a pipe, to train for architectural restoration. He'd gotten the basics in a minor at MIT while working on his electrical engineering degree. He should have switched majors, he now knew. But jobs in architectural restoration were hard to come by. Journeyman electrician would provide him a comfortable living. And it had, at least for the past twelve years.

This building, he discovered, had seen the worst of experimental treatments for the insane. Although the area's powerhouse in electrical contracting had eagerly agreed to rewire all the other four buildings on the new campus, they'd declined to include Gravely Hall. Too massive a project, they'd whimpered.

Daniel, as well as Conner and Jacob, knew better. None of them had the balls to tackle the job.

But hiring a woman as their fourth member? What was Conner thinking? Daniel was in no way anti-feminist and didn't mind working with Mercedes. In fact, he imagined her presence would be kind of refreshing. He spent most of his time these days with his coworkers, or with his basketball sparring buddies. His nephew as well. All guys. It was safe, but sometimes, the loneliness ate at him. And spending time with his sister did nothing but convince Daniel he was much better off keeping it that way.

She said she liked to be called Mercy. He'd never worked with a female journeyman and was sure they weren't numerous in the field.

Mercy had shocked him with her knowledge and efficiency. She definitely knew her stuff. Been an electrician, she'd said, all her life. She and her husband were a team in Atlanta.

So, what happened there, he wondered?

She wasn't too bad to look at, even in her baggy Carhartts. With her dark hair always coiled around her head and hidden under the safety helmet, she almost looked like one of the guys.

Except for those eyes, twinkly pale ones that threw out sparks when she was angry. Were they blue or green? He couldn't tell. And what the hell difference does *that* make?

She was tall and slender. How the hell was she going to handle the ladders they'd need to reach the vaulted, two-story ceilings in the place? Most of the old metal conduit ran up high. Probably to be sure it was out of reach of the crazies they had locked up in there.

Gravely Hall was sure to be infested with everything from mice and rats to spiders—and God knows how women usually reacted to creepy-crawly things. Not to mention the rumors about the old place. Daniel made a silent bet she'd run screaming out of the building before the end of the first day.

What he didn't expect was that she'd nearly get fried.

Not to say it was her fault. Conner was good about safety precautions, and he'd radioed in not once, but three times to campus security to be sure the power had been shut off at the main. But nobody knew there was a separate trunk line. Nobody, not even the tech school's maintenance department, knew there was a hidden passageway connecting the building to what had been now renovated into administrative offices.

A tunnel. Underground. Complete with its own, separate power supply.

So, after the new girl had nearly singed off her fingers, the team spent half of the first day tracing the conduit through the tunnel to be sure they'd disabled every possible electric source. Daniel followed Conner to the east end, where the passage curved around and rose to follow the contour of the hill leading up to the administration building. When they reached the end, they discovered a heavy steel door with hinges. An ancient lock rusted it shut.

An old fuse panel hung on the wall just inside the door. Daniel reached up with his tester, which glowed at the touch. "Hot as a fire-cracker," he said.

Conner lifted his cell and called campus security.

"Didn't you guys ever wonder what was behind the steel door on the east side of the admin basement?" he barked into the phone. After a pause, he said, "You're shittin' me." He hung up and turned to Daniel. "There's no door on the basement side. The whole west wall's been bricked up."

Daniel threw the main switch and the tunnel went black. Snapping on his flashlight, Daniel tested the feed again. "She's dead now."

Conner slid his eyes up to meet Daniel's. "And almost, so was our girl," he muttered.

Our girl? He didn't mind working with a woman but had to admit his hackles raised a bit to realize that his boss was acting as if she were some freaking mascot or something. But it appeared Mercy hadn't even heard him. She'd already taken off back toward the stairwell.

They followed their flashlight beams up that way to where Jacob waited, having donned his lighted helmet. "Well? What's the deal?" he asked.

"Nobody even knew this tunnel was here," Conner said. "There's a whole separate panel down that end." He peered up the narrow stairwell. "Mercy go back up?"

Jacob shook his head and motioned over his shoulder with his thumb. "She went exploring down thatta way."

Gutsy little imp, Daniel thought. Even he was creeped out down here, along with feeling just a bit claustrophobic. And now everything was pitch black.

"I'll go fetch her," he said.

DANIEL FOLLOWED the tunnel as it sloped down and curved off to the north.

"Mercy," he called out. His voice landed flat, muffled by all the stone surrounding him. It was colder down here, too, and smelled moldy and wet. "Mercy, you okay down there?"

Then he saw the bright circle from her flashlight crawling over a smooth wall in the distance.

"Here," she called back. "Hey, come take a look at this wall, Daniel. I've never seen concrete blocks like this before."

"This blockwork is old," Daniel said, running his fingers along the smooth, elongated rectangles much smaller than modern concrete blocks. "Must have sealed this end off back in the forties or fifties, way before they closed the place up," he said. "I wonder if it originally connected all the buildings."

"I'm guessing you found the power source?" Mercy asked.

"Yeah, we found it. All shut down now."

"I figured," she snorted. "Either that or I'd gone blind."

She was a feisty one, he'd give her that. Not many women would have ventured down into this place, let alone gone off on their own. And she didn't even shriek when the lights went out.

"Sorry about that," Daniel said. "I didn't realize you'd wandered off."

"Like an unattended child, huh? No problem. I don't scare that easy," Mercy snapped. "I'm a mother, remember? I learned to roust monsters out from under the bed a long time ago."

They heard Conner's voice then, sounding echoed and far away. "Come on, you two. We got work to do. You can go ghost hunting on your own time."

"Not likely," Mercy said before stepping around Daniel to head back up the incline. "If you don't mind, though, I'll go ahead of you."

Ah, Daniel thought, a dent in the armor. She talks a good game, but let's see how long she holds up with the macho act.

"Geez, Mom, I don't know how you can work in a creepy place like that. Aren't you afraid of ghosts and stuff?"

Reagan spoke between and around huge mouthfuls of the pizza he was devouring as though he hadn't eaten in a month. Mercy had gotten in late . . . again. On nights like this, her expected transformation from electrician to Paula Deen just didn't happen. Thank God for takeout and home delivery.

"Well, the ghosts were actually the least of my problems today. I hit a live line that almost fried me." She blurted out the words, and then winced. Why, oh why had she let that slip?

Reagan's eyes flew open wide as he stopped chewing and stared at her for a long moment. He grimaced as he swallowed an obviously not-properly-chewed mouthful.

"What happened? Did you get hurt?" The little-boy tone of panic quickly morphed into anger. "What kind of an asshole is this guy you work for, anyway?"

For a split-second, Mercy saw her husband, Luke, sitting there in Reagan's skin. Quick- tempered, judgmental. Then came the jab of pain in her heart. She shook off the image.

"Now don't go freaking out on me, Reagan. Conner's very competent. He was working right there in the same room. It could have happened to any of us."

But Reagan wasn't listening. He was shaking his head, staring down at his half-eaten slice of pizza as though it had turned into a pile of dog crap. Slowly, he raised furious, narrowed eyes to hers. "Dad would never have let that happen," he growled.

Stab. Jab.

"Don't start. It wasn't Conner's fault. It just happened, and I'm fine. I'll be needing a new pair of gloves, but no damage done other than that." Mercy pushed away from the table and threw her paper plate with the half-eaten slice into the trash. Her appetite was gone, and she needed to pedal past this moment before her own pain brought on another episode of her son's.

"Tell me how your GED class went tonight. How's your instructor? What is it, Mr. Wright?" Mercy chuckled to herself. "How could he possibly be bad with a name like that?"

Reagan's lip twitched as though he'd like to smile but didn't. "Yeah, Mr. Wright. He's okay."

Mercy waited, but her son offered nothing more. She watched him refold his pizza and take a bite. As he chewed, she asked, "Sooo, how many are there in your class?"

Reagan swallowed and lifted his can of Coke, draining it. "Five of us," he said, wiping his mouth on a napkin. "Two Hispanic housewives, an older dude, and another kid. Chris is a year older than me."

"Two nights a week? Tuesdays and Thursdays, right?"

"Uh-huh."

"Did you get your book yet?"

"Yup."

"Is there a lot of homework?"

"Uh-huh."

Mercy knew when Reagan's sentences deteriorated into single words, he was done. He'd retreated into that dark, hidden place where he lived most of the time since . . . then. Even with constant counseling, Mercy had figured out the more she tried, the further Reagan shut down.

In the few months they'd been in Corby, Reagan had seen three different psychotherapists. Although the Boston area had more than its share, they just hadn't found the right match yet. But Massachusetts had a historically strong reputation for mental health care— just one of the reasons she'd chosen to move back when she realized they couldn't stay in Atlanta.

In Atlanta, the ghosts were everywhere, and not just walled up inside an old state hospital building.

CHAPTER 2

*T*here was no denying it. Working on this old building gave Mercy the creeps. Most of the electrical work she'd done back in Atlanta on Luke's crew had been on new construction. Within the first week of starting at her new job in Massachusetts a month ago, Mercy had found herself missing the sharp, piney fragrance of fresh lumber and the whine of the skill saws. Conner seldom wired buildings going up for the first time. His team's specialty was refurbishing old structures, which made perfect sense to him.

"We get paid for two jobs this way," he'd explained. "First everything's gotta come out, all the antiquated, worn and out-of-code stuff that the building inspectors would never pass. Then we start from scratch and make it all shiny, new, and legal again."

The Corby Technical Institute's campus center was only their second job since Mercy came on board. The house they'd done before that was a turn-of-the-century colonial donated to the town for their new library. There, most of the work had been in replacing light fixtures and running new lines for computers and printers. The building was old, but well maintained and held an innocuous history. Compared to Corby's new library job, the renovation on the old asylum complex seemed not only insurmountable in complexity, but eerie, since the building seemed to have memories of its past life.

Conner's team was experienced and efficient. The first week on Gravely Hall the team's work progressed without further mishap or surprises. It only took two days to strip the old wiring and boxes out from the ground-floor rooms, and then Daniel and Mercy moved to the basement while Conner and Jacob started on the upper levels. The early spring weather had boiled up into a summer-like heat in a hurry. New England experienced an unseasonable string of days with thick humidity and unseasonably high temperatures for early June.

Mercy was grateful to be working in the basement, even though it was definitely creepy. It was damp and musty, but at least it was ten degrees cooler than the vast upstairs rooms. On the upper floors, sunlight streaming through the iron-gridded walls of glass turned the dusty air into a sauna before noon. She also didn't mind working with Daniel, whose quiet manner and methodical mode appealed very much to Mercy.

Which scared her, a little. She felt way too comfortable around Daniel, and she couldn't deny her attraction to him. He was a good-looking man, probably a few years younger than her. He wore no wedding band, but that meant nothing. She liked the fact that he treated her as an equal, not any differently than the way he treated Jacob, their other peer on the team. But still, she had to maintain her distance. Keep her concentration focused on doing a good job, getting settled in here in Corby. Giving Reagan the solid base he so desperately needed.

They had both had endured enough uncertainty and disorganization in their lives over the past two years.

The basement rooms were, well, *basement*: all concrete, floor to ceiling, with only a few small, rectangular windows along the ceiling in places where the landscape dropped lower than the foundation. Rusted bars gridded every one of these. Several of the smaller rooms looked like prison cells, spaces no bigger than closets. Each was equipped with a discolored, antique porcelain toilet in one corner. The largest, and by far the creepiest room, lay directly under the great hall on the main floor, nearly matching its dimensions. It was eerily furnished with a half-dozen old footed bathtubs lining the back wall, their white porcelain coating chipping away from the metal along the top edges.

"This is an odd place to bathe the patients," Mercy commented that first day she and Daniel were taking inventory of their next tasks.

Daniel just chuckled quietly, pulling on his straggly, reddish beard with his ungloved right hand. "They brought 'em here to clean them up, alright," he said in an ominous tone. "They thought they were cleaning up their muddled minds."

"What do you mean?" Mercy asked.

"I've done a bit of reading on these old mental hospitals," Daniel said. "Their version of 'treatment' would now be considered torture." But Mercy never got any more information out of him because he quit the line of talk right there. Slipping the notes about the wiring patterns he'd been scribbling into his back pocket, Daniel slid on his other glove. "Got a big job here. Better get started."

The day passed uneventfully except for a call Mercy got from Reagan shortly before quitting time. Reagan was home alone and sometimes even his homework, his guitar, the television, and his video games couldn't keep his troubled mind busy enough.

"Mom, sorry to bother you."

"What's wrong, Reagan?" Mercy could tell from Reagan's casual tone that there was nothing really wrong. She tried to keep the impatience out of her voice. Daniel, who was busy at work across the room unscrewing metal wire brackets out of the concrete, stopped and glanced back over his shoulder. Was it curiosity, she wondered, or admonition in his look? She lowered her voice. "Everything okay, Reagan?"

"I have class tonight, Mom," Reagan stated, a little annoyance creeping into his own tone. "Are we gonna eat dinner together or what?"

Mercy glanced down at her watch. Four thirty-five. Reagan's GED class started at seven, and the school was practically around the corner from the house.

"We quit around five, Reagan. You know that," she replied with a small, exasperated sigh. "What do you want for dinner? I'll stop and pick us up something on the way home."

After the call Mercy's head began to pound with tension as she finished detaching wire harnesses in the tiny cell off the main room where she'd been working all afternoon. About five minutes before five, Daniel appeared in the open doorway. None of these little ante-rooms had doors on them anymore. They were just gaping holes, like empty eye sockets peering in on the large room with all those big bathtubs.

"Everything okay, Mercy?" Daniel's voice rumbled soft, a sound standing perpendicular to the physical persona of the tall frame of a man with unkempt hair in grubby Dickie overalls. It wasn't only his beard that seemed ill-attended. His hair, a rusty tone a few shades darker than his beard, looked as though it might have once been trimmed into a neat style—maybe three months ago.

Mercy was looking back at him over her shoulder as she stepped down off the low stool she'd been working from. She started gathering her tools into her belt.

"Yeah," she replied quietly, "as good as can be expected for now."

"With your son, I mean," Daniel probed.

Mercy avoided the tall man's penetrating gaze. "Like I said, as good as it's been. Nothing different." Mercy wasn't sure if Daniel was trying to be nice, or just being nosy, but his questions annoyed her. She hoped her irritation hadn't leaked too badly into the tone of her reply. "Long day," she chirped brightly, and smiled up at him as she finished slipping tools into her belt. "Glad it's quitting time."

A few minutes later, the four electricians were climbing into

Conner's van and heading out. The parking lots were abandoned except for a lone black and white patrol car in front of the small brown building on the corner. Campus Police kept one security guard on duty round the clock.

Mercy and Reagan's rental home was less than a half-mile off the campus. Although the other men always met in the parking lot of the tiny office Conner rented in Corby Center, Conner saw no reason for Mercy to have to drive three miles in the opposite direction. They drove right past her house on the way to and from the campus. That night, like every other since they'd started this job, Conner pulled up close to the curb at 344 Elm Street. Daniel reached down and unlatched the van's sliding side door.

"G'night, guys. See you in the morning," she called.

As Conner's van pulled off, Mercy heard the screen door squeal, and she looked up to see Reagan standing on the front porch of the old Victorian-style house.

"What'd you bring for dinner?" he asked accusingly, seeing she obviously bore nothing except her tool belt around her waist.

Mercy glanced down at her watch and replied, "Plenty of time, Reagan. How about you go with me to the Bridge Street Café?"

Mercy had found it increasingly difficult to maintain conversation with her son, especially since the move. Reagan had always been a quiet kid, introverted and moody. But now, since their whole life had undergone a major revision, it was as though she didn't even know him anymore. He spent too much time alone during the day since he'd dropped out of school in his junior year.

Mercy wouldn't allow Reagan to get his driver's license until he finished his GED, even though Luke had let the boy drive his work vans on the back roads around Atlanta since he was fourteen. Reagan had left all his friends behind, yet he didn't seem interested in making any new ones since they had moved. He had grown beyond the age where he wanted to spend any time with his mother. Mercy sometimes felt as though Reagan hated her.

The time they spent at the café grabbing burgers was the longest hour Mercy had spent all day. They ordered and sat in complete silence across from each other until Mercy asked, "So what did you do today? Get all your homework done?"

Reagan's eyes lifted to glare at Mercy. "Yes, Mother," he sneered. "Aren't you interested in anything else about me except whether or not I've done my homework?"

Mercy closed her eyes and sighed. "Yes, Reagan, of course I am. I just don't know what else you do all day. Are you reading anything? Watch any movies?"

Reagan sat hunched on his side of the booth, speaking down to his lap when he answered. "You know I don't like to read much. I'm playing in a tournament online, though."

Mercy knew absolutely nothing about the video games Reagan played almost constantly except for how much they cost. But she tried to sound enthusiastic.

"Oh yeah? Which one? That one you got for Christmas? Killer's Mantra, or something?"

Reagan snorted and shook his head, a look of annoyed disgust on his face. "Assassin's Creed, Mom."

Mercy was relieved when the waitress interrupted them, clicking their plates down on the table. Reagan hunched over his plate like a defensive dog protecting his prey, and the meal continued in complete silence.

She was almost relieved to drop him off at Corby High School for his class. Reagan climbed out of the car without a word. Before he flung the door shut, Mercy barked, "Hey!"

Reagan tipped his head back towards her in silent insolence, one eyebrow raised.

"I'll be here to get you at ten. I have my cell phone if you need me. I don't expect a hug, but 'goodbye' would be an unexpected gift."

Reagan mumbled something that sounded vaguely like goodbye and slammed the door in Mercy's face. No hug. She sighed, closed her eyes, and laid her forehead down atop the steering wheel. This was getting harder every day.

It was then her eyes flew open as she thought, *cell phone*. Where the hell did she leave it? She groped in the multiple pockets of the overalls that she hadn't even bothered to change out of before going to dinner. She reached around for her purse, tucked behind her seat, the one she never carried to work. No phone.

Damn it, she thought. *I've left it at the job.*

Not that it was a big deal. The campus was only a mile away, and she knew security was on duty all night. All she had to do was stop in at their make-shift office in the little brown house, ask for access permission to Gravely Hall and find her phone. No big deal at all.

It was almost dark by the time she pulled up to the Campus Police building. The sleepy-looking young officer who accompanied her back out into the parking lot seemed almost grateful for the distraction. He tailed her car in his cruiser to Gravely Hall. Mercy followed him up onto the mildewed steps as he used a key from a huge metal ring to open the padlock.

"Do you have a flashlight, Miss?" The young patrolman stepped aside as the door opened, seeming reluctant to accompany Mercy into the old building. The long shadows of evening had already stamped the interior into dense gloom.

"Yeah, no problem," she grinned at the greenhorn cop. "I'll be back in just a minute."

The musty smell and odd air quality seemed amplified in the growing darkness. Mercy strode confidently toward the broad staircase at the end of the great hall and snapped on the flashlight she always kept hooked to a loop on her overalls. She must have left her phone in the small anteroom, she thought. She must have laid it down after Reagan called her earlier that afternoon and failed to pick it up when she was packing up her tools.

Access to the lower level was at the far end of the great central room, and some pale light still slithered in through the greenish glass panes of the windows near the head of the stairs. As she descended the creaking boards, a smothering calm increasingly muffled all sound. Mercy felt an instinctive impulse to reach for a light switch, but of course, there was none, at least none in working order.

In the waning glow of daylight seeping in through the high basement windows, she could make out the shapes of the porcelain tubs, standing in a sentinel row. A damp shiver ran up and down her back. Mercy straightened her shoulders and cleared her throat.

I'll just go directly into the anteroom where I'd been working, she thought, and retrieve my phone. Then I'm outta here.

She'd gotten to the open doorway of the small space when she heard the sound. A water sound, almost like waves lapping at the edge of a pool. Or on the sides of a bathtub: that soft sound of liquid kissing its solid prison walls. The tubs along the back wall weren't even connected to a water source anymore. They'd been dry and littered with small chunks of dusty debris when she and Daniel worked around them earlier today. Some still wore their mildewed, leather coverings.

Mercy hurried directly toward the room she'd last worked in, her light flashing wildly through the mostly empty space. She aimed the beam into the gaping hole of the toilet, but it was as dry as it had been earlier in the day. Struggling to ignore the increasingly loud sloshing sound, reverberating now louder and louder all around her, she located the black wedge of her cell phone. It was lying abandoned on the concrete windowsill. She snatched it up, clutching it tight to her chest. The hard-plastic case felt reassuring in her grasp.

As she crossed the central room, the water sound echoed in the space around her, seeming to get louder with every step. Her heart hammered in her chest, and she quickened her pace. Almost there.

Mercy.

Resonating above the sloshing sounds, she could swear she'd heard her name. Mercy jolted to a stop and spun around. The sound had come from behind her, it seemed. Or had she imagined it?

It must be the security officer. He must be calling from the head of the stairs.

"Hello?" Mercy called out. Her voice reverberated so loudly it startled her. "I'll be right up," she called again, and flashed her light beam in a path straight toward the stairs.

Mercy!

The voice came again, louder now. Wheezing and feeble, it sounded like that of a very old man, or a very sick one. Had one of the homeless sought refuge here for the night? A jumble of thoughts tumbled through Mercy's mind, panic obliterating the logical portion.

How would anyone even know her name?

A veil of clammy perspiration blanketed every inch of her skin. Dank basement air threatened to seep right through her. Clutching her phone to her chest, she jabbed the flashlight beam wildly with her other hand, back and forth across the wide expanse of the room. The ray glanced off the white porcelain shapes, transforming them into hulking ghosts standing in ominous formation.

"Who's there?" she shrieked. Her voice echoed and bounced back to her in empty coldness.

Mercy...

This third time the voice was faint, fading, melting into the mysterious water sounds that ebbed like the receding of an ocean wave. Silence ballooned around her, black and deafening, enveloping all sound except for the wild pounding of her pulse in her ears. Mercy fought the panic rising into her throat and broke into a full run toward the steps. To the exit, where the officer was waiting for her. Toward safety.

She stumbled twice on the stairs, dropping to one knee the second time, her phone clattering from her grip. Mercy scratched frantically on the wood riser, scuffing her knuckles on the rough edge and driving splinters and grit under her nails as she snatched the instrument up. When she stepped at last onto the old tile of the ground floor, she took a deep breath and slowed her steps, basking in a wash of relief to see the shadowy silhouette of the security guard in the open doorway. His flashlight beam snapped across her face, blinding her.

"Everything all right, Miss?" The officer stood stiffly just outside the door of the building. It was almost as though he'd been afraid to step over the threshold.

"Yes. Yes, I'm fine." Mercy's voice was trembling, but she cleared her throat in an effort to hide her panic. "I found my phone. Thank you. Thank you for letting me in."

CHAPTER 3

 s she pulled out onto Route 30, the sudden buzzing of her phone in the breast pocket of Mercy's overalls nearly sent her through the sunroof of her Camry. On reflex, she snatched the thing out in a trembling fist, mashed the green button with her thumb and barked, "Hello?"

A split-second of silence ended with the chiding voice of her ex-husband. "Well that's certainly more friendly than the usual 'What do you want, asshole?'"

Mercy took a deep breath, scrambling to center her fried nerves. "I obviously didn't look at the caller ID, Luke, or that's exactly what you'd have gotten."

"Look Mercy, I'm not trying to be an asshole. I'm just calling to make sure Reagan is okay." He sighed, and Mercy could tell his demeanor was more hesitant than usual. "You're both just so far away. I can't help but worry."

Mercy snorted. "You should have thought of that a couple years ago when you started banging your cute little blonde bimbo." Her patience had run out about two hours ago, and for Luke, at least two years back.

She heard his exasperated huff on the other end. After a long pause he asked, "How is Reagan doing with his new therapist?"

Mercy knew she had no choice but to communicate with Luke, for Reagan's sake. Luke had turned out to be a very bad husband, but she couldn't deny he'd tried to be a pretty decent father. She was about ready to credit him that, even now, until she recalled how once Reagan's problems had been formally diagnosed, Luke had backpedaled. Her irritation flared anew.

She tried to tamp down the cynicism in her tone. "You know Reagan," she said. "He doesn't talk much. Least of all to me."

"He hasn't called me either. It's been a few days. That's why I was worried."

Mercy squinted against the glare of oncoming headlights. She knew she should end the call while she was driving, but she was almost home.

"How often has he been calling you?" She knew the words came out indignant, but hell, the kid barely said ten words to her in a day. Yet he'd been calling his cheating, lying, son-of-a-bitch father on a regular basis? She couldn't help feeling slighted.

Another long pause. Then Luke snapped, "I didn't think you'd mind him calling his own father, Merce."

"That's not what I meant. I don't care if he calls you every day, ten times a day. He needs a man to talk to. I get that." Mercy turned into the driveway of her rental home and pulled up close beside the porch. When she killed the headlights, darkness dropped over her like an ebony blanket.

"Shit," she mumbled, forgetting her words flew effortlessly over the hundreds of miles to Atlanta.

"What's the matter?" Luke barked. "What did I say now?"

Mercy dropped back in her seat and groaned. "Nothing, Luke. I'm just getting home and it's freaking black as pitch. Look, I'll have Reagan call you, okay?" she growled through gritted teeth.

Damn, she thought, stepping out into the darkness. She'd meant to

change that porch light bulb two days ago. She reached for the flashlight she'd carried with her to the job site and snapped the switch.
Nothing. She shook the cylinder, rattling the batteries inside and
muttering, "What the hell? You worked just fine a few minutes ago."
Then she pushed the switch back and forth frantically with her
thumb. "Great. Just great."

Mercy groped her way up the three steps to the porch, wishing
she'd left a light on in her living room. Or the kitchen. Somewhere.
She'd never been afraid of the dark before. Having worked in the sole
company of males for the last twenty years, she'd absorbed some of
their fearless, macho ways by osmosis.

But tonight she was shaken, and Luke's call hadn't helped. She felt
the hair on the back of her neck rising and a chill rippling across her
shoulders as she fumbled with her keys. Her hands were shaking as
she tried to blindly fit the key into the lock.

The flash of headlights behind her sent her shadow skittering over
the side of the house. Mercy whipped around and blinked into
blinding light. Did Reagan get a ride home? No, his class didn't get out
for another two hours. She straightened her spine and palmed the
keys so hard they nearly cut into her skin.

"Who's there?" she called as a tall figure stepped out of the vehicle.

"Mercedes?"

She recognized Daniel's voice, and her shoulders immediately
relaxed.

"Wow, I sure am glad you happened along about now," she said.
"Not only is my porch light out, but my flashlight died too." She
paused, cocking her head as he approached her. "What are you doing
here, anyway?"

She couldn't see his face, silhouetted as he was in front of the
headlights, which he'd left on so she could see to unlock the door.

Why didn't I think of that?

"Just driving by. Thought I'd stop in and see if you wanted to grab
a sandwich at the pub."

Mercy's hands were still shaking as she turned the key and swung the door wide. She snapped the wall switch and proceeded to work her way around the living room, turning on every table and reading lamp she had. As her panic subsided, her brain gradually registered Daniel's words. She turned and saw him standing on the threshold, watching her.

"Is it alright if I come in?" he asked, a grin splitting his straggly beard. He looked like an ill-groomed Cheshire cat.

Mercy lifted one hip to sit on the arm of her reading chair, regarding him through narrowed eyes. She folded her arms across her chest. "Why would you stop in when there were clearly no lights on? How'd you know I was home?"

Daniel pushed his hands into the pockets of his nicely fitting jeans and leaned a shoulder on the doorjamb. "Why ESP, of course. I can read every thought in that pretty head of yours, too, so be careful what you think."

She wanted to be annoyed, angry even. This was simply a guy she worked with. Hadn't known more than a couple of months. But Mercy's brain couldn't tamp down how the rest of her body was reacting. A warm flush gradually replaced the icy jitters that had consumed her just minutes ago. She attempted a scowl but ended up quirking a half-smile at him.

"Very funny. You look like an idiot trying to play door. Shut it and come on in."

He did, then replaced his hands in his pockets and leaned back against it. His gaze on her was steady, unnerving. Mercy didn't exactly feel as though he was mentally undressing her, but more as though he was looking clear through into her mind. Even more unnerving. She looked away, fluffed a pillow she kept propped in the chair.

"I'm serious, Daniel. What made you stop?"

His slow, warm smile preceded his words. "I was right behind you, silly. Saw you pull out of the job site. Forget something?"

Mercy sniffed and felt the flush rise into her cheeks. "Yeah. My stupid phone."

"Any problems?"

Even as she shook her head, Mercy relived the wash of terror she'd felt down in that creepy basement. The water noises. The voice calling her name. She always did have a vivid imagination. She hid the shiver with a twist of her shoulders.

"No. The place is just way spookier at night."

Daniel nodded sagely, never taking his eyes off her. "What about that sandwich? The pub makes a great turkey club."

"I ate earlier with my son," she replied quickly, but then hesitated, blinking down at her now twisting fingers. Did she really want to sit here alone in this empty house until it was time to go pick up Reagan? After the night she'd had? She raised her eyes to his, took a deep breath, and huffed it out. "Normally, I don't socialize with the guys I work with after hours."

She said it, but knew it was a bold-faced lie. Hell, she'd been married to the foreman last time around.

"Aw, come on, Mercy. No hidden agendas here. I just don't like to eat alone. I was supposed to take my nephew out tonight, and he bailed on me." He took a step forward and held a hand out towards her. "I won't try to get into your pants, I promise."

A spontaneous laugh burst from Mercy as she sputtered, "Okay, okay, you got me on the honesty factor." She stood then, reaching forward to take his hand, dropping into her best serious mode. "Against my better judgment. Just this once."

A few minutes later Daniel was pulling out a chair for her at a window-side table in the Post Office Pub. Mercy had been there once before for lunch, but she'd sat with Reagan in the dining room. The bar area was large and glitzy, shiny wood everywhere with a half-dozen TVs mounted along the wall.

She glanced around and noticed the other women in the room. Cleaned up, dressed up, made up. Designer jeans and heels. Sparkly stuff swinging from their ears, jangling on their wrists. Jewelry, for God's sake.

I must look like a bag lady.

She snatched her grubby ball cap off her head. "Hey, um, I'm gonna just go and like, freshen up, okay?"

Daniel's smiling eyes never left her face. He said nothing, just nodded.

Dear God in heaven, she thought, looking at her pitiful reflection in the ladies' room mirror. What's happened to my sense of feminine pride? Mercy still wore her work clothes, baggy Carhartt overalls and a sensible polo, the long sleeves of which were now, she noted, horribly smudged with dust and grime. There was even a smudge on her cheek, which she frantically swiped away with a dampened paper towel.

Unwinding her hair would help, she thought. Well, maybe not. After twelve, humid hours wound into a French braid and stuffed under her safety helmet, she knew quite well her freed locks would burst out into a mass of dark, kinky waves. Crap.

At least with her hair down she would look like a girl.

She untwisted the braid, then ran dampened fingers through the mess. Holy hell, she looked like the Bride of Frankenstein. Her hair, the color of aged mahogany, was incredibly thick and had a soft natural wave of its own. But after the extended confinement, its mass exploded into alarming volume.

A young woman wearing a bright pink skirt suit clicked in through the ladies' room door, her Coach purse clutched under her arm. She started toward one of the empty stalls, then glanced back over at Mercy. Their eyes locked in the mirror.

"Scary, huh?" Mercy moaned. The woman's own hair, an expensive looking blonde-on-blonde highlighting, fell to her shoulders in obedience-trained waves that looked like they knew better than to move. The woman stopped, her mouth twisting into an appraising scowl. She lifted one hand to her hip.

"Honey, if I had hair like that I wouldn't spend a paycheck a month at the salon." She yanked her purse out from under her arm and opening it, extracted a plastic-tined brush, its handle folded neatly back on itself. Clicking it open, she handed it to Mercy. "Here," she said. "Comb through the mess and I'll be out in just a minute."

Mercy looked at the tool, then up at the door of the stall that closed behind her. She ran the brush under hot water and began working her way through her mass of rumpled waves.

By the time the blonde emerged, the water and the tines of the brush had tamed some of the chaos. As she washed her hands, the woman scrutinized Mercy in the mirror. Her brows knitted together. She dried her hands on a paper towel, replaced the brush in her purse and pulled out a small, tortoiseshell clip.

"Here," she said, handing it to Mercy. "Take some of those side pieces," she motioned, her hands hovering over her own hair as if afraid to touch it. "Twist them and clip them at the base of your neck." She grinned. "You'll look just like Maid Marion." Then she turned and before Mercy could say another word, pushed out the door.

Mercy rejoined Daniel at the table to discover he was hovering over a half-empty mug of beer. There was a full one sweating on her side of the table.

"I'm so sorry, Daniel. I'm kind of embarrassed. I went right from work to feeding my kid to driving him to school. I guess I forgot what I looked like."

Why am I apologizing to him? He's my coworker. And he just happened to stop by unannounced. Why should I care what I look like?

But Daniel's eyes just twinkled as he studied her face and hair, and she felt the flush rising again. "You're a might pretty thing under all that macho armor, aren't you?"

He had perfect white teeth. His hazel eyes sparked to silvery-gold when he smiled. And as he leaned across towards her on elbows resting on the table, she could feel something inside her coiling and heating up, like the element on an electric stove.

"I wasn't sure you drank beer, but I figured if you didn't I'd be having another one anyway," he said.

Wow, that voice. Why was he an electrician and not some late-night radio host? John Tesh's brother?

Mercy raised her eyebrows and kept her eyes trained to the mug in front of her. "I do," she said. "This is fine. Thanks."

Daniel ordered a sandwich and convinced Mercy to share an order of onion rings with him.

"They really do make the best, but an order could feed half the city." He took a long draw from his mug and wiped the froth off his mustache with his napkin. "Now tell me what's got you so rattled tonight."

Mercy met his eyes and wondered, why should you care? Why are you being so nice to me? And why does my heart rate skyrocket when I hold your gaze for more than ten seconds?

She blew out a breath. "Tired plus stress equals overactive imagination, I guess. I imagined I heard water sloshing around in those tubs down in the basement of Gravely Hall." She slanted him a look. "They really do look like hulking ghosts in the dark, you know."

Daniel nodded. "Why didn't you ask the security guard to go down there with you?"

"Ha! That nerdy kid? He wouldn't even set foot over the threshold, let alone go down in the basement. He looked so scared when I came back out I was afraid he might have peed his pants just waiting for me."

Daniel chuckled and shook his head. "Well you're a braver man than either of us going down there after dark all alone."

Mercy shot him a resentful scowl. "Gee, thanks. So much for looking like Maid Marion."

Daniel cocked his head. "Huh?"

"Never mind." Mercedes switched gears. "So, tell me about your nephew."

Daniel's gaze dropped to his mug. "Davin is sixteen. My younger sister's kid. Kim's raising him alone and I do what I can to help them out. There's no dad in the mix. I try to give the kid a male role model."

"That's nice, Daniel," Mercy said, feeling a warm fist clutch in her chest. Maybe he really was as nice a guy as he seemed.

Wait. Way too soon to be making that kind of assumption. I've been fooled by the nice guy act before.

Mercy squared her shoulders. "No kids of your own, then? Not married, I assume?"

Daniel shook his head. "No, no kids. Never married, either, although I came close once." He slid his gaze away. "My fiancé . . . she was killed in an accident. I was only twenty-three. Hit me pretty hard."

A stab of pity shot through Mercy and she was suddenly over-whelmed with the desire to wrap her arms around this big, kind man. "I'm so sorry, Daniel. I . . . I can't imagine."

The waitress arrived and interrupted them, setting down plates of food and a bottle of ketchup. "More beers?" she asked.

"I'll have one more," Daniel said. But Mercy shook her head, then glanced at her watch.

"I've got to pick up my son in less than an hour," she said quietly.

"How old is your son, Mercy?" Daniel asked.

"Almost eighteen. And I know exactly what you mean about the role model thing. I'm having the toughest time relating to him since we left Atlanta." Mercy hadn't meant to spill any of her personal life over into her working realm. But Daniel's story, the casual setting, the beer perhaps? A few bricks had come loose in her carefully constructed wall of defense.

Daniel finished chewing a bite of his sandwich, regarding her. Quietly he asked, "How long ago did you and his father split?"

"Two years this June. I tried to stay in the area, you know, so

Reagan could still see his father on a regular basis. Stay in his familiar environment, with all his friends. But it just wasn't working out. And Reagan has had, well . . . some issues."

Daniel reached forward and plucked an onion ring from the dwindling stack between them. "So, he was what, sixteen when you guys split up?"

Mercy nodded and sighed. "Just turned sixteen. He took it hard."

"I'm sorry to hear that. It's a tough age for a kid. The transition from boy-child to man-boy looks like the Grand Canyon to them."

Mercy looked off into the dark outside the window. "If I can just find a therapist who can help him cross that canyon," she said, almost more to herself than to Daniel. Then, blinking back behind her wall she turned to him. "So, you started telling me what they used those bathtubs for. In the basement. Finish."

Daniel's one eyebrow shot up and he huffed. "Psychotherapy, in those days, was a little different than it is today."

Mercy tipped her head. "I figured that, but why bathtubs in the basement?"

Daniel threw his napkin down on the empty plate and pushed it off to the side. "Back in the early twentieth century, mental health treatment was a bit crude, you might say. It was more like management. Water therapy meant they fairly boiled the poor bastards."

Mercy eyes widened. "You mean, like torture?"

"They didn't see it that way. And they didn't exactly scald them. If they got a patient who was violent, unmanageable, they'd chain them in a tub of really warm water, sometimes for days."

Horror brought Mercy's hand to her throat. "Why?"

Daniel drained his mug and clanked it down on the table top. "You know how relaxed you feel after a long, hot bath? Well, that building was for patients they called *excitable*. The hardest to handle. Thus, the bars on all the windows. Soaking them in hot water was one way to take the fight out of them."

.   .   .

THAT WORD STUCK in Mercy's head as she waited in her car in front of Corby High. *Excitable.* She wondered what word they would have used to describe Reagan's illness.

A minute or two past ten, Reagan filed out of the side door of the building with his other four classmates. He climbed in and didn't say a word as he buckled his seat belt.

"How'd it go?" Mercy asked as they pulled out onto Rt. 122.

"Great." Reagan spat out the word, filled with cynicism.

"Did something happen? What's the matter?" Mercy asked, glancing back and forth between the road and her son's face, dimly illuminated by the lights on the dash. Reagan kept his eyes straight ahead, his face rigid as stone.

"Nothing, Mom." He'd raised his voice, a little more than Mercy usually accepted from him. When she snapped her head in his direction, he continued, his words a bit softer. "It's just not my thing. I hate school. You know I've always hated school."

Mercy let the statement float in the stale air between them and said nothing for a few minutes. As they approached their driveway, she looked at him again.

"Look, Reagan. A high school diploma is not an option. You are going to earn one. Once that's done, I won't push you to do anything else."

He glared at her. "You can't. I'll be eighteen before I take the test. You can't even make me finish this GED crap." Then he stared straight ahead again. Into nothingness. His future, Mercy thought with a shiver.

"As long as you live under my roof, I can. And I will," she said flatly. "Your father called tonight. He wants you to call him," Mercy said as she pulled into their driveway and parked. Light spilled all over the porch, as Daniel had insisted on replacing the bulb for her before they'd left for the pub.

"Yeah, okay," Reagan mumbled as he climbed out and slammed the door. Mercy watched him drift away toward the house. Leaning her head on the steering wheel, she fought the lump in her throat and lost. The tears came, and she let them run down her cheeks unchecked.

This was turning out to be a harder transition for her too, she thought, remembering Daniel's words. For Mercy, adjusting from married to single mom, from loved partner to alone, was a wider leap than even the Grand Canyon. She lifted her head and gazed out toward the rising half-moon. Light years, she thought. That's how far my journey stretches out in front of me.

Somehow she made it through the week, but for Mercy, Friday wasn't a day to look forward to anymore. Instead of a family-fun weekend, Saturdays and Sundays had become an endless string of laundry loads, juggling the budget, and lonely hours. Reagan wouldn't have dared stayed stowed up in his room when Luke was around. But Mercy had a hard time dragging him down to eat even one meal with her.

Mercy silently unloaded her belt into her toolbox just before five that Friday, so lost in her own thoughts she didn't hear Daniel's footsteps behind her. She jumped when he touched her arm.

"I'm sorry. You must have left the job site already, huh?" he asked, tapping his temple.

Mercy smiled, embarrassed. "Guess so." Then she glanced over her shoulder at him. Over and up. Man, he was tall. "Any plans for the weekend?"

Daniel shook his head. "I usually like to do something with my sister and nephew. How about you?"

Mercy shook her head. "Just the usual. Laundry, grocery shopping. Fun, single mom stuff." She wondered if her grin looked more like the sneer she was trying to suppress.

Daniel crossed his arms and leaned on the door of the van. "I'd like to meet your son, you know. I was thinking maybe we could have lunch somewhere tomorrow. What do you think?"

Narrowing her eyes, Mercy regarded Daniel suspiciously. "I told you, Daniel. I don't like to socialize with the team. It's just not a good idea."

Especially since every time I get within an arm's reach of you, my brain melts and drains into a warm puddle in my belly.

"Look, I think it might be nice for your son to meet my nephew. They're a year or two apart in age, but we live close. They probably could both use a friend." He grinned at her, that Cheshire cat expression splitting his mustache in a way that made Mercy smile even though she tried not to.

She didn't know why she said yes. Reagan, however, didn't respond to the idea with any kind of enthusiasm.

"Why do I have to go eat lunch with some guy you work with? I'll be bored to death, Mom. No. I'm not going." Reagan was sprawled on his bed that night, his eyes never leaving the TV screen where some horrifically volatile video game was booming and crashing.

Frustrated, Mercy leaned over and pushed the power button on the monitor. Reagan came up off the bed with such speed, Mercy almost cringed. This is my son, she reminded herself. I am not afraid of him. I am the boss here.

"Look, Reagan. Daniel is a really nice guy who just wants to meet you and have lunch with us. His sister has a son about your age. They're going to join us. Can't you please humor me for one single hour of my weekend?"

Reagan had thrown his controller down on the bed next to him and was glaring at Mercy through narrowed eyes. "Is this guy hitting on you?" He almost hissed the words.

Mercy pinched two fingers to the bridge of her nose. "I work with him, Reagan. He's a nice man. His nephew doesn't really have a dad, and Daniel spends a lot of time with him—"

"What the hell do I care?" Reagan barked. He was actually curling his lip.

"I'm not asking you to care. I'm asking you to go to lunch with me and a man I work with. A friend, maybe. That's all."

Her self-imposed rule about not getting involved with a coworker be damned. Mercy found herself spending an extra-long time primping after her shower Saturday morning, in between running up and down the stairs to shift laundry from washer to dryer. She didn't want to admit it, even to herself. But she was excited.

WHEN DANIEL PULLED up into their driveway just before one o'clock, Reagan was shooting a basketball at the rusted hoop mounted on the outside of the shed flanking the house. Daniel got out, slammed the door of his crew-cab pickup, and leaned against the fender.

"Got a pretty good eye there, kid," he said after watching Reagan for a minute or two. A boy, Daniel noted, who had failed to even acknowledge his presence.

At his comment Reagan stopped, cradling the ball against his hip and turning. Daniel recognized the cocky, squinted glare of a slightly pissed-off teenage boy. He'd seen that look on his nephew. Hell, it wasn't all that long ago he'd been wearing that look himself.

"Hey," Reagan barked. Then, as if he suddenly remembered the manners-training that most obviously had been drilled into him, he stepped forward and offered his hand to Daniel.

"Hi. I'm Reagan."

"I'm Daniel Gallagher. I guess your mom has told you we work together."

Reagan nodded, gripping Daniel's hand and eyes just a little bit longer than he expected. "Reagan Donohue. Mom said you were taking us to lunch." Reagan dropped his head and muttered, "I hope she told you I'm a pretty hungry dog."

Chuckling, Daniel said, "I'd be disappointed if a guy your size and age didn't eat four times as much as an average human being." He held out his hands for the ball. "You mind?"

Daniel dribbled the ball a few times on the blacktop drive, watching Reagan begin to slowly shift between him and the hoop. The kid's a natural, he thought, watching the crouch and the bounce in his knees, movements that seemed almost reflexive. When Daniel faked left and turned to shoot, Reagan sprang into the air and snatched the ball in flight. He spun on his heel, aimed, and made the shot. It swished through the net.

"Shit," Daniel mumbled, even before Reagan could turn back towards him.

"You let that happen, dude," Reagan smirked.

"Yup. Uh-huh. Sure, I did."

The screen door squeaked open and Daniel turned to see Mercy standing on the top porch step. She might as well have punched him full in the gut.

She was wearing jeans, the soft faded denim hugging every line of her curves from the hip down. She'd topped an ivory, lacy blouse thing with an open, sky-blue sweater. Her hair flowed down over her shoulders in mahogany waves that Daniel was sure felt as soft as they looked.

Shit, he thought.

Mercy perched both fists on her hips. "I take it you two have met?"

"Yup." Both man and man-boy answered together, as though they'd rehearsed it. Mercy chuckled.

"Alright then, well, I'm starving. What's for lunch?"

CHAPTER 4

The questions kept rolling over again and again in Daniel's mind as he navigated his truck along the highway, headed for Newton. It had been almost a month since Mercy joined Progressive Electrical's team. How had he not noticed? How had he not become aware of this gorgeous creature he'd been working elbow-to-elbow with every day? The one hiding underneath the safety helmet and Carhartts?

The beautiful female who also today, he noted, smelled like a freshly baked vanilla cookie as she sat on the bench seat in the front with him. Her son, in the back seat, hadn't shut up the entire drive.

"Do you go to any of the games, Daniel? It's okay if I call you Daniel, right?" Reagan asked, leaning forward as far as the seat belt allowed.

"Sure, Reagan. And yeah, I've been to a few," Daniel replied. He glanced up in the rearview and saw the spark of interest in Reagan's eyes. "Maybe when the season starts up I'll get tickets, if your mom will let you go with me."

He saw Mercy shoot him a glance. "I'm sure Reagan would like that just fine," she muttered.

Wow, what was that scent she was wearing? It reminded him of the sugar cookies his mom used to bake around the holidays. But instead of his stomach rumbling, the chaos was emanating from just a little farther down.

Daniel cleared his throat, slid his gaze over to Mercy, and then back to the rearview. This was her son, he reminded himself. He could only imagine what they'd been through over the last few years. It must have been rough. He needed to tread very lightly.

"In the meantime, maybe we could shoot some hoops once in a while. I sure could use the exercise. You're taking night classes though, right?"

Reagan barked back almost before Daniel had finished his sentence. "Only two nights a week. Tuesday and Thursday."

"Duly noted. Maybe one night next week." He grabbed Mercy's gaze, who was watching him carefully, though not with exactly what he could call a glare. More of an amazed stare. "Would you like that?" Daniel spoke to the rearview.

"That would be awesome," the boy shot back.

Saturday traffic in Newton sucked. Daniel checked his watch repeatedly as they waited for the light in the center of town for the third time. "I'm sorry. I had no idea it'd be this bad," he apologized.

"Where are we going?" Reagan piped up. "Mom didn't feed me this morning, so I'm starved."

Mercy's head snapped around. "Don't play that card, Reagan. I'm more than willing to make you breakfast any morning you roll out of bed before eleven o'clock.

Daniel played ref. "This place is awesome. It's Italian mostly, but they have everything. From pizza to burgers to grinders. Bartucci's. Ever been there?" No verbal response, but Daniel caught the shake of heads both in the rearview and his peripheral vision. "You're gonna love it."

The place was bustling when they got there, and Daniel had to circle the parking lot twice before he found a spot big enough to fit his pickup. Surprisingly, the wait wasn't bad. Within fifteen minutes of walking through the door, the three were seated in a large booth against the back wall. Daniel announced, as though it were fact, his sister would most certainly be late.

The waitress, however, was interested in quick turnaround on her tables. Before they'd even settled in she popped up, pad in hand and pen poised, ready for drink orders.

"We're expecting more to join us," Daniel said, holding up two fingers to the waitress. At her undisguised scowl, he added, "They'll be along any minute now."

The server hadn't even returned with their drinks when Kim arrived, breathless, dressed in a too-tight and very low-cut sweater dress in a shade of pink Daniel had only ever seen lining the edges of a birthday cake. She was, however, alone.

"Sorry, bro," she said as she leaned in to kiss his cheek, giving him a way-too-close-up view of her very full breasts. "You know me," she added with an impish smile and shrug.

"It's okay, Sis. If you weren't late, I'd think something was wrong." He grinned, then ducked to glance behind her. "And . . .where's Davin?" he asked.

"Isn't coming." Her brightly painted lips twisted. "Said he had plans with a buddy of his this afternoon. Some video game tournament, or something."

Daniel's jaw tightened. He'd been afraid Davin would cop out. Again. Moving past his annoyance, he said, "Kim, I'd like you to meet Mercedes Donohue. She joined Conner's team a few weeks ago. And her son, Reagan. This is my baby sister, Kim Gallagher."

Bubbly as always, Kim flashed a huge grin and reached forward with both her hands to grasp Mercy's. "It's so nice to meet you. I just wish Davin would have come. He's probably about your age, Reagan. Davin will be seventeen this fall."

Daniel noticed Reagan had looked up at the mention of video games. "What games does your son play?" he asked.

Kim shrugged again, lifting both hands up along with her shoulders. "Couldn't tell you. But next time we get together, I'll hogtie him and insist he comes along."

His sister slid into the booth beside him and commenced her most practical talent—conversation.

Daniel knew that hiding in his sister's shadow was the least awkward way to manage what he was hoping would be a sorta kinda first date with Mercy. He couldn't explain why, but there was something about her he couldn't resist. Even with her femininity masked under work clothes and a safety helmet, his blood heated up just being in the same room with her. He hadn't felt that way about a woman in a long time.

Plus, he had to admit, he admired her. She'd moved from Atlanta to Massachusetts to start over with her boy and talked herself into the job with Conner's team. That was something he never expected to happen. Conner was a bit of a dinosaur and, equality be damned, still thought there were certain professions women should stay out of. Like, any kind of trade.

But Mercy had the license, the experience behind her, and she knew the lingo. She dug in like a trooper from the first day. He'd heard her say she'd been born in New England, but he couldn't help thinking the transition had been hard for her. Pulling up stakes must have been difficult after so many years in someplace so different, both culturally and weather-wise, from Massachusetts.

Kim managed to get more information out of Mercy in an hour's lunch than Daniel had in several weeks of working beside her. It was easy, though, to see how the two women were as different as day and night. All he knew was Mercy was divorced, and that her kid needed some kind of therapy.

"So, just you and Reagan moved back to Mass?" Kim asked.

Mercy nodded. "Yup. This is where I was born. At Mass General in Boston. I grew up here. My parents decided to move to Atlanta when I was fifteen."

Kim raised an eyebrow. "No other folks here?" she asked, swirling the ice in her diet cola with a straw.

Mercy sighed and cut her eyes to the side. "I was adopted. My new family was . . . older. They're both gone now."

July 14, 1970

Boston, Massachusetts

Breanna and Devlin Doherty set down their suitcases just inside the door of their second-floor apartment in Old Colony, South Boston. The small space was dimly lit, cramped and meagerly furnished, but it would have to do. They'd come with little more than the clothes on their backs, lucky to have been able to afford two tickets to America.

Breanna strode across the small living room to peer out of the single, dingy window. The view was uninspiring, depressing even. It overlooked a narrow alleyway between the closely packed brick buildings that defined the housing development. Across the way, she noticed, the window facing theirs had been dressed with a pretty lace curtain.

Little things, Breanna thought. I can do the same. In time, I can fix up this little flat and make it feel like home.

"It isn'a bad, now is it, Bree? I mean, it's really the best we can afford right now until—"

She spun on her heel, rushing back to him. Putting a finger to his lips, she whispered, "It's fine. Even if it's not so grand as our cottage in Kilkeel. To be sure, there'll be none of The Troubles to contend with here."

Breanna shuddered as she remembered the terror they'd left behind them. It hadn't been safe to go into the village alone anymore, especially after dark. Too much turmoil and tempers and fighting. All she wanted, she thought, was a chance for a peaceful life with her beloved husband. And their unborn child.

But she couldn't tell Devlin about the baby just yet. Not until they'd settled in to this, their new home in a new land. Not until he'd gotten his feet under him at his job down at the docks. Not until his worries subsided some.

Besides, it was early times yet. She could lose the child like she had the first. The last thing Breanna wanted to do was to heap any more worry on her husband's head.

Breanna knew, love him though she did, what happened when worries mounted and times got tough. Her husband was a good man, a hard worker, and faithful as an old hound. But common sense be damned, Devlin did like the drink.

IT SEEMED to Daniel as though the clattering of glasses and silverware in the restaurant had suddenly kicked up a notch. Or was it just the silence hanging over their table? He watched as Mercy crossed her arms, her gaze wandering out the window. He cleared his throat.

"How about Reagan's dad? He still in Atlanta?" Kim fiddled with the silverware as she spoke. Never one to keep still, Daniel thought.

"He is." Mercy stiffened, and Daniel could see her shutting down again. "We split. About two years ago."

Ouch. Okay, Kim, let's steer this conversation in a lighter direction, Daniel thought.

"Oh, hon, I'm so sorry." Kim reached over and patted Mercy's arm. "But you have a good job here, so it looks like you're doing well at starting over." She turned to Reagan. "And how about you, my man? Graduated school yet?"

Reagan shifted in his seat and looked away. "Soon."

The waitress returned to their table again, pad in hand and pen poised. Thank God, Daniel thought.

"Ready to order?"

They did, although Daniel's usual healthy appetite seemed to have evaporated. Even with his chatterbox sister sitting across the table, huge chunks of silence still hung in the air like a damp mist. Until Kim took charge of the conversation.

Okay, so maybe this wasn't such a good idea after all. Without Davin there, talk as they ate drifted into a definitely feminine direction. Kim chattered on about her salon, which was located in a fairly upscale strip mall in Westborough. She invited Mercy to come by when she was ready for her next styling, on the house.

"We do manis and pedis too," Kim chirped. "My makeup artist, Loraine, is amazing."

Daniel watched Mercy glance down at her grubby workman's hands and discreetly tuck them under the table. "With the kind of work I do, I can't really spend a lot of time on stuff like that," she murmured.

"Oh, and we have a psychic come in, two evenings a month. She does tarot cards, palm readings, that kind of stuff. I don't particularly believe in the paranormal, but my clients love it."

Mercy smirked. "I don't believe in it either."

An awkward silence after Daniel saw Reagan's eyeroll told him it was time to change the course of the discussion.

"So hey, did Davin have a good time at the game the other night?" Daniel interrupted. "I know the kid can put away some hot dogs. I lost count after his third one."

Reagan looked up from his double bacon cheeseburger. "There's nothing like a stadium hot dog. My dad and I used to get 'em at the Hawks' games all the time."

Uh-oh. Another touchy subject. Navigating this conversation was like walking through a minefield, Daniel thought.

He cleared his throat. "I'll bet you really miss him. It won't be the Hawks, but as soon as the season starts, I'll take you with us. You can let me know how our team compares." Reagan's quick smile was a joy to see. "As well as the hot dogs."

By the time lunch was over, Kim had managed to get Davin on the phone, actually handing the device to Reagan and introducing them, virtually. Daniel shook his head. He was never very outgoing when it came to social situations, and it was little wonder. He was sure in his family all those genes had gone to his younger sister.

Kim had also convinced Mercy to make that appointment for a free trim and style. Mercy had accepted with a small, shy smile. Daniel figured the two women didn't have a whole lot in common, but perhaps at least they would become casual friends. When they parted in the parking lot, he was not at all surprised when Kim wrapped both Mercy—and Reagan—in huge hugs. That was just her way. He was even more surprised, and pleased, that neither had refused her gesture.

As they headed back to Mercy's house he asked, "So what are your plans for the rest of the day?"

She quickly folded her arms across her chest.

"Got a bunch of laundry still. And Monday is the first of the month. Might as well get out the old checkbook and divvy up my bank account between the vultures."

Daniel glanced over, carefully measuring his next words. "Are you doing okay? Since the move, I mean."

The look that Mercy shot him clearly said *back off*. There I go showing off my foot-in-mouth capabilities.

"I just meant, well, I don't know how the salaries up here compare with down south. I know living expenses are higher."

Mercy shifted in her seat and turned just a bit more away from him. Daniel was no body language expert, but her message was coming through loud and clear.

"I can't deny that. But we're okay. And my ex sends some money. Got real lucky renting the little house."

Perhaps, at least budget-wise, she had. The tiny, two-story Victorian sat flanking a bend along Route 30. Too close to the road, Daniel thought, and sandwiched behind by the commuter rail tracks. But that probably made it a renter's deal of a lifetime.

"Do the trains bother you much?" he asked.

49

Mercy tipped her head and quirked her lips. "Takes some getting used to."

Reagan barked from the back seat, "Dude! The first week I almost fell out of bed when the early train went by. Not only does the rumbling come right through the walls, but the whistle scared the crap out of me."

They all got out and Daniel could see Mercy had no intention of inviting him in. Her arms were wrapped across her chest as she took a step back toward the porch. "It was really great of you to take us to lunch, Daniel. I enjoyed meeting your sister." She was avoiding his eyes, her words spilling out quicker than they had all day. She glanced over her shoulder toward her son. "Bring down the rest of your laundry, Reagan. Please."

The kid stepped forward to shake Daniel's hand without prompting. Her knitted brows seemed at odds with the pride Daniel saw in Mercy's eyes.

"Real nice to meet you, man," Reagan said.

"Same here," Daniel replied. "Maybe Wednesday. I'll come by, we'll shoot a little one on one."

Daniel spent the entire drive back home berating himself. Why had I even bothered, he wondered. Mercy made it pretty obvious, right from the start, that she was not interested in a relationship. He worked with her, for Christ's sake. What kind of trouble was he getting himself into by even considering a relationship with a coworker?

But no matter how hard he tried to concentrate on the Red Sox game that night on ESPN, he somehow couldn't help the images that kept floating back into his brain. Her long flowing mane of chestnut hair. Those clear, pale eyes that said more to him than she ever did with words. There was a softness about her, wasn't there? Or do I just imagine there is?

And yet he saw the fire in those eyes, an independent determination to do things her own way. Daniel shook his head. He'd made the mistake of falling for a woman like that once before. And considering he worked with her, he would be foolish—emotionally suicidal—to do the same thing again.

THE WORK in Gravely Hall progressed at a snail's pace, at least compared to the other jobs Daniel had worked on since joining Conner's team. Deconstruction took twice as long as installation of new, same as in any phase of construction. People asked him all the time why remodeling cost more than building from scratch. This project, he thought, was the perfect example.

He and Mercy had already been working in the basement for almost a week. Although the demolition team had promised to remove them by now, the bathtubs remained. It was a pain to work around them, but Daniel volunteered to do the wiring on that side of the wall since he knew the tubs spooked Mercy. Besides, he was taller than she was. Bending over the tubs was no problem for him. Mercy would have been perching on a ladder or step stool between each one, reaching around them to run the new conduit and receptacle boxes. Basement level meant the boxes had to be at least four feet off the floor.

Although he'd never been one to chat much while he worked, Daniel had to admit, the basement was an eerie place to work in silence. The buzzy blaring of a small portable radio running on battery power was just plain annoying. Sports talk, like he'd usually share with Conner and Jacob, didn't seem appropriate. Mercy's son, he knew, was a topic she might be willing to talk about.

"I really enjoyed meeting Reagan, Mercy. He seems like a good kid. Certainly a little tamer than Kim's boy." Daniel shot her a glance as he rolled his eyes.

Mercy sighed. "He is a good kid. Always has been. He's just been out of sorts since the divorce. Came at a bad time for him. He and his dad were pretty close." She was silent for a beat, the sound of her electric screwdriver echoing as she worked on one of the last outlets. "Kim's boy is a hellion, huh?"

Daniel chuckled and shook his head. "Guess I shouldn't be surprised, as wild as Kim is. He's hanging around with some trouble-makers this last year in school, though. I've been worried about him. I finally convinced Kim to take him to see a good friend of mine. He's a therapist. I think it's helped him some."

Mercy stopped what she was doing and turned toward him. "A therapist, huh? I've been trying to get Reagan with a therapist he likes since we got here. What's your friend's name?"

"Ian McGuire. His office is right on the square in Corby. Maybe you should give him a call. He does well with teenagers. I mean, really *gets* them."

At this Daniel heard the creak of Mercy's ladder, and she turned to face him. She looked adorable, a strand of her dark hair clinging wet to her sweaty cheek. Her overalls were covered with concrete dust, and a dark grey smudge swept across one cheek.

Another cobweb encounter, he thought, and he couldn't help but smile. Mercy's frantic swatting always left the telltale evidence plain on her soft-looking skin.

She nodded, thinking. "I might just do that. He's been so distant, so angry since we moved here. Maybe this doctor will be able to get through to him."

THAT AFTERNOON, Conner called a meeting as the team packed up their tools. Jacob stood beside Daniel, and Mercy folded her arms and leaned against the rear door of the van.

"How far along are you two down in the basement?" He directed his question to Daniel.

"We're about done. Conduit's all run, boxes hung. Just need a cleanup and an inspector's permission to let us screw everything down tight."

Conner nodded. "Third floor's 'bout done too. I'd like to get started down in that tunnel next."

"Did we ever find out why they had those tunnels, Conner?" Mercy asked, lifting her boot up onto the bumper of the van to retie her shoelace.

"Couple o'reasons. First, transportation between the buildings, in bad weather or when they were moving one of the feisty ones." He sent a stream of tobacco juice into the gravel next to the rear tire. "And you saw them chains, that bench. I guess you could call it their 'time-out' room."

Mercy shuddered. "Alrighty then." When she glanced up she saw both Jacob and Conner glaring at her with their strangely matching, cool blue eyes narrowed.

"You're not goin' to get all jumpy on us down there, are you Mercy May?" Conner's tone was half-jesting, half-threatening. He pulled off his cap and scratched his balding head with dust-covered fingers. "You and I both know the most dangerous working partner, in our field, is a jumpy one."

Mercy scoffed. "Conner, this isn't my first pony ride," she snapped, unable to stifle the anger. "You should know that by now, no?"

He held her gaze a long moment, and then turned away, his heel crunching in the gravel. "We'll start down there tomorrow then."

As Mercy climbed out of the van in her driveway, she nodded to the men, deliberately avoiding Daniel's gaze. Today was Wednesday. Hadn't he told Reagan he was coming by to "shoot some hoops" tonight? He hadn't said a word about it all day. Shouldn't be surprised, Mercy thought. She could blow it off. She knew Reagan wouldn't.

She was dead on. The very first words out of Reagan's mouth when she came through the kitchen door were, "What time is Daniel coming over?"

Mercy headed straight for the stairs, pulling the band out of her braided hair. "I don't know, Reagan. He didn't mention it to me today. He might have forgotten." She paused before she reached the landing and turned. "Could you please start the grill for me, son? I'm gonna grill those chops tonight."

Nothing, absolutely nothing felt as good as a shower after working in that dirt and grime all day. She stood under the hot water an extra-long time, knowing full well she'd regret it when the electric bill came. She was rinsing the last of the conditioner out of her hair when she heard the knock on her bathroom door.

"What is it, Reagan?"

"Daniel's here. Do you still want me to start the grill?"

Mercy turned off the spray and grabbed a towel. She couldn't help but smile. So, he'd remembered after all. "No, hold off for now. We'll eat after you guys get done with your one-on-one."

She came trotting down the stairs after pulling on a pair of white sweatpants and a faded Atlanta Braves tee shirt. She'd left her hair soaking wet, reveling in the cool trickle down her neck. Even though it was early evening, the air was still and warm. It was starting to feel like summer, she thought.

She padded barefoot into the kitchen, a cozy but incredibly serviceable space Mercy was rapidly becoming very fond of. The house, although it had been built almost a hundred years ago, had been completely updated. Quartz countertops sparkled beneath warm pine cabinets and atop the center island. It was Mercy's favorite spot to enjoy her first cup of coffee as the morning's earliest, purest rays spilled over her through the east-facing window above the sink.

Mercy pulled the chops out, rinsed and patted them dry, and sprinkled them with Cajun seasoning. As she slid them back into the sparsely stocked fridge, she heard the thumping of the basketball in the driveway. Teasing male banter and laughter floated through the open window.

Quick tears filled Mercy's eyes as her throat tightened around a memory. Reagan had been so close with his father, and they'd often played ball in the driveway while she fixed dinner. It was a routine she'd taken for granted, the security in the comforting sound of her man and her boy laughing together. She doubted she'd ever feel that secure again.

But it sure was nice to hear Reagan having a good time. He was young, and strong. And Daniel was good with him, probably from having to help raise his sister's boy.

Mercy poured herself a glass of iced tea and headed for the porch. The guys looked up when the screen door slammed.

"This boy of yours is kicking my butt, Mercedes," Daniel called out, a little breathless. "And I am finding out how considerably out of shape I am." He grinned, a flash of perfect white teeth shooting straight into her gut.

He certainly didn't look out of shape to her. His black sleeveless jersey showcased nicely sculpted biceps and revealed just a tuft of curly, tawny chest hair above the neckline. His matching shorts fit loosely around narrow hips, and his long legs were banded with hard, corded muscle.

Mercy held the sweating glass of tea to her temple. She was all for Daniel developing a relationship with Reagan, to help him out of his shell and get him back on the right track. But she needed to keep her distance. And if she wanted to stay in control of her life in this new situation, she was going to have to keep the bad-girl thoughts at bay.

She had the feeling the task might be more difficult than she'd anticipated.

CHAPTER 5

*G*etting Reagan introduced to Daniel, although he'd had fought it so hard, had really been a good move. Since lunch that day, and then their hour thumping a basketball on Wednesday, Reagan seemed more congenial than Mercy had seen him in months.

It frightened her how distant he'd become, especially after a phone conversation with his father. Mercy knew Reagan had idolized Luke, and how devastated he'd been when the truth about what his father had been doing came to light. Now, he was confused, still wanting to love and respect a man who had betrayed both him and his mother as horribly as he did.

Getting Reagan to talk it out with a therapist, though, had been an uphill battle. She'd taken him to two so far, and neither had been able to do anything except make him angrier and more distant. At times, Mercy felt as though her son was rapidly spiraling out of her reach.

When Reagan heard, though, that Dr. Ian McGuire was a personal friend of Daniel's, he perked up.

"Really? Well, he might be a cool dude, then. Yeah, Mom, I'll go talk to him."

The problem was, Mercy soon discovered, that Dr. McGuire's office wasn't open Saturdays or evenings. Mercy was on the clock with the team until five. She finally secured an appointment for him, the last of the day at 4:30 that following Thursday. She'd have to leave work early. And if Reagan and Dr. McGuire hit it off, that would mean leaving work early *every* Thursday.

"I have no problem helping you out on this, Mercy," Conner said, "but we all work a solid forty here. I'll have to dock you, otherwise it's not fair to the rest of the team."

Mercy struck a bargain with Conner, giving up her one-hour lunch break on Thursdays. That first day, she drove her own car to the job site so she could leave early. She'd told Reagan to be ready to go by four-fifteen.

It got worse for Mercy once they moved to re-wiring the tunnel. Not only did that part of this job kick up her claustrophobia, but her imagination as well.

Weather wise, the tunnel wasn't such a bad place to be. Summer had officially arrived in New England, and Thursday morning dawned sunny and humid. The tunnel's thick block walls acted like an old-time root cellar. Although damp, the temperature stayed a cool sixty-eight degrees. Mercy was glad, because setting conduit wasn't easy. The metal tubing was made of aluminum, so although it wasn't very heavy, it was unwieldy. Its helical coil construction gave the stuff a mind of its own.

When the guys loaded into the van around noon or so to head for Burger King or Subway, Mercy stayed and worked on. The agreement was, for safety's sake, she handled no live connections while they were gone—although as they'd discovered that first day on the job, determining what was completely safe on this job was difficult at best.

Mercy had just reached the bottom of the stairway into the tunnel when she heard the roar of the work van, then the engine fading away. She was startled to hear Daniel's voice.

"I'm not going with the boys, Mercy." She turned to find Daniel at the top of the stairs. "I brought a sandwich. I'm gonna eat and take a nap under that big tree out behind the building."

Mercy nodded but said nothing. She wondered if Daniel's staying behind had anything to do with worrying about her working alone. Had Conner put him on babysitting patrol? The boss was obviously worried about Mercy being skittish in the tunnel. Or maybe it was all Daniel's idea. She wasn't sure whether to be flattered or annoyed.

"If you need me, just holler. Really loud." Daniel's smile lit up his whole face, his row of perfectly white teeth peeking through his beard. She decided to bypass both flattery and annoyance and go with relieved.

Try as she might to deny it, the tunnels really did creep her out.

"Okay," she called back. Then she hiked the roll of conduit up over her shoulder and headed down toward the south end of the tunnel.

This line was to replace the tarnished old steel snakes they'd yanked off the stone walls a few days ago. This was the trail of the "hidden power source" that had almost fried Mercy on their first day. Discussion had gone back and forth between Conner and the architects for several days on the matter, but in the end it was decided to retain the separate line running directly from the Security Building to the new Campus Center. Eventually, this trunk would be linked to the school's gigantic generator. It would carry in emergency power.

This part of the subterranean passageway actually broke above the surface of the ground for a few yards about halfway down to the next building beyond Gravely Hall. A row of ancient glass block lined the outer wall just below the ceiling. The thick and irregular greenish glass allowed filtered light to infuse the blackness, but didn't provide nearly enough light to work in. Mercy's battery-powered lantern took up the slack.

Mercy began connecting metal hangers for the conduit high on the wall. The going was slow, since she had to drill into the mortar between the stones and set lags to hold the screws. Then came the tricky part—wrestling the unwieldy metal tubing off its spool and convincing it to hold still while she set the fasteners around it.

The squeal of her portable screwdriver pulsated through the tunnel with rhythmic regularity. It was hard work, and every twenty feet or so, she paused to stretch out. She stepped down off the stool and twisted at the waist, the leather of her belt creaking as she swiveled from one side to the other.

She heard the clank of metal and assumed she'd dropped a tool. The sound echoed eerily all around her. Mercy checked the slots on her leather belt, but nothing was missing. Then she turned to check the floor behind her. That's when a flash of movement caught her eye.

The north end of the tunnel was shrouded in darkness, since it gradually crept deeper and deeper under the ground as it headed north toward Building 21. The window blocks ended just ten feet beyond where Mercy stood. She blinked, then shoved her lantern to one side with her booted foot and squinted into the darkness.

"Daniel?" she called. "What'd you do, swallow your sandwich whole?"

Silence. Mercy blinked into the clouded air, watching dust motes glow putrid green as they floated past the mildewed glass blocks. But down beyond where the light could reach, she saw—or more like *sensed*—movement. Squinting, she saw a pale shape in the distance.

A disturbingly human-like shape.

A sense of dread draped over her like a cold blanket, and for a moment, she froze. Was she letting her imagination spook her again? She had to stop this. She was a sensible, logical woman, not a timid teenage girl.

Mercy clutched her drill and grabbed the handle of the lantern. Staring into the shadowy blackness, she called, "Who's there?" though she couldn't quite suppress the quiver in her voice. "Security? Conner?"

With her heart slamming double-time against her ribs, Mercy held the lantern higher, but the dusty darkness swallowed the light just feet in front of her. She stared at the pale shape, and for long seconds, it didn't move.

It's probably just a ladder, she thought, releasing a whoosh of relief. One draped with a drop cloth or something else the guys had carried down here. She shook her head and chuckled to herself and was just about to turn back to her work when the figure moved.

It drifted, silently, from one wall of the tunnel to the other. She heard no footsteps, no crunching of boot on broken concrete. What she did hear sent chills skittering down Mercy's back—the sound of metal against stone, like something was being dragged.

It had to be Daniel, come back from lunch early. "Daniel, if this is some kind of joke I'm not finding it very funny."

Mercy hadn't heard him come down the stairs, and he'd been at lunch barely twenty minutes. Would he be so cruel as to try to scare her? Certainly not. She was being ridiculous. There was nothing down here that could hurt her. And Daniel was still here, stretched out under the big maple behind the building. Just a few feet on the other side of those mold-covered glass blocks.

If she screamed, would he hear her? And wouldn't this be exactly the weakness, the skittishness, that Conner was waiting for Mercy to exhibit?

No, she had to go down there and defy her ridiculous imagination. Face this absurd phobia by herself.

Her hand quaked so badly her lantern sent dizzying waves of light flashing on the wall and ceiling, but she held it high as she moved down the tunnel. She had her drill pointed like a gun straight out ahead of her.

Don't get scared. Get mad, she told herself, over and over again.

Taking long, bold steps, she headed straight toward the shape, her boots crunching on scattered fragments of broken concrete. The sound was solid, real, and reassured her. She passed the foot of the stairway, where the pile of debris was deeper. The roll of conduit she'd left there blocked her path. Rather than set down her lantern and electric drill to move it, she lifted a foot to step over.

But as her foot landed, Mercy's heel slid forward on the inches-thick accumulation of broken stone, skidding as though riding an avalanche. She pushed off of her back foot, struggling to avoid landing open-crotched on top of the metal coil. Momentum thrust her forward, and when she managed to bring both feet to the other side, she'd lost her balance and stumbled sideways. The lantern swung and she pitched sharply, her left elbow smacking against the rock wall, hard.

Pain shot up her arm, all the way into her jaw. Her screwdriver went tumbling down ahead of her. The lantern hit the floor, fell on its side, and went out.

"Damn it," she screamed, then sucked in a breath against the sharp pain searing her arm from elbow to shoulder. Almost immediately the sound came again, the distinctive clinking of heavy metal, like chain links, clanking against one another.

"Who the hell is there?" she roared.

Even without the lantern's glow, she could still make out a pale form. About ten feet from her, it was misty and seemed to glow and fade, changing shape. Mercy squinted, unsure if her eyes and imagination were taking her on a field trip, or if the pain in her arm was making her delirious. The pale figure was large, and for a second, its outline glowed brighter, making it appear even more human in form.

Mercy reached down with her good arm and grabbed the drill. Holding the injured arm close to her middle, she held her breath and waited. Without her lantern, there was no way she was venturing down the tunnel any farther. Not only would that be scary as hell, but it was dangerous.

Within seconds the figure faded into the blackness without making a sound.

Mercy stood rigid, her shoulders quaking from the fear, the damp chill, and the pain. She swiped angrily at the tears streaming down her face. She hadn't realized she'd been crying. Probably all this damned dust, she thought. The stairwell—the only way out—was several yards behind her, but she wasn't about to turn her back on whatever lurked down the end of the tunnel. One boot at a time, she slowly stepped backwards. One step, then two, then a half-dozen more, until she felt the stir of air tickle her neck. The stairwell must be right behind her.

"What the hell are you doing down there?" Daniel's voice boomed, and Mercy screeched and spun around. In three strides, he was down the steps and had Mercy by the shoulders. "What's wrong? What happened?"

His grip on her upper arm caused the pain to peak unbearably, and she whimpered, her knees wobbling. A wave of nausea twisted her stomach, and her mouth felt sour.

Please, God, please don't let me vomit all over his boots. Or worse yet, pass out.

"What happened, Mercy?" Daniel's voice was softer, and he eased his grip but pushed her gently until her back rested against the cool stone wall. "Are you hurt?"

Mercy swallowed hard, forcing back the nausea, and then dragged in a shaky breath. "I'm sorry, I'm sorry, you just startled me, that's all." She started waving the drill around toward the north end of the tunnel. "I heard something. An . . . an animal, or something. I was headed down there to investigate and I slipped." Her face crumpled, and she doubled over against the pain. "I whacked my elbow pretty hard," she moaned, her resolve shattering. She let out a garbled sob.

A HALF HOUR later and in the face of her adamant protests, Conner sent Daniel with Mercy to the local emergency clinic to have her arm x-rayed.

"I pay a pretty penny for liability, Mercy. May as well get some use of it," Conner said. "Jacob and me, we'll scour that tunnel real good, make sure there's nobody—or nothin'—came creeping in there from the north end. Don't you worry about anything."

Mercy was shaken and hurting and just plain pissed off at herself. She wouldn't respond to Daniel in more than one or two clipped words as she dug her car keys out of her purse. She tossed them in his direction with more force than was really necessary. Daniel snatched them out of the air, and then reached out to put one arm around her good shoulder, which she quickly shrugged off. He opened the passenger side door and she plopped down into the seat without a word.

Once they were out on Route 30 she turned to him and snapped, "This is ridiculous, and you know it." Then she slammed her back against the seat and glared straight ahead for the entire ten minutes it took for them to reach the Emergency Clinic in downtown Corby.

Fortunately, it was a slow afternoon at the clinic. The paperwork took more time than the actual radiograph and exam.

"There's no fracture," a tall, white-coated young man reported, speaking more to the films stuck up on the glow-board than to Mercy. "But you've got a hell of a bone bruise."

She groaned. "Does that mean a cast?" she asked.

The doctor shook his head. "No, there's no displacement. We'll immobilize the joint with a brace, and I'd advise you ice it every couple hours for the next two days. We'll fit you with a sling."

"How long will I be out of commission?" she asked.

"If you rest your arm, and don't try to do more than you should, you'll be back at work within a few weeks. Maybe three," the doctor replied as he typed furiously on a keyboard. "They'll give you a full set of instructions when you check out. And they'll set you up with an orthopedic doctor for a follow-up." He paused and turned, peering at Mercy over the tops of wire-rimmed glasses. "I suppose you'll also need a work release form." It wasn't a question, and Mercy nodded miserably.

The form might well double as an involuntary resignation. This would probably mean the end of her job. She certainly hadn't been with Conner's team long enough to have earned sick time. He'd balked about letting her leave early for Reagan's appointments. He certainly wouldn't be happy about her taking two, possibly three weeks off, even if the injury did happen on the job.

Daniel was waiting for her in the lobby and rose to his full six-plus feet when she came around the corner. He held his cap against his chest as he studied her, his gaze flashing from her face to her sling and back. His tawny, wavy hair was sticking out over his ears in awkward, hat-head angles, giving him the look of a little boy. And those eyes, those compelling hazel eyes, were filled with such concern, Mercy knew she couldn't look at him for long, or she'd start crying all over again.

"Uh oh," he said quietly. "Broke, huh?"

She shook her head. "Might as well be, though," Mercy mumbled.

"How long will you be out of commission?" he asked as they left the clinic and headed to Mercy's car.

"Long enough to where Conner will probably end my employment," she said.

"He won't do that, Mercy. He can't. This happened on the job. Workman's comp would go nuts if he laid you off due to an injury."

"No, but he'll find some other reason once I'm back," Mercy said miserably. She was fumbling to latch her seat belt, almost impossible around the bulky bandage and sling.

"Need help?" Daniel asked as he slid behind the wheel.

"No. I got it," she snapped. She'd made a complete fool of herself not once, but twice since she started with this new team. The last thing she needed was to play damsel in distress.

ON THE WAY back to the job site, Daniel probed Mercy to open up about what had happened in the tunnel. "Was it an animal, you think? I know there's a bunch of raccoons living out behind that building across the street. I've seen them rustling around early in the morning when we unload."

"Not unless this one is about six feet tall and wears ankle chains," Mercy said. "I heard this thing more than saw it, Daniel. I could hear it dragging something, something metal. And I got to within fifteen feet of it. It was big. And pale. Almost like, glowing fog or something."

Mercy realized the minute she finished her description how ridiculous she must sound. The last thing she wanted to be labeled was a skittish woman. Especially in her line of work. She dropped her head forward and pinched the bridge of her nose between two fingers.

"Look," she continued, "I got spooked the other night down in the basement when I went back for my cell phone. I mean, the security guy wouldn't even step across the threshold after me. I'm sure today, the noise I heard was just an echo from conduit—you know how sometimes the stuff kinks and pops back on its own, making an eerie sound."

But she'd seen *something*. The pale shape. The figure that drifted from one side of the tunnel to the other. Mercy twisted her shoulders to throw off the chill. She looked over at Daniel. "You think my job is toast, don't you?"

Daniel pulled Mercy's car back into the spot behind the work van and handed her the keys. Then he locked eyes with her.

"No, Mercy, I don't think so at all. You've earned Conner's respect for your experience already, even though you've only been with us for a few weeks. He knows you're under a lot of pressure. He knows you're worried about your son. He's got a couple of kids too, you know. They're grown now, but still. He's been there."

Reagan. Mercy suddenly remembered it *was* Thursday. Reagan's first appointment with Dr. McGuire.

"Damn," she muttered. "What time is it, Daniel? Reagan's got to be at the therapist's at 4:30."

He fished a pocket watch out of his overalls and glanced down at it. "A little before four. You've got time. His office is right in town."

Daniel followed her down the steps to the tunnel where they could hear Conner and Jacob busy with power tools. Dust floated thick in the air in the narrow space, and the stronger bands of afternoon sun oozing through the glass windows tinted the fog puke green. Jacob appeared from the end of the tunnel where Mercy had been working, toting his lantern on the same side as the loop of conduit slung over his shoulder.

"Well, is it broke?" he asked.

"Nope. Bad bone bruise," Mercy replied. "Where's Conner?"

"Ouch," Jacob said with a grimace. He tipped his chin toward Conner who was slowly appearing out of the eerie dust cloud, lantern in hand.

"What's the verdict, Merce?" Conner asked.

She handed the doctor's note to her boss without saying anything and waited as he read it. When he looked up she asked, "I'm finished, huh?"

"Hell, no," he said, a grin revealing a row of crooked, yellow teeth. "What kind of a guy do you think I am, Mercy May?"

"I don't expect sick pay, but will I have a job when I get back in a few weeks?" Mercy asked.

Conner studied her, his pale blue eyes watery from the dust. He swiped a hand down his face and then riveted her with a look with brows drawn together, as though he were genuinely concerned. Maybe he was. Maybe she would get lucky.

"Listen," he began, folding the note up and shoving it his breast pocket, "you obviously can't work on the site. At least not until you're healed up. But nothing says you can't fill in someplace else. In the office, maybe."

Mercy groaned. "Conner, I can't even type. Especially with one hand."

Besides, I'm no damned secretary. I'm an electrician. A professional tradesman, just like you.

Fortunately, Conner interrupted her irritated thoughts. "We can talk about this tomorrow." He shifted around and peered down into the tunnel. "And listen, Jacob and me checked out that end, and it's sealed up tight. I doubt anything could have gotten in, not even a rat." He turned and started walking, holding up his lantern. "But, were you doing some measuring or anything?" Conner's one eyebrow lifted and his voice trailed off.

"No, why?" Mercy asked.

"There's some numbers been scratched on the wall down that way. Hadn't noticed them before. Looks to be fresh chalk." Conner's eyes strayed to where Mercy's tool belt lay on the bottom step. She'd unbuckled it and dropped it there before she'd left for the clinic. "And I notice your chalk plug's missing from your belt."

"That's odd," she said, tilting her head. Had she dropped it? "I didn't use the chalk at all today. What kind of numbers?" Mercy tilted her head and took a step in Conner's direction. "Show me."

The group followed Conner back down toward the north end, Jacob flicking on a second lantern to help illuminate the space. The hundred feet or so of tunnel very gradually descended, and the further they went the more choking the dusty dampness became. About thirty feet down, Conner stopped abruptly, raising his light and flashing it back and forth along the wall. It took him a minute or two, but then he stopped.

"Here," he pointed one finger. "And all along here too."

The numbers were scratched in white chalk, just like the kind the team used to mark out measurements on sheetrock or wood. In places, the trail of the white dust cut through an ancient covering of moss that thinly patched the stone in irregular shapes. The marks did, in fact, appear fresh, the white lines not yet having had time to absorb the dampness of the stone. The chalk was not at all discolored along its edges.

The number was scratched in shakily inscribed numerals about five to six feet off the floor, not more than a foot under the ceiling. In places, smaller and in more irregular, misshapen numerals, the number appeared to have been written by a child. The same number was scrawled dozens of times, at odd slanted angles, covering a space on the wall wider than a man could span with outspread arms.

1033.

A chill washed over Mercy, and her stomach twisted again. She swallowed back the bile rising in her throat. "Did you find my chalk?" she asked, almost in a whisper.

Conner nodded. "Yup. It was dropped right here, underneath all this crazy scrawl." He produced the white plug, now coated with concrete dust and half the size it was when Mercy slipped it into her belt that morning. An icy bolt ran between her shoulder blades like frozen lightning.

Conner was staring at her as though questioning her sanity. "You sure you weren't figuring something? Measuring for the conduit?"

All Mercy could do was shake her head. She'd not reached that end of the tunnel earlier. Horror and dread stole her ability to speak.

Whoever—or whatever—had scribbled this number with the chalk had been trying to make a point. Communicate. Send a message. The number appeared on the wall almost a hundred times.

CHAPTER 6

*M*ercy's car had barely driven out of sight when Conner reached out to grab Daniel's arm, pulling him around the backside of the van.

"What do you think of this gal?" he asked. "Seems awful skittish. I'm not sure I made the right choice hiring her. Not sure at all."

"Now just a minute, Conner. You know as well as I do this place is creepin' us all out."

Conner pulled off his grimy Red Sox hat and scratched a patch of balding head with calloused fingers. His words rumbled around the lump of tobacco that perpetually lived in his cheek. He spat off into the weeds, mumbling, "Yeah, but none of us have gotten hurt. Not on any of our jobs. It's been twice now in two weeks Mercy's gotten herself into some sort of scrape."

Daniel sighed and rubbed the back of his neck. "I don't know her all that well, Conner. I do know she's got some issues with her kid."

"I know that," Conner shot back, glaring at Daniel. "The boy's seeing a shrink, right?"

"She went through a bad divorce, Conner. So hard she had to

move clear out of the state to start over." Daniel's voice grew quiet. "And her boy took it hard too. I think you should give her a break."

Conner stared off over Daniel's shoulder for a few moments, thinking. Then, with a decisive nod he said, "Guess you're right." He slid his cap back on and regarded Daniel through squinted eyes. "Timing's good anyway. Darcy's going out on family leave next week. I'm putting Mercy in the office until we get done on this job."

Daniel was surprised to see Mercy's car pull up behind the van the next morning just after the guys got to the job site. When she'd left last night, Conner had told her to take the next day off—it was Friday. He raised an eyebrow, but then kept his eyes on his task of stocking his tool belt.

"Did you forget to pick me up, Conner?" she asked. Daniel could hear the edge in her voice.

Conner squinted up at her over the top of the blueprints he was studying. "Now Mercy, I thought we had this all worked out. I said you'd be filling in at the office for a couple weeks. Starting Monday."

"But what about today? Isn't there something I can do here today to help? I've got one good arm. I can carry conduit, fetch supplies—"

"You've got to be in some pain with that arm. Why don't you just go home and take it easy for today?" Conner said.

She's a tough one, Daniel thought. She really did have to be in some pain, and he knew she hadn't stopped for a minute since the incident yesterday. She'd grabbed her keys and dashed off to get her son to the therapist, just minutes after Conner showed her those weird chalk numbers in the tunnel.

Now those were creepy. No wonder Mercy was jumpy working down there.

He stood by silently as Mercy huffed and pinched the bridge of her nose. "Conner, you don't understand. I just can't afford to take time off right now. My son's seeing a new doctor, and my insurance doesn't even kick in for another two months, right?"

"I won't dock you for today. I already told you that." Conner's tone was placating, as if he were speaking to a small child. He shooed her away with one hand and said, "Go on now."

Daniel watched the color creep up Mercy's neck and her eyes flash. He was afraid she was getting ready to explode any minute, and he knew Conner would definitely not take kindly to that. He might take it from his brother, but not from anybody else, Daniel was sure. It was time for him to break the tension. He took a step closer to her, putting himself between Conner and Mercy.

"How'd it go with Dr. McGuire anyway?" he asked quietly. "He and Reagan get along?"

It took a full three seconds, but Mercy finally closed her eyes and drew in a breath. She gets it, he thought. She realizes what I'm trying to tell her.

The rigid set of her jaw relaxed, and she looked up at him, an invisible smile playing at the corner of her eyes. "Thanks for asking. They did. I think, thanks to you, maybe Reagan has finally found somebody he can talk to."

Then she did smile, and God, was she beautiful. She was one of those rare women who was an impossible combination of sweet femininity and pure steel. Her pale eyes—he still couldn't tell if they were blue or green—threw off rays of electricity all on their own. And those rays hit Daniel right in the gut, or maybe a bit farther down. He shifted from one foot to the other and cleared his throat. "That's great, Merce. I'm glad," he said, turning his attention back to his tool box.

"So, listen, Mercy May," Conner said, "Monday morning, you go on into the office. Around nine. My niece, Darcy, will be there. Get you situated."

It seemed to Daniel he could sense the fight going out of her now. Mercy realized she wasn't going to win this one. Her shoulders sagged and she sighed.

"This is just temporary, right, Conner? I mean, I'm no secretary." She still couldn't keep the tiniest tinge of indignation out of her voice. Daniel could tell she was struggling to control her temper.

Conner didn't hesitate in his reply. "Didn't you say you handled all the business end of things for your husband's team in Atlanta?"

Daniel winced. Yeah, he thought, she probably did. But that was apparently a very sore, very volatile subject. A big chunk of her life, gone.

Thanks for reminding her, asshole.

Mercy straightened, her hands flexing into fists. "I did. But this isn't my family business, and I'm an electrician, Conner. That's what I'm trained for. That's what you pay me to do."

Conner cleared his throat and leveled his gaze at her. "Don't go worrying over your pay rate, Merce. Nothing is gonna change. You'll just be working for me in air-conditioned comfort for a few weeks. Maybe you can get the paperwork in order for me. Darcy's good but sometimes . . . "

She's good, Daniel thought, but she's also your niece. And you'd pay her no matter how badly she screws up the records, the accounting, the supply orders, her life—

"Well I appreciate the accommodation, Conner," Mercy measured her words, and her tone, carefully, "but let's be perfectly clear here. When this thing comes off," she tugged at the sling supporting her left arm, "I'm back to being one of the boys. Are we clear?"

Conner paused to spit into the weeds lining the driveway. He didn't look up. "Be at the office at eight on Monday," he said.

Oh honey, you are a feisty one, Daniel thought as he watched Mercy turn on her heel and stalk back toward her Camry. Her firm, rounded bottom pumped against the denim of her overalls deliciously, and he thought she looked even sexier in them than in the girly clothes she'd worn to lunch last weekend.

Daniel shook his head and turned away from the team as he buckled on his belt, tamping down a fresh wave of desire. No ma'am, Mercy Donohue. I, for one, will never be able to consider you one of the boys.

. . .

TEN MINUTES later when she slammed through her front door, Mercy found Reagan slumped in the corner of the living room couch.

"What happened? No work today?" he asked. But he sounded distracted and hadn't even taken his eyes off the TV screen. Mercy snatched the controller up off the coffee table and the screen went black.

Reagan came up off the couch with his fists clenched. "Hey, I was watching that," he said, just a little too loud and a little too threatening. Mercy refused to be intimidated.

"You," she said, pointing a finger, "are about to become a grown man. It's time you started acting like one and not some vagrant dropout."

Reagan's eyes narrowed, a smartass smirk twisting his lips. "I am a dropout, remember?"

"But you don't have to end up like most of them. I've been easy on you for too long, Reagan. It's time you went out and looked for a job."

Reagan dropped back down on the couch and folded his arms, glaring at her. "And just how am I supposed to get a job if I don't have a license? Or a car? What, is Mommy going to drop me off and pick me up like she does for school?"

The facetious singsong in his voice made Mercy want to slap him. She knew part of her anger had nothing to do with her son. She was taking out her own frustrations. With work, with her injury, with her asshole ex-husband. But she had issues with her son too. This show-down had been a long time coming. Reagan didn't have his dad around anymore, at least, not close by. She wondered if, under the circumstances, that was a good thing or a bad one. One thing she knew for sure: Mom was going to have to get tougher and play the role of both parents, alone.

"There's a pizza place a half a block up the street from here. I passed there just now, and saw they've posted a Help Wanted sign." Mercy took a step back and folded her arms over her chest, refusing to look away from Reagan's death stare. Then she pointed up the stairs. "You get yourself upstairs, clean up, and go down there and put in your application."

The one piece of advice Dr. McGuire had given her when they met privately after Reagan's session was this: it's been long enough, and you're being too easy on the boy. He's got to learn to respect you as much as he did his father. Once upon a time, anyway.

"A big part of Reagan's problem," the doctor had said, "is that he had the utmost respect for his father. Now he's questioning whether anyone deserves to be respected. Unfortunately, that includes you."

The staring match between mother and son stretched out into what felt like forever, but Mercy held her ground. Finally, uttering a growl she chose to ignore, Reagan heaved himself up and took the stairs in four strides. She heard the bathroom door slam just before the spray of the shower.

She was trembling and there was a lump in her throat, but she wasn't sure if it was from her confrontation with Reagan or with Conner. Or from the damn pain from her elbow shooting up her arm so far that her jaw ached. She searched the kitchen counter for the bottle of prescription pain meds she'd filled last night on the way home from Reagan's appointment. She hated taking anything that might impair her, but the pain was even worse this morning than it was last night.

She shook out one of the pills, noting how few the doctor had prescribed. He either thinks I'm tougher than I look, she thought wryly, or expects me to heal mighty fast. Let's hope he's right on both counts.

The meds did two things—dulled the pain and knocked Mercy out. After Reagan came barreling down the stairs and slammed the door behind him without saying a word, Mercy propped herself up in the corner of the sofa. With a pillow under her sore arm and a paperback in her other hand, she'd really just intended to rest for a half-hour or so before tackling the weekly chore of stripping beds and washing sheets. She would need the rest, she thought. She could pull the sheets off with one hand. Remaking the beds, however, might be dicey with only one usable arm.

This was the last thought hovering between her brain and the words on the pages of her romance novel. A moment later she jolted awake to her son's excited voice over her.

"I got the job, Mom," he said. "Just bussing tables . . . but it's a start, right? I start training tonight. Can you believe it? They need somebody really bad."

His earlier, snarky tone was gone, replaced by an enthusiasm that made Mercy's heart leap with hope. She struggled to sit up, wincing when she accidentally placed too much pressure on the braced elbow. Still groggy from the pill, her head spun a little as she swung her feet onto the floor. She didn't attempt to stand.

"That's fantastic, Reagan. How long did it take you to walk down there?" she asked.

"Not long at all. Ten minutes, maybe? Listen, I gotta go make sure I have black dress pants and a white shirt. That's what I'm supposed to wear," he said as he climbed the stairs.

Mercy hoped he did. There was no way, with that pill making her head spin and her eyes cross, she'd be able to drive him to the mall.

"What time do you go in?" Mercy called, realizing she had no idea what time it was or how long she'd been passed out on the couch. She fumbled on the end table for her phone.

Half past two. Seriously? She'd lain down around ten-thirty. The pill had knocked her out for over four hours.

"They want me there at three," he called back, "so I have to hurry."

It took a few minutes for Mercy to realize how much time really had passed since Reagan slammed out the door on his way to the restaurant. Where had he been all this time? Surely, the interview hadn't taken this long.

She waited until he came down the stairs, dressed in a white, short-sleeve shirt and black pleated trousers. His hair was combed back from his face, rake lines still apparent. Mercy felt a jab of pride in her chest. He looked so grown up. Taller even. The hunched, leave-me-alone teenage slump vanished.

"You look great, Reagan," she said. She glanced down at the phone in her hand, noting one new message. "Where were you all this time? You were gone four hours." Mercy tried to keep her tone light. The last thing she wanted to do now was to make Reagan feel as though she was interrogating him.

Reagan had pulled open the fridge and was pouring himself a glass of milk. "Oh, yeah. After the interview, I bumped into one of the guys in my night class. He was picking up a pizza." He drained the glass of milk in three swallows and grabbed a paper towel to wipe his mouth. "We went back to his place and I ate lunch with him and his buddy, Jim. I sent you a text. So, I look okay then?" He came around the end of the counter and stood there, one hip cocked, and arms folded across his chest like he was posing for the cover of GQ.

Mercy shook her head, unable to suppress the smile she felt start in her eyes and warm her all the way to her heart. She nodded and gave Reagan a thumbs-up. "Awesome."

What happened next hadn't happened in so many years, Mercy couldn't begin to count them. Reagan strode across the room, bent down, and kissed Mercy on the cheek. "I get off at ten. I'll see you then," he said, smiling down at her.

Surprise and a warm tingle wedged a lump in her throat so she couldn't answer right away. She nodded and swallowed, but by the time she'd recovered enough to speak, Reagan was halfway out the door. "Good luck," she called after him.

He hesitated in the half-open doorway. "Thanks, Mom."

The screen door's hinges squeaked as it bounced twice on its spring. Then it latched with a quiet click.

It took Mercy twice as long to perform simple tasks with the damned sling on her arm. It was almost six by the time she'd tidied up the house, emptied the dishwasher and stripped the beds. Inching her way down to the basement, where the washer and dryer were, was a real challenge holding the basket in one arm.

She was out of breath, frustrated, and her arm throbbed like a metronome. This one-armed-bandit gig sucked, she thought bitterly. When she heard the distinctive growl of a diesel engine pulling into her driveway, she wondered for only a moment who it might be. As she crested the basement stairs, she recognized Daniel's red truck. Groaning, she realized she neither looked, nor smelled, very appealing.

But why should she care? She silently chastised herself. He was a coworker. A friend. Maybe a male role model for her kid. Nothing more.

That's not how her body reacted when she found him peering at her through the screen, filling the doorway with his lean, muscular body. Instantly, her heart rate skipped up a notch. Self-consciously, she pulled on the band securing her crazy, wild hair and tugged at the hem of her tee shirt.

"Hey there," she said. "Come on in."

Things got worse once he was standing inside, just a few feet away, and she could smell his clean, musky scent. He'd obviously showered and changed after getting off work. Faded Levi's fit him snugly in all the right places, and a crisp, plaid shirt open at the neck revealed a tuft of tawny chest hair.

"Hey. Thought I'd stop by and see how you were feeling." He peered over her shoulder toward the living room. "Reagan around?"

Mercy shook her head. "He got himself a job today," she said, tipping up her chin. "Down the road at Anzio's. I, on the other hand, slept away the first half of the day and then spent the last three hours playing one-armed house maid." She swept a loose strand of hair from her cheek. "I'm sure I look a fright."

His eyes scanned her, and the edge of his lips quirked. "You look pretty good to me."

It was those tiny, auburn hairs straying down from his mustache, she thought. The way they curved defiantly over a full, soft, sculpted upper lip. Bet they would add a delicious tickle factor to a kiss.

Okay, no sense denying it. She was really attracted to this guy. She was a normal female in her sexual prime, and it had been awhile. A long while. Too freaking long.

Daniel's grin spread wider when she didn't say anything for long seconds. She realized she'd been staring and was so glad he couldn't hear what she'd been thinking. She cleared her throat and shifted from one foot to the other. "Have a seat."

"Didn't take Reagan long to get himself hired down there," Daniel said. "That sign only went up yesterday, I think. He's a good kid, Mercy. You've done a good job with him."

"Thanks," she said, heading for the kitchen. "I've done the best I could under the circumstances. Can I get you something to drink?"

"No, I'm good," Daniel said. He plopped down on the couch and leaned back, crossing his arms behind his head. "I'm headed down to the Corby library to do some research on the building we're working on. Thought you might want to tag along."

Mercy reached into the fridge, intending to grab a bottle of water, but came out instead with a beer. She stared at it, momentarily surprised by her own impulse. But hell, it'd been plenty long enough since she'd taken the pain pill, and there was no way she'd be taking another of those now.

"Are you sure you don't want one of these?" she asked, waving the bottle in the air. "I hate to drink alone."

Daniel laughed and the sound danced on Mercy's skin, sending a shiver down her spine. His voice was deep and rumbling, so incredibly masculine, his mirth so genuine. "Well if you put it that way, what choice do I have?"

He rose and joined her at the counter, his arm brushing hers as he reached for the bottle. She felt the tingle as the hairs on her arm rose, though not in a bad way. Her face flushed hot, and she hurriedly pulled open the fridge to fetch a second beer, lingering in the coolness for a few seconds longer than necessary.

I've got to get hold of myself, she thought. This is ridiculous. I feel like an oversexed, horny teenager. Maybe those pain pills aren't just for pain . . .

But wait, Daniel was speaking. He'd opened both beers and was holding his bottle up in a toast. She needed to stay in the moment here.

"Here's to debunking the haunting of Gravely Hall," he said, grinning.

Mercy lifted her bottle, clinked it to his, and took a deep drink. When she looked up, he'd stepped a little closer, so close her sling was brushing the buttons on his shirt. He was looking down into her eyes, his gaze steady and shining and silvery-green. She blinked but didn't pull away as he brushed a calloused finger along her jawline.

"How's the arm?" he rumbled.

"Sore. Made carrying a laundry basket a real bitch. But the pain meds they gave me? Crap, I think I almost killed myself taking one earlier."

A flash of concern twisted his features and he reached to snatch the beer out of her hand. "How long since you took one?"

"Don't worry, silly. I'm not stupid. It's been almost nine hours. I only took the one. Won't make that mistake again. I'll stick to Tylenol next time."

His shoulders relaxed. "Okay. I guess I don't have to remind you how much your son needs you."

Mercy's gaze slid off toward the window, where the rays of an early evening sun were slanting across the countertops. "Yeah, I know he needs me. But he needs his father, too, unfortunately." She lifted her eyes to his. "Not the best role model I'd like to have for him. At the same time, I also know a boy his age needs a man in his life."

Daniel took a long pull on his beer and leaned back against the counter. "Copy that. Kim's kid has the same problem. I'm filling in on that role for Davin. Trying, anyway. I wouldn't mind helping you out with Reagan either."

Mercy set down the bottle on the counter and hugged herself, turning away. "Yeah, but Davin never really knew a dad, did he?"

"No, he never did. His biological father never wanted to have anything to do with him. Doubt Davin's ever met him. But what about Reagan? I'm guessing it's a different scenario."

Mercy began pacing up and down along the countertop, arms still tightly folded across her middle. "Yeah, lots different. Reagan idolized his dad. At least, until . . ." She stalled in front of the window looking out over the parking area and makeshift basketball court.

"It's okay, Mercy. If you're not ready to talk about it, there's nothing I need to know. I just want you to know that I'm here for Reagan, and for you, if you need me." His already deep baritone had dropped lower, to almost a rumble.

She felt his big, strong hand on her shoulder then, and her throat tightened. Every cell in her body was screaming, "Turn around and put your arms around this beautiful man!" But her gut knew better. He was her coworker, for heaven's sake. And she hardly knew the man. He seemed like a nice guy, but who knew? For almost twenty years, she thought Luke Donohue was a Greek god in Dickies. How wrong had she been about that?

"Look," Daniel said, "I'm headed to the Corby library. Want to look up some stuff on the old mental hospital. See if that number—1033—see if it means anything. Wanna go with me?"

The library in Corby was old—really old. Mercy read the plaque beside the front door: *Est. 1864*. It might have been a mansion at the start, a regal Victorian with gingerbread decorating the wraparound porch and more gables than Mercy cared to count. A labyrinth, she thought as they pulled into the parking lot. A place to explore and get lost in other worlds, other times. Mercy had always loved libraries, especially old ones.

The librarian on duty was ancient too. Her nametag, hand

inscribed with black, fine-tip Sharpie, said AGNES PINCHER. She looked up as they pushed through the heavy oak door, studying them over a pair of tortoiseshell readers tethered to her neck by a purple beaded chain. Her expression went from blank to beaming when she recognized Daniel's face.

"Danny," she said quietly, in a typical librarian's purr, "so good to see you." Then her gaze shifted to Mercy and one eyebrow lifted. "You've brought us a visitor, I see."

"Hey, Agnes. Yeah, this is Mercedes Donohue. She and her son just moved back here from down south. We work together."

Agnes' overgrown, straggly white eyebrows drew together, and her eyes narrowed as she stared Mercy down.

"I, um, I guess I need to apply for a library card, too," Mercy stammered.

Agnes lifted a hand to her chin. "You ever hold a card here, Miss . . . ?"

"Donohue. Mercedes Donohue. And yes, I did have a library card, but it's been . . ." Mercy glanced up at the ceiling, "over twenty years? And my last name was different then. Time for a fresh start."

"Welcome to Corby," she said, and slid a card across the desk toward Mercy. "Just fill this out and we'll give you a temporary pass you can use today, if you find anything you want to check out."

As Mercy scribbled on the form, Daniel asked, "Agnes, the Reference Room. Is it open today?"

Mercy glanced up to see the flat line again press out the creases in the woman's upper lip. She was shaking her head. "Sorry, Dan. You know the rules. Materials in the Reference Room are only available when an attendant is working." She paused dramatically, looking from one side to the other, and then holding her hands up. "As you can see, I'm the only one here tonight."

Daniel nodded as Mercy handed the card over.

"We'll just browse a bit then. I'll bring Mercy back when Reference is open," Daniel said.

"What's up with her?" Mercy whispered after she and Daniel had climbed the steps to the second floor and rounded the corner. "What's so precious about the books in the Reference Room?"

Daniel cleared his throat and leaned in close to Mercy's ear. She tried to ignore the zing his closeness sent down her spine.

"The Corby Mental Hospital has a history that many of the old town residents aren't proud of," he murmured. "All the records, of everything that ever happened there, are kept under lock and key. Even when there's an attendant present, they limit the amount of stuff you can see, or take notes on. And they never, ever let anybody make photocopies of anything."

Curious, Mercy thought. Very curious, as she wondered if this news or Daniel's touch was the cause of the shiver rippling across her shoulders.

CHAPTER 7

*D*aniel was pleased when Mercy didn't hesitate on his offer to grab dinner on the way back from the library. They stopped in the Bridge Street Café around six. The dining room was packed, but there were two empty bar stools. They sat side by side, both ordering the meat loaf special. For a comfortable hour, one filled with easy conversation and lots of laughter, he could swear he and Mercy had known each other all their lives.

But now, here they sat in her driveway, and Daniel hesitated before turning off his truck's engine. He didn't want to assume anything. He didn't want her to *think* he assumed anything. He wavered between disappointment and relief when the moment stretched out, awkward silence between them.

Mercy reached down to the floor to retrieve the three books she'd selected at the library, along with her purse—not an easy feat with only one good arm. Daniel mentally smacked himself in the head.

She's gonna need help getting inside, dumbass. What a gentleman she must think you are.

He quickly pulled the keys and opened his door, saying, "Wait, Mercy, wait. I'll help you with those." But by the time he got around to the other side, she was already standing, books balanced on her hip, purse over her wrist, and house key in her hand. She scowled up at him.

"I can get this, Daniel. I'm a pretty tough chick, if you hadn't realized it by now. I can take care of myself."

And one with a pretty quick temper too, he thought, catching the flash of defiance in her pale eyes. The sun had just set, leaving bright flaming streaks across the sky behind her. Flames that might well be coming off her.

Okay, well he tried. He nodded solemnly, not knowing what to do or say next. He cleared his throat.

"So, Tuesday then? Agnes said the Reference Room is open from six to eight, I think. I can pick you up—"

"I'll meet you there. I have to drop Reagan off at school first. I won't be able to get there until seven." Her voice was cool, almost clipped. She turned and headed toward her porch, calling over her shoulder. "Thanks for a nice evening, Daniel. I guess I'll see you Tuesday."

Damn, what the hell happened in the last ten minutes?

He followed her, reached her in two long strides and laid a hand on her shoulder. "Mercy, wait. What's wrong? What did I do?"

She didn't face him right away, but her shoulders rose and fell before she let out a sigh. Then she did turn, gazing up at him with much gentler eyes. Darker too and soft, like a doe's.

"Daniel, I really did have fun tonight. Too much fun. It feels like we've known each other forever, and I've only worked with you for a few weeks. That scares me. This whole situation scares me."

He wasn't sure if it was just the way the fading sky reflected in her eyes, but he could swear they were glazed with tears. His stomach clutched. He never could think very clearly once a woman turned on the waterworks.

"Look," he said, and reached up to stroke her cheek with the back of his hand, "I'm not putting any pressure on you for anything. But I enjoy you. Your company—both at work and afterwards. And your son, too." He hesitated, holding her gaze. "Hell, I'm really going to miss you these next few weeks."

Then Daniel took a chance. He leaned down, very slowly, ready to back off if she shrank away from him. She did not. He planted a gentle kiss on her forehead, lingering there long enough to breathe in the scent of her. Damn, she smelled good. Always sweet and hot, like cookies baking in the oven. Like dessert.

And she *hadn't pulled away*. Hadn't even stiffened in that way he'd seen her do before. In fact, unless it was wishful thinking or an overactive imagination, he could have sworn she leaned into him.

He stepped back, digging his keys out of his pocket. "I'll wait until you're inside and the door's locked. And I'll see you Tuesday night." He turned quickly before his instincts took control and he did what he really wanted to do, which was sweep her into his arms and carry her inside. And lay her down right there on the living room carpet and—

"Thank you, again," she said as she mounted the porch steps.

He climbed back into his truck and the diesel engine roared to life, but he sat there watching, as he'd promised, until she got inside. One handed, books balanced on the railing, she struggled to unlock her door. He shook his head. She's a stubborn one. The toughest, sweetest cookie he'd ever met.

MONDAY MORNING ARRIVED with a bang—one that literally jolted Mercy awake ten minutes before her alarm. A thunderstorm was rolling in, with window-rattling thunder and flashes of lightning heralding its arrival. She ran to her car between downpours and drove at an agonizing snail's pace through the deluge to the office. When she got there, her umbrella stuck and proved to be practically useless. It took her more time to struggle the thing open with one good hand than it would have to run straight to the covered sidewalk. When she stumbled through the glass door stenciled with *Progressive Electrical*, she felt more like a drowned rat than a temporary replacement for the smartly dressed lady in shocking pink who sat at the office's only desk.

Darcy, Mercy brooded, must have come in way before the first raindrop fell.

"Good morning. You must be Mercedes," Darcy said brightly, then winced. "Ooh, I see you weren't as lucky as I was with the rain this morning, huh? Sorry about that. I'm Darcy."

Mercedes stood inside the doorway dripping onto the carpeted mat. Her hair was drenched, and water streamed in icy rivulets down her neck. Good thing she didn't wear makeup, she thought. If she'd done her eyes like Darcy's she'd look like a Halloween ghoul by now.

"Yeah, bad morning," she grumbled. "I'll dry off in the rest room and then we can get started."

Mercy struggled to blot her face and smooth her hair in the smudged, distorted mirror of the tiny half-bath. It needed cleaning badly. A typical workman's bathroom, she thought. She'd have to remember Lysol and a toilet bowl brush next trip.

Minutes later she emerged to find Darcy sitting at her desk, legs crossed at the knee, which brought her too-short skirt thigh high. Didn't think they made maternity clothes like that, Mercy thought. Darcy's eyes were glued to her cell phone. She was so intent on her texting that when Mercy stepped up beside her, Darcy squeaked and jumped.

"I'm sorry. Didn't mean to startle you."

"No problem. I'm just used to being here alone," she snapped. Then she tucked the phone under a shelf on one end of her desk and swiveled to face her. "Dried off a bit?"

Mercy soon learned that Conner's niece, Darcy Stevenson, was twenty-two. She was hired on originally through a work-study program Conner arranged with the community college. When the program was over, Conner kept Darcy on. No surprise there.

The girl was pretty and had a pleasing telephone voice. Mercy had heard Conner remark on more than one occasion how Darcy had better luck pulling permits down at the county office than he or Bill did. Conner was convinced it was due to Darcy's negotiating talents. Mercy was more inclined to believe it had something to do with the revealing cut of her outfits.

Now, however, the short pink mini dress Darcy wore strained around a huge baby bump. It pulled the already low-cut neckline down to where Mercy was afraid she might get a peek of nipple if the girl leaned over too far. Darcy was no doubt due any day.

"Conner says I need to teach you everything I do around here in just one day," she exclaimed, lifting both hands in the air. "I don't know if that's even close to possible."

Mercy struggled to keep from rolling her eyes. She took a deep breath and closed them instead. Then she said on a sigh, "Why don't we start with a list of suppliers Conner orders from?"

The next eight hours lapsed so quickly Mercy wondered if time hadn't spontaneously sped up. Darcy, though seeming at first merely an attractive airhead, was quite well versed on the tasks she'd been performing for the past year and a half. Invoices were up to date and although not as succinctly organized as Mercy would want them, they were not in the state of disarray Conner had intimated. The supply lists were fairly complete, and Darcy had organized a master list of their most commonly used vendors.

Payroll was the weak link. Hourly records were sketchy and hadn't been entered into the spreadsheets for almost two months. Mercy secretly wondered how promptly the quarterly payroll taxes were being paid.

They took a twenty-minute break around one o'clock to eat the lunches they'd both brought—fortunate since the rain hadn't abated much. The rest of the afternoon flew by. Mercy was so engrossed in her note-taking, she was surprised when a band of sunlight fell across the desk. The storm had moved on through.

"Well," she breathed out, "at least we won't have to drive home in the rain. You usually close up here at five, Darcy?"

"My hours are pretty flexible," she grinned sheepishly, "since my uncle's the boss. I usually try to get here by nine, and yeah, lock up at five. I'm usually long gone before the team gets back to pick up their vehicles."

Mercy nodded. "Okay, nine to five, then. Easy enough."

"But today, I've got to leave early. Do you have any other questions before I take off? I have a doctor's appointment at four-thirty."

"I don't think so, Darcy. I think I can handle this. When are you due, anyway?"

The younger woman smiled and blushed, one hand smoothing instinctively over her impressive bump. "Doctor says next week, but I'm already having Braxton-Hicks contractions," she said. "It's a girl," she added, beaming proudly.

"Well, best of luck to you. Picked a name yet?"

Darcy grinned sheepishly. "Lou Ellen. My new boyfriend's name is Lou. Being he's not the baby-daddy and all, I thought I'd like to bond them by name. Right from the start, you know?"

Mercy struggled to hold down the eyebrow that itched to lift up into her hairline. "New boyfriend, huh? Baby-daddy's not involved?"

"Nope," Darcy shot back and shrugged. "Better this way."

Mercy cleared her throat and switched gears. "Well, you be sure to bring that pretty bundle in here just as soon as you can get her out and about." She paused, uncertain about asking the main question she'd been dying to ask all day.

Better get it out in the open. I need to know what my own future looks like.

"Darcy, how long do you plan on staying home with your daughter?"

The girl half-turned away from Mercy and shot her a sidelong glance. Then she leaned closer and whispered, "Well, Uncle Conner doesn't know it yet, but I'm probably not gonna need to come back at all. My new boyfriend? He's Louis Carson, a big-wig down at Security Bank." Darcy struggled to her feet awkwardly and threw Mercy an exaggerated wink. "I might just have landed me a big fish this time. Louis is adopting Lou Ellen, and he wants me to be a stay-at-home mom."

As the door swung closed behind the waddling Darcy, Mercy dropped her forehead into her palm. She'd had a feeling this was going to happen. Conner may not yet know his niece wouldn't be returning to office duty. But even if he did, Mercy felt pretty damn sure he had no intention of letting her back on the job site anytime soon.

DANIEL'S MONDAY started as badly as Mercy's, but not entirely because of the weather. He'd slept poorly, thoughts of Mercy haunting his dreams. This hadn't happened to him in a long, long time. In fact, he couldn't remember the last time a woman had enough influence over his mind—and body—to follow him home like that after a date.

Hell, it wasn't even a date. Just a friendly evening together. Daniel reminded himself that he mustn't think of their time together any other way. At least, not yet.

His wall was pretty solid. Ever since he'd stood over the coffin of his beloved at the tender age of twenty-three, he'd kept his emotions out of the few, lighthearted relationships he'd had over the years. He was a man, after all, with all the normal desires and needs. Fortunately, there were plenty of women around these days who didn't mind carrying on an affair consisting of no more than a few fun evenings, dinner or a movie, followed by a raucous roll in the sack. In fact, most of the women he'd dated made it clear right up front they didn't want him to hang around long enough to get attached.

Fine with him. Yeah, he got lonely sometimes. But one, weeklong tryst every few months was enough to keep him from even considering opening his life, or his heart, to a woman again.

Yet he couldn't help the clutch of panic in his chest when he stepped out of the shower this morning to a boom of thunder.

God, I hope Mercy doesn't have to drive to the office in this. Or be foolish enough to use an umbrella with this lightning. She probably wouldn't be able to use an umbrella with only one usable arm, anyway.

He agonized over that thought again and again as he sat in his truck in front of Progressive Electrical's darkened office windows. It was a good two hours before Darcy, or Mercy, would be opening the office. Another lightning flash made him jump, followed almost simultaneously by the ground-shaking thunder. He was sure the strike hit close by. He blew out a ragged breath.

Hopefully the worst of the storm would be passed by the time Mercy had to leave her house.

Mooning over a woman. This was so out of character. What was wrong with him? A little too young for mid-life crisis. Maybe a full moon is coming up.

Mondays were always the longest of the week, but this one threatened never to end. The rain continued throughout the day, peaking and waning as one storm cell followed another in an endless parade. And Daniel was working alone in the tunnel.

Sometimes the thunder booms shook the ground with such intensity, chips of loose mortar broke free from the battered walls around him. The pattering sent chills up his spine, sounding like a thousand tiny feet running beyond where the light of his lanterns reached. In the rainy gloom, so little light leaked in through the few window blocks along the upper edge of the outer wall, it could pass for twilight. Daniel had two lanterns lit, one on either side of where he was working, drilling to set the lags. Then came the tussle with the unwieldy conduit—alone—causing him to swear under his breath more than once.

But with only three of them, this is how it had been before Conner hired Mercy. It was one of the reasons Daniel had pushed for a fourth team member. Electrical, especially in old buildings, was not the kind of work that should be done alone.

But who was Daniel fooling? It wasn't just the extra work or working alone down here in the tunnel eating at him. He missed her. He wondered how Mercy's first day at the office was going. He hoped the arm healed quickly, and that Conner didn't really have intentions of moving Mercy into a desk job. She was a damned good electrician, and the team, especially on jobs like this one, certainly could use her expertise.

His stomach started grumbling around noon, and he figured he'd climb up to the second floor where Conner and Jacob were tearing out old boxes. Time to suggest a lunch break. As he climbed the stairs, he could hear the annoying drone of Conner's ancient portable radio over the brothers' banter. They were arguing about whether Kyle Busch would win the NASCAR Sprint Cup over Jeff Gordon. Daniel shook his head and smiled.

But when he reached the second-floor hallway, a long corridor that was once a long lineup of patient rooms, Daniel stepped into a pocket of decidedly cooler air. Not a breeze, just a pocket, as if he'd passed through the door of a walk-in cooler. He wondered if the guys had found a way to open a window up here. But why? Rain continued to pound down on the roof, and the air outside had remained chilly and damp.

Daniel turned the corner into the large common room where his colleagues were working. Jacob perched on a ladder, removing the screws on the conduit set along the top of the wall. Conner, down on his knees, was doing the same along the baseboard. He turned and looked up when Daniel stepped in.

"'Bout ready for lunch?" Conner asked.

"I know I am," Jacob chimed in.

Jacob holstered his screwdriver in his tool belt and began making his way down the ladder while Conner clambered to his feet.

"What's it going to be today, boys? I'm in the mood for some Mexican," Conner said.

It was then that Daniel felt it again, a chill that crept up behind him, making the hairs on his arms stand up. He glanced down the hallway, noticing that all of the heavy doors to the patient rooms stood open. He rubbed his arms.

"Did you guys open a window up here?" he asked.

Conner snorted. "Ain't no way I can see of opening any windows in this place. It's locked up tighter than a—"

Bam! Bam, Bam! Bam Bam Bam!

A horrific bang shook the building, and all three men jumped.

"Holy shit," Jacob muttered. "Did you see that?"

Almost simultaneously, every single door to the patient rooms had swung on its their hinges and violently slammed shut.

THEY SAT at table in the bar at El Bandido, Corby's Mexican restaurant. Although Conner had a strict rule about alcohol consumption on the job, Daniel wished for once he'd make an exception. He didn't.

"This job is really creeping me out," Jacob said, stirring what must have been the fifth packet of sugar into his iced tea. "Some weird shit goes on. I don't like it."

Conner scowled at his brother. "Quit being such a pussy, bro. It's an old building. We've worked on plenty of them. They shift and creak all the time."

"There's got to be a window open in one of those rooms," Daniel said. "It's windy today. You know what a draft can do sometimes. Hell, I've been convinced I have a ghost in my own attic when the wind whines and moans in the eaves."

"Well I'm sure as hell checking every single room when we get back," Jacob spat. "None of us, with the kind of work we do, needs a jolt like that." He hesitated a moment, then looked up and smirked. "No pun intended."

CHAPTER 8

*M*ercy was relieved to close up and lock the office door at five o'clock. She'd never been an indoor kind of gal. Which worked fine when she lived in Atlanta. Well, yes and no. The weather down there was blazing hot most of the time, so most folks didn't spend much time outside of an air-conditioned building. Mercy had worked on newly constructed houses, way before any HVAC went into place. So sometimes, it was like working in pine-scented hell.

Still, sitting in an office all day wasn't going to cut it for her for too long. She prayed that's not what Conner had planned for her.

As she climbed into her car she glanced at the dash clock and sighed. Monday, so no night class for Reagan. That would mean she'd have no excuse not to cook dinner. What did she have in the house to cook, she wondered? Okay, some ground beef in the freezer, which she could defrost in the microwave. There was a box of taco shells with seasoning mix in the cabinet. She'd stop by the farmer's market on the way home and pick up lettuce and tomatoes. There. Dinner's done.

After making the stop at the market—then at the grocery for some sour cream and salsa—it was after five-thirty when Mercy pulled into her driveway. Behind a big, red Ford pickup. Daniel's pickup.

She sat in her car for a few moments after killing the engine, watching the two handsome males banter on the makeshift basketball court in front of the shed. Mercy couldn't decide if this warmed her heart or froze it in fear. After all, Reagan had idolized his father. She didn't need him latching onto another male role model just to be disappointed. Again.

Reagan saw her first and paused to wave, ball on his hip, wearing a huge grin. She hadn't seen that boyish exuberance in quite a while. Okay, so maybe this was a chance worth taking. Mercy had to admit; it was kind of nice to come home to find Daniel there as well.

"How was your first day in the office?" Daniel called. "And how's that arm? Missed you today." He paused, glanced over his shoulder at Reagan, then added, "On the job, I mean."

Mercy climbed out, hefting the bag of groceries out with her good hand. "Okay, for a desk job. Got a crash course in bookkeeping, Darcy Stevenson style." She shot him a look.

Reagan handed the ball off to Daniel and ran over to grab the bag from his mother. "Let me get this Mom. I'll be right back, Daniel."

As the porch door slammed, Daniel moved close to Mercy, studying her eyes. "So really, how's the arm? You whacked it pretty good last week."

Mercy twisted the sore shoulder in a semi-shrug. "It's getting better. With a little help from Dr. Tylenol, that is." She smiled up into his hazel eyes. He was close enough for her to catch his scent—not exactly a freshly showered one. "What'd you do, come straight from the job?"

He nodded. "I wanted to get Reagan out of the house. From what you've told me, all he does is hang in front of his video games most of the time. That hasn't done my nephew any good."

The screen door banged behind them and Reagan re-emerged carrying two glasses of iced tea. Mercy's eyebrows lifted. Hadn't seen him this considerate since the days when he and his father hung out together.

"Sorry, I couldn't carry three of them, Mom. Do you want some?"

"I can get my own, Reagan. I've got to start dinner anyway. Tacos tonight. That okay?"

"All right!" Reagan pumped a fist in the air. "My mom makes wicked good tacos. Can Daniel stay for dinner, Mom?"

"Wicked good, huh? Isn't that New England lingo? I thought you were from down South?" Daniel asked with a smirk. He turned to Mercy. "And if you've got enough, yes, I'd love to stay."

Mercy fried the ground beef and chopped the vegetables, all the while watching Reagan and Daniel work up a sweat in her driveway. Damn it, she had to admit that the sight did warm her heart. She was surprised when, after turning to drain the meat, she glanced back to see two more faces added to the pair. Squinting through the glass, she recognized Kim, Daniel's sister. Standing next to her was another teen, a little taller and lankier than her own son, with a buzz cut of sandy red hair.

Must be Davin, Kim's son.

Kim chatted for a second with Daniel before turning toward the house. She rapped lightly on the jamb and called through the screen. "Mercy?"

"Come on in, Kim," Mercy said. "What are you guys doing here? I'll have to ask Daniel to run out for more taco shells if you're staying for dinner."

Kim slipped inside, shaking her head. "Daniel asked me to bring Davin down to meet Reagan. I hope you don't mind. I've got to run down to the shop and close up. I'll swing by and pick him up on my way back."

Mercy pondered this. What exactly were Daniel's motives here? Was he really, truly interested in his nephew and her son getting acquainted? Keeping both boys outside and away from the video games? Or was there another, more self-serving motive?

Who is he really interested in getting to know better—Reagan, or me?

Still, she couldn't help the warm knot that formed in her chest at the thought. Either way, or both, Daniel really did seem like a nice guy. Too bad they worked together. Mercy had been down that road before, and it had a rocky end. One she'd had to flee over a thousand miles to escape. God knew, she didn't want to have to uproot her son, and herself, again.

"No problem. There's probably enough here to feed Davin, too, if he likes tacos. Can I get you a cold drink?"

Kim hoisted her purse up higher on her shoulder and glanced at her watch. "No, thanks, I really do have to get back down to the shop."

Mercy nodded and smiled. "I hope our sons hit it off. Reagan is still trying to get his footing under him up here. I mean, I grew up here. I've been gone a long time, and most of the people I knew have moved on, but . . . well, you know what I mean. Reagan was born and raised in Atlanta. A whole 'nother world."

"I'll bet," Kim said, glancing back through the screen at the three bouncing a basketball on asphalt. "I hope they get along too. Davin could use a friend. A *good* friend. One who's been raised right and won't guide him down any dark alleyways." She sighed. "Gotta run. See you in about an hour. That okay?"

After Kim left, Mercy had to wonder what she'd meant by the dark alleyways comment. Had Davin been in trouble? She knew the school system here in Corby had a pretty good reputation, but for a moment, she was kind of glad Reagan was finishing his GED at night. She made a mental note to ask Daniel what Kim had been referring to.

An hour later Mercy had the taco meat warming on top of the stove, the shells on warm in the oven, and the bowls of fixings chilling in the fridge. She was starving and wondered if she should just go ahead and call the boys in to eat. There was enough for Davin. She could always have hers as a taco salad without the shell.

Just as she was about to do that, she heard Kim's car pull into the driveway. Wiping her hands on the kitchen towel, she pushed through the screen door.

Kim didn't even get out of the car, just waved and then motioned for Davin to get in. Mercy watched as the boy awkwardly started backing away with a weak wave before Reagan stepped forward and extended his hand. Davin hesitated. Then he took it but seemed uncomfortable at the gesture. He tipped his head at his uncle before climbing into his mother's car.

Hasn't been taught a whole lot of manners, she thought. Wonder what other aspects of his education are lacking?

Daniel and Reagan stomped in through the door minutes later, both of them red-faced and sweaty. Mercy fisted her hands on her hips and looked them up and down.

"Reagan, you need to go shower off before you come to the dinner table." Then she looked at Daniel and continued, "and you can jump in right after, if you're quick. There are plenty of towels. But hurry. I don't want the taco shells to turn into Tupperware lids."

"Thanks, Mom," Reagan said.

And then her son did something that shocked Mercy to her core. He came to her and, careful not to soak her with his sweaty clothes, kissed her cheek. Over his shoulder, Daniel grinned at the owl eyes she knew she was wearing.

After the upstairs bathroom door slammed shut, Mercy looked at Daniel and said, "Wow. I guess it really was a good idea for you to meet my son. He's already a different kid than he was a week ago."

Daniel's grin split his beard and seemed to light up the whole kitchen. "He's a nice young man. I do get the feeling he's feeling pretty out of sorts, though. I'm hoping I can get him back on track." He paused, his eyes flashing to hers, embarrassed. "You know, after the move and all."

Mercy regarded him for a long moment. "And bringing Davin tonight? Same purpose?"

His eyes slid away, and he folded his hands behind his back. "I hope so. Davin needs a friend too. A *good* friend."

There it was again. Daniel placed extra emphasis on the word *good*, just as Kim had done. She wondered exactly what he meant by that. Good as in "really close," or . . .

"Your sister said the same thing. Has Davin been in some kind of trouble? I got the feeling—"

"Let's just say Davin's got in with a pretty rough crowd at school. Corby is a small town, but every school has them. I guess because he's alone so much, and because he doesn't have a father in the mix, he's been drifting off course lately. I'm worried about him."

"I guess I should be glad Reagan is finishing his degree in night school, huh?"

Daniel nodded. "It's certainly not a bad thing. Teenagers, well, you know how they can be."

Mercy knew all too well how unstable, as well as unpredictable, teenagers could be. At least, her teenager. They could be uber-sensitive and ultra-dramatic and would do just about anything to draw attention to themselves. Young bleeding hearts. Or worse.

She spun away from Daniel, suddenly feeling the need to shut down. She bent to check the taco shells in the oven. Without looking at him, she said, "You've got to be parched. What will it be? Iced tea? Lemonade? Water?"

"Water's fine." Daniel paused, seeming to sense her discomfort. "Hey, I don't want to stink up your table with my funk. I only live about ten minutes away. Why don't I run back home, shower, and come back all clean and shiny? I promise, I won't take long enough for dinner to be ruined."

He left toting a red plastic cup full of ice water and promised to be back within a half-hour.

And he was. He rapped on the screen door as Mercy was getting the chopped vegetables out of the fridge. She noticed the six-pack of beer hanging from his other hand.

"Come on in. And how did you know I could use a cold beer tonight?" She grinned.

"Coors Light, right? Isn't that what you ordered at Bridge Street the other night?"

Sweet that he remembered, she thought. But ooh mama. The beer might have been cold, but the man toting it was anything but. Daniel had changed into a pair of jeans that fit him just right, in all the right places. His Red Sox tee-shirt snugged enticingly around sculpted upper arms.

And I don't have any business noticing anything like *that*. Not at this point in my life.

"Have a seat," she said as she took the beer from him. Then she turned and called up the stairs. "Reagan, dinner's on."

This is nice. That's the thought that kept running around in Mercy's head as the three of them sat at her small dining table. It brought on bittersweet emotions in a variety of flavors. Up until a few years ago, at least once or twice a week, she and Reagan had enjoyed a family dinner with his father. Then the frequency of those meals had begun to taper off, since Luke had started working later and later at the office.

Working. Or so he'd claimed.

She shook off the memory and the anger and resentment it caused to bubble up in her chest. That was then, and this is now. New town, new home, new life. And even though she didn't want anything more from Daniel than to be a male role model for her son, it was enough. She smiled as she watched the two men banter over their meal.

"Dude, you can't possibly eat a taco without sour cream. I think there's a law against it," Reagan said as he spooned enough of the white cream over his to obliterate all else. "Besides, it sort of glues all the other stuff inside. Keeps it from falling out when you eat it."

Daniel's lip curled. "Not a fan, my man. So, you make fun of me all you want when I scatter tomatoes and lettuce everywhere. Pass me the salsa, would you, Mercy?"

With a mouth full of taco, earning an arched eyebrow from his mother, Reagan brought up a subject Mercy never expected from him.

"So, Mom. Dr. McGuire, who," he glanced at Daniel, "is a really cool guy, by the way. Well, he was asking about my family situation and all." He shot a pointed look Mercy's way. "I told him about what happened. You and Dad splitting up. But then he was asking about extended family. Grandparents, aunts, uncles. I don't have any, do I?"

Mercy shifted in her seat and cleared her throat. "You have your father's parents in Atlanta. But no, not on my side. My adoptive parents were older when they took me in. They're both gone now."

Reagan nodded slowly, chewing. "Did you ever try to look up your *real* parents? You were born up here, right? Wouldn't there be some way for you to find out who they are? Why they gave you up?"

Mercy knew that at some point in his young life, Reagan would start asking questions about his heritage. Her heritage. It wasn't a subject she liked to talk about. But apparently, she was going to have to share what information she knew sooner or later.

"My adoptive family told me that my real mother died giving birth to me. They were immigrants, from Ireland. Hadn't been here more than a year or so. My birth father, I guess, just couldn't face raising a baby girl on his own. That's why he gave me up for adoption."

Reagan's eyes widened and he lowered his overstuffed taco to his plate. "That's really sad. So, do you know anything about your father? Is he still alive? Could we try to find out and maybe I could meet him?"

Mercy shook her head. "He's gone too. I did try to find him once, when I was about your age. The records weren't sealed, so I do know his name. But he sort of fell off the map about a year after I was born. Nobody really knows what happened to him."

Daniel had been silent throughout this exchange. Mercy could feel his eyes on them, ping-ponging from one to the other. When the conversation stalled, he blotted some salsa off his mustache and took a pull from his beer. "What was your father's name, Mercy? Was he local?"

"Doherty. Devlin Doherty. And no, they lived near Boston. He was a dock worker."

Mercy managed to pick her way through only one taco, a challenge with one arm in the sling. After the uncomfortable turn in the conversation, though, her appetite evaporated anyway. Still, it didn't take long for the two hungry males to demolish every single scrap of food on the table. When she rose to clear the dishes, Daniel held up his hand.

"Oh no. The lady cooked. The men clean up." He turned to pull another beer from the fridge and handed it to Mercy. You go chill out while Reagan and I get this."

Fifteen minutes later, Mercy was enjoying the cool of early evening in one of the two Adirondack chairs in her dooryard when she heard the screen door slam.

"Hey Mom? Is it okay if I go over to Davin's house for a couple hours? He's got Dead Space 2, man, and an Xbox 360. My controller will work with it." Reagan was standing on the steps with said controller in his hand, the cords dangling from the thing like black tentacles. Mercy's eyebrows rose.

"Dead Space, huh? That some war thing?" she asked.

Daniel followed Reagan down the porch steps. "No, it's an outer space thing. Humans versus the Necromorphs. It's pretty cool."

Damn, the man looked good in jeans. And why did he look so right coming out of her door? Why had it felt so right to have him sitting at the dinner table with them?

And why the hell wasn't he already spoken for? Mercy wasn't sure whether the clutching in her belly was her body reacting to the man, or her visceral instincts warning her to steer clear.

"How are you going to get there?" she asked. "Where do Kim and Davin live, anyway?"

"I'll drive him. It's only a few miles down 30 toward Westboro. I live right around the corner. Why don't you take a ride with me and I'll show you my house?" Daniel suggested. "We'll give the boys an hour or so to battle the Necromorphs, and then I'll bring you both home. What do you say?"

Mercy knew she shouldn't. But it warmed her heart to see this new attitude of her son, happier than she'd seen him in months. And yeah, okay, he would still be playing a video game, but he'd be getting out and doing it with a companion. Socializing. Maybe making a new friend.

At least, that's the excuse she used to justify climbing into the truck with the hot guy she worked with intent on spending the evening—yet *another* evening—with him.

After a moment's hesitation, she said, "Okay."

CHAPTER 9

*K*im Gallagher lived in one unit of a duplex just off Rte. 30 on a dead-end street surrounded by woods. She had the entryway decorated nicely, Mercy thought, with hanging baskets of fuchsias on either side of the porch steps, and a planter spilling over with pansies next to the front door. Inviting, cozy, it looked like home.

Where does she find the time, Mercy wondered? She's raising a son alone and working full-time, just like me. She made a silent vow to visit the local nursery this weekend. It's about time Mercy did a few things to her own house to make it feel more like home.

Reagan barely threw a goodbye over his shoulder as he clambered out of Daniel's truck and trotted up the steps.

"Did you at least call Kim and warn her she was having a guest?" Mercy asked.

Daniel grinned as he folded his arms atop the steering wheel. "I did, although Kim's used to unexpected guests all the time. Davin is a pretty free spirit." He sobered. "I'm sure she'd rather have him in his own bedroom with a friend than out with a bunch she doesn't know."

As he backed out of the driveway, Mercy asked, "So, what kind of trouble has Davin gotten himself into? I'd like to know, seeing as he's taking my son on as a friend."

Daniel's shoulders rose and dropped on a deep breath. He reached up to pull on his beard. "Nothing serious. Skipped out of school a time or two. He's never been arrested or anything. To my knowledge, he's not dabbled in any drugs."

Nodding, Mercy considered this. "Well, that's good, Daniel. Because my son has his own emotional issues." She shifted her gaze out of the window, away from him. "I guess you already know that. Thanks, by the way, for recommending the therapist. Reagan seems to like him. So far, anyway."

"I'm glad," Daniel said. "Ian is a really great guy. I went to high school with him. Comes from a good family."

Mercy sighed. "Yeah, well, I'm hoping he can bring some stability to Reagan's life. The divorce rocked him. Hard."

"Are you ready to talk about it?" He reached over and laid a hand on her arm. "Or is it none of my goddamned business?"

Mercy turned to look into his eyes. "Maybe."

Daniel was right—he lived literally around the corner from Kim's place. His house, though, was totally not what Mercy expected. She'd assumed, him living alone, that it would be a duplex, like Kim's. There were a lot of them in the area, especially because the tech school was so close. They didn't provide dorms for their students, so local rentals were all that were available for housing.

He pulled the truck into what looked like nothing more than a pine-needle strewn path into the woods. It wound to the left, then the right, in a tight serpentine curve. Coming into the clearing, Mercy saw a cute farmhouse, two stories, complete with wraparound porch. It wasn't huge, but had to be at least a two-bedroom, maybe three.

"Wow," she breathed. "Do you own this place? Or rent, like me?"

He killed the engine and ran his hand through his hair. "Nope. Own it. Well, the bank does, anyway. For at least the next ten years or so. I got a hell of a deal on it when I was in my early twenties. It was a fixer upper, and I, well, fixed it up."

They climbed out and Mercy surveyed the surroundings. A neatly trimmed lawn ringed the house, but there were no flowers like at Kim's. Simple, evergreen shrubs lined the foundation. A man's house, she thought.

As if he'd read her mind, Daniel said, "I haven't done much to fancy it up. With flowers and stuff, like Kim did. But it's home. It's close to work, and it's quiet back here."

"How much acreage do you have?"

"Almost an acre. Most of it's wooded, and I like it that way. I like my privacy." He met her in front of the truck and reached for her hand. "Come on. Let me give you a tour."

The interior was clean, uncluttered, and definitely male. Wide-board floors gleamed, dotted here and there with strategically placed area rugs. Vaulted ceilings hovered over the open plan. There was a dining area to the left, with a living room taking up the bulk of the space. A burgundy leather sofa and recliner flanked a fieldstone fire-place that looked like it had been used—a lot. No decorative birch logs here, just a well-swept clean grate. The window treatments were the only incongruous feature. Sheer panels drawn back at the sides graced every one of the paneled windows.

"This is gorgeous, Daniel. A lot of space, though, for, what? Just you?"

Daniel sighed and hunched his shoulders. "Well, that's not how it started out. I actually bought this house when I was engaged to be married." Daniel cleared his throat. "How about some iced tea? I made some sun tea yesterday. Would you like some?

They sat on his porch, at the rear where the only view was the woods. There were two classic rocking chairs with a small wooden table between. Mercy settled herself in one of them and sipped her tea. She felt as though she might have opened up a rather sensitive topic after his last comment. Wait, she thought. I'll just wait to see if he wants to share more.

Daniel came out and dropped into the other chair, draining his glass by half. He turned to look at her, a contemplative expression on his face.

"I guess we both have some backstory to share, it seems. Who wants to go first?"

Mercy laughed, although even she could hear how little humor there was in it.

"Mine is probably way uglier than yours, so I'll let you go first."

Daniel drained his glass and set it on the table, then leaned forward, elbows on knees. "Mine isn't very long, just very sad." He turned and riveted her with his hazel eyes. He began without preamble, without apology. "I fell in love at nineteen, got engaged at twenty-one, and was a mourning pseudo-widower by twenty-two."

Mercy blinked and dropped back in her chair. "Oh my."

He rubbed both hands down his face. "Okay, well, Keelin was the most beautiful woman I'd ever seen. I'd had a crush on her in high school, but it wasn't until I got accepted into MIT that she even considered dating me." He smirked. "It was instant. Love at first sight. At least in my book. But damn if she wasn't Irish, to the core." He leveled a somber gaze on her. "It killed her, that stubborn streak."

Mercy felt her chest clutch and reached out, laying a hand on his arm. "Oh, Daniel, I'm so sorry."

He snorted. *"I might be a woman, by God, but I can drive in New England weather as good as any man. Any man at'all. Even the likes of you."* He covered his face with his hands, and his next words came out thick. "Those were the last words she ever said to me."

The stab of pity took her by surprise. Mercy was up and out of her chair before she knew even what was happening. She knelt down in front of Daniel, cupping one of his cheeks in her hand.

"I'm so sorry, Daniel. Auto accident, then?" she whispered.

He nodded without looking up. Then he dragged in a deep breath and heaved it out, his shoulders shuddering.

"Noreaster. Worst one we'd had in years. She had only a mile to go —a freaking mile! But she never made it to her Mom's house. If she'd only listened . . ."

Mercy rested her head on Daniel's knee. "Okay, I give. Your story is much uglier than mine. Mine is based on human error—"

His head snapped up, and she could see the pain, as well as the sheen, in his eyes. "So was mine. Human error. Stubborn, pig-headed, I'm-perfectly-capable-of-driving-myself, error."

They sat that way a long time, with Mercy's head resting on Daniel's knee. When she thought she couldn't sit on those hard, cold porch boards any longer, she felt his fingers under her chin. Even she was surprised to feel the wetness on her cheeks.

"It was a long time ago. I should be over it by now," he murmured into her eyes.

She shook her head. "No. That kind of loss is beyond your control. Devastating. Fate taking a whack at you. With a baseball bat."

"Maybe," he said, looking deep into her eyes. "But everything happens for a reason. Even if it's a knife to your heart, your life, when it does."

Mercy climbed up onto her knees then and shimmied up between his legs. "Maybe that's true." She held his gaze. "Maybe that's why I ended up back in New England after all. And just for the record, seems I'm really full-blooded Irish, too. Second generation."

Daniel hunched his shoulders and tipped his head. "What can I say? It's one of my weaknesses." Peering deep into her eyes, he murmured, "I think I started falling for you even before I knew you were a Colleen."

He lowered his face to hers and kissed her, softly, cupping her cheeks in his big hands. Chaste, at first, soft lips rimmed with bristly stubble. This, Mercy thought, was different. Luke had been clean shaven. Different, but tantalizing. New. She couldn't help the fire the sensation erupted low in her belly.

Alarm bells were clanging in Mercy's head. *Don't get involved with a coworker. This is such a bad idea. You hardly know this man.*

But her body was speaking much louder than her mind. Screaming, in fact. It didn't matter. She parted her lips and invited him in anyway.

Arm sling be damned, Mercy laced the fingers of her untethered hand around Daniel's neck and tilted her head to probe deeper into his hot kiss. He smelled like spicy cologne under musky male sweat. He tasted like lemony tea and temptation. It was nearly a full minute before he broke the kiss, looking away.

"I'm sorry," he murmured, embarrassed. "You've made it very clear that you want no part of a relationship, or . . ." He hesitated. "Or anything up close and personal with a coworker. I get that. It's probably not a good idea."

He was right, of course, but Mercy just couldn't help the subtle deflation she was feeling. Her shoulders slumped and she dropped her chin to her chest. Had she initiated the kiss, or had he? Horrified, she was sure it was she who made the first move.

I'm only human. A lonely human. A woman who's in need of a little . . .

"I'm sorry," Daniel repeated, tucking one strand of her hair behind her ear. Mercy sighed.

"No, it's not a good idea." She glanced at her watch as she climbed to her feet. "It's been almost an hour. Shouldn't we be picking up the boys soon?"

IT DIDN'T OCCUR to Daniel until he'd pulled into Mercy's driveway that he'd never had the chance to hear *her* sad backstory. Damn it. He'd really hoped he could glean some information about her's as well as her son's past, so he could position himself in a helpful manner.

Reagan leaned forward and rested a hand on Daniel's shoulder.

"Thanks for bringing me over to Davin's tonight, Daniel. That game he has rocks. I hope we can do it again."

"We will," Daniel replied. "Real soon."

After the boy had climbed out and slammed the truck door—a little harder than necessary—Daniel turned to Mercy.

"We never got to your baggage tale," he said sadly. "I guess I got derailed with my . . ."

"No. No, it was me who came on to you, Daniel Gallagher. I'm guilty and I'll take full responsibility for it." She nervously twisted her hair into a tail at the base of her neck. She was deliberately avoiding his gaze. "I hope you won't hold it against me. I'm not a tease, I promise. I've already told you, I'm not ready for any kind of . . . thing. Especially with a coworker."

Daniel placed a hand on her leg, down close to the knee where it couldn't be misread as anything sexual. "I hope we can become really good friends, Mercy. I'm lonely, you're lonely. Your kid could use a little male mentoring, I have free time on my hands. I think we could both use a good friend. It's all good." He patted her leg briskly and grinned. "All good."

Her slow smile made him feel warm from the inside out. *Now if only I can keep my own thoughts—and libido—in check.*

"Library tomorrow night?" he asked.

She nodded. "I'll drop Reagan off at the high school and meet you there at seven."

CHAPTER 10

*D*aniel's truck was already in the library parking lot when Mercy pulled in a little past seven the following night. In fact, the lot was filled with way more cars than it had been when she'd come with him on Friday. Must be open late tonight, she thought. Maybe the Reference Room would be open too.

She didn't realize until she'd climbed out and locked her car that Daniel hadn't yet gone inside. His truck door slammed, and he emerged from between the parked vehicles down the end of the lot wearing a broad smile.

"You made it," he said. "I'm glad. I think Tiffany is working the Reference Room tonight, so we might actually make some progress. Find out some stuff."

Daniel fell in step beside Mercy as they made their way to the side entrance.

"So . . . why is it so important to you to find out the history of the old building?" she asked. "Is this a personal quest or—"

"No, no. Nothing personal. Just some creepy legends about the old place. You know, mental healthcare back in the day was sorta like medieval torture." He arched an eyebrow at her. "The bathtub story should have told you that."

Mercy remembered Daniel's tale about "hydrotherapy." Then she thought about her eerie encounter in the basement the night when she'd gone back to retrieve her cell phone. A shiver ran down her spine.

She nodded. "Yeah, it creeped me out. But medicine has come a long way in the past hundred years. Hell, in the past fifty."

Daniel opened the glass door and they mounted the stairs that would take them to the main level of the building. The basement area appeared to be mostly storage.

The head librarian, Agnes, was at her post this evening, and greeted Daniel with a warm smile. Danny, she'd called him. Mercy wondered if this was a personal endearment. No one on the team referred to him that way. He'd introduced himself as Daniel. She'd have to ask him.

"Danny. So nice to see you again. And . . . was it . . . Mercedes?" she asked, nodding to Mercy.

"Mercy is fine. How are you this evening, Agnes? Working late tonight?" Mercy asked.

Agnes' head bobbed. "Yup, Tuesdays and Fridays. Not too bad, all things considered. She turned to Daniel. "And you're in luck because, as you probably already know, Mr. Smarty Pants, Tiffany is manning the Reference Room tonight." She beamed. "Or should I say, *womaning*?"

Hmm. Tiffany. Wonder just how well old Danny boy knows Tiffany?

Stop. You're being ridiculous. What has gotten into you, crazy woman? This is your coworker. A friend. Nothing more.

The Reference Room was located in the rear corner of the ground floor of the building, its doorway obscured by the stacks of popular fiction. No wonder Agnes worries stuff will go missing, Mercy thought as they made their way in that direction. It wouldn't be hard for someone with a large purse or a roomy overcoat to make off with what might be irreplaceable documents.

But what big secrets were hiding inside the records of the Corby Mental Asylum? Mercy wondered. And why was the town so protective of them?

Mercy rounded the corner into the room and stopped in her tracks. Tiffany immediately smiled as she saw Daniel.

"Hey, Daniel. Back to do some more grave digging?"

Tiffany looked very familiar. It took only a moment before Mercy realized—she was the same, neatly groomed blonde who'd helped her freshen up that night in the ladies' room of the Post Office Pub. When their eyes met, her smile broadened.

"And hey there, pretty lady who borrowed my hairbrush."

"Thank you for that. I was feeling mighty grungy and out of place. You saved me," Mercy said.

Tiffany crossed her arms over her chest. "I didn't realize I was fluffing you up to be with Daniel. I might not have been so willing to lend a hand." She narrowed her eyes, then winked.

So maybe there's more to Daniel's obsession with the Reference Room than just history.

Mercy raised an eyebrow, but said only, "Daniel and I work together."

Yet even as she said the words, Mercy knew there was more to her relationship with Daniel than coworkers. If not, then why the flare of jealousy in her chest? Her eyes flashed to the woman's left hand, where she was relieved to find an elaborate and very sparkly wedding set.

"So, what are you after tonight, Dan? Oh, and I found another folder on the place after the last time you were here. It's just a bunch of newspaper clippings, but it might have some information you'd be interested in."

Tiffany turned toward a small but very neat desk behind the counter and retrieved a manila folder. She handed it to Daniel gingerly, holding the edges closed with both hands.

"Be careful. This stuff should really be in an envelope or laid out in a scrapbook. I made a hell of a mess when I pulled it out of the file drawer the other night."

"Thanks, Tiff."

He nodded toward the lone table in the room flanked by two folding chairs. They certainly didn't appear to want anyone to get too comfortable in here, Mercy thought.

They sat, and Daniel drew a small notebook out of his back pocket that Mercy hadn't noticed before.

He turned and waited until Tiffany had disappeared between the two lone stacks in the room. He ducked his head close to hers. "No photocopies allowed," he murmured conspiratorially.

The man's breath was minty and hot on her cheek, and Mercy felt her face warm. As well as in places farther down. Damn this attraction, she thought. But there was no denying it. Pheromones, maybe. It had to be as simple and scientific as that.

Daniel flipped open the folder and carefully began spreading the yellowed newspaper clippings out on the table. Mercy leaned forward and silently began arranging them in chronological order. The headlines were varied and banal, for the most part. But just seeing the photos of the old building the team was renovating, *in its prime*, so to speak, gave her chills.

Daniel began a mini-lecture in a hushed voice. "So, back in the day, even up until the late 1900s, mental illness was rather *loosely defined.*" He put air quotes around the words. "Women suffering from depression were admitted for a condition known back then as *melancholia.*" He ducked his head and whispered into her ear. "Or when their husbands got sick of them and wanted them out of the way. Without killing them, anyway."

Mercy blinked in shock. "Holy cow."

"Yeah, holy cow is right. I did a survey once of the list of diagnoses the patients up there at Corby were admitted under. A lot of them were conditions not well understood back then. Epilepsy. Diabetes. Even alcoholism was considered a mental illness."

December 24ᵀᴴ, 1970

It seemed as though he'd been listening to his wife scream for days, though it'd only been about eight hours. Devlin paced back and forth across the small living room, raking his hand through his hair. Every few laps, he pulled the silver flask out of his back pocket and took a pull. He knew his lovely wife was going through hell, but this waiting was hell too. And the wondering. He prayed the midwife knew what she was doing.

There was no money for a hospital or a real doctor.

Abruptly, at ten minutes before midnight—before the dawn of their first Christmas morning in their new land—Breanna's screams diminished to whimpers. Seconds later, he heard the indignant howl of his firstborn, echoing from the tiny bedroom on the other side of the door.

Was it a boy or a girl? No matter. Thank God, it was over. The baby was wailing holy murder and sounded strong. Hot-tempered little thing. Wondered if the babe would have the same cap of bright red curls as her father . . .

Devlin ached to open that door, step through and reach for the child. Reassure himself that Breanna was okay. But he was afraid. Birthing, that was a woman's realm. Lifting the flask from his pocket, he drained it and swiped his lips across his sleeve.

The baby's cries continued, muffled at times, then rising to a frenzied crescendo at others. Minutes passed, then half an hour. What was going on in there?

He had dozed off at the small kitchen table, his head pillowed on his arms, when the creaking of the bedroom door awoke him. The midwife, a stout woman in her sixties, stepped out. In her arms she held a swaddled bundle, wriggling and whimpering. Mrs. Fitzpatrick wore a grim expression, and Devlin's heart sank.

"What's happened? What's wrong with the babe?" he asked, jumping to his feet. "Tell me, woman," he demanded.

The midwife held the writhing bundle out toward him. He shrank away when he saw that the woman's hands and sleeves were stained with blood.

"You've got a fine, healthy baby girl, Mr. Doherty." Her voice was thick, and a fat tear slid down her beefy cheek. "But I'm a-feared I couldn't save her momma. The bleedin'... it just wouldn't stop."

DANIEL CAREFULLY LEAFED through the odd-shaped scraps cut from local papers, yellowed now and brittle. They really should be in a scrapbook, Mercy thought, or within another few years, they would crumble to dust. Most of the headlines boasted of some celebration the town hosted for the patients of the hospital. Thanksgiving feasts, Christmas dinners, and Fourth of July picnics. But as Daniel flipped deeper into the pile, some disturbing headlines emerged.

Patient Death Ruled Accidental

Corby Hospital Attendant Questioned About Patient Injuries

Escaped Patient Apprehended by Local Police by Force, Later Dies of Injuries

Daniel skimmed the first of these before handing them to Mercy. They were not related, and all appeared on different dates between 1925 and 1973. There were dozens of them.

"My god," Mercy breathed. "Were the patients in that place really that violent?"

Daniel shook his head and sighed. "It wasn't about treatment back then, Merce. It was about containment, controlling them."

Mercy pointed to a commonality she spotted in at least half of the newspaper reports. "The cause of death was listed as either *unknown*, or a fractured skull. How can a fractured skull possibly be an accident?"

Daniel's shoulders rose. "Some were falls, to be sure. The stairs in that place are steep and narrow. Wouldn't be hard to crack your head open on a windowsill after tumbling down a flight."

Mercy picked up one of the smaller clippings, squinting to read print that was already fading, bleeding into fuzziness on the old paper. "What about this? Broken arm . . . fractured mandible . . . dislocated shoulder . . ." She looked up, wide-eyed. "Were they all that clumsy?"

He shook his head. "Electroshock therapy. Now it's called ECT—electro-convulsive therapy. They deliver a jolt of electricity to the brain. With paddles, here," he placed his fingers on Mercy's temples. "The treatment was supposed to correct imbalances in the brain. More often, the patients instead suffered amnesia and memory loss."

"What about the broken bones?"

"Convulsions, Mercy. They could be quite violent, depending on the voltage administered and the duration. It wasn't uncommon for the patient to thrash about enough to break a bone."

A shock wave of ice shot up Mercy's spine. "Oh my god. I had no idea—"

"Most people didn't. It was considered treatment, back then. Now it almost seems like a form of medieval torture." Daniel scribbled a few dates with accompanying phrases into his notebook. Without looking up, he murmured, "They still do it, you know."

"Do what?"

"ECT. The treatment is still used to treat conditions like depression. In a much more controlled, scientific way, of course, but still . . ."

Mercy wrapped her arm around her middle, cradling her sling. Is this what could await her son if his depression didn't abate? Would he actually be in danger of being subjected to this barbaric treatment?

Daniel glanced over at her and, reading the expression on her face, laid his hand over hers. "Hey. Don't be getting all freaked out about your son's depression. I'm fairly certain Dr. Ian McGuire isn't an advocate of ECT. Reagan is young, and he's strong. I'm sure a traumatic life event is the cause of his . . . issues." He tipped up her chin.

"Which, of course, I still have no knowledge of. But since it's none of my business, I won't ask until you're ready to share his story. And yours. I'm here when you're ready. Okay?"

Mercy felt the sting of tears behind her eyes and suddenly, urgently, wanted to spill out the whole ugly story to somebody—anybody. But especially to Daniel. To this kind, caring man who'd already taken her son under his wing without even knowing what his demons were.

She held his gaze. "I'm ready now," she said flatly. "Whenever you're done here, anyway."

DANIEL FOLLOWED Mercy back to her house, less than two miles up the road. She pulled in beside him, and before he'd had a chance to kill the engine and climb out, she was climbing into the truck next to him. Okay, he thought. She doesn't want me to come in. But what's this?

She was rubbing her arms as if she were cold, yet the evening had remained balmy. Hunching her shoulders, she kept her eyes trained on her feet as she chuckled.

"Still gives me goosebumps just to talk about it. I don't think I'll ever get the memory out of my head. I have nightmares, still."

He laid a hand on her knee, patting it. "Sometimes bad memories can do that to you. They fade, but they never quite go away. Like ghosts that stay invisible until you close your eyes."

She grabbed his gaze then, her eyes glistening. "Yes. Like that. Exactly like that." Her eyelids fluttered and she heaved a deep breath. "I should start at the beginning, but I think it's more important for you to hear about the end first."

"However you're more comfortable telling it, Mercy."

Turning to stare straight ahead, her body went rigid beside him. Her fingers balled into tight fists, and her jaw clenched.

"About a year ago . . . it was last June, right after school let out. I came home from work to our house—Reagan's and mine—and he didn't answer when I called out for him. That wasn't too unusual since he plays those blasted video games. Sometimes he wears headphones, and if he's alone he's got the volume up so damned loud he can't hear me if I scream bloody murder. But the house was quiet. Too quiet." She lifted her eyes to his, and now there were tears, running unchecked down her cheeks. "Except for the sound of trickling water.

"I found Reagan sitting in a bathtub full of water. Overfull. The tap was still running, with rivulets streaming over the side of the porcelain. I thought, a bath? Reagan never takes a bath. And what kind of funky bath salts is he using—"

Daniel didn't need her to finish the telling. He slid across the seat and pulled Mercy into his arms. She buried his face against his shoulder and sobbed, her body heaving.

"The water looked like Cherry Kool-Aid, Daniel. He'd slit both wrists with a straight razor. One of his goddamned father's goddamned straight razor blades. One the bastard left behind in the medicine cabinet. Thank god the kid didn't know enough to slice the veins vertically, or they'd not been able to save him." She was shaking all over now, and Daniel wrapped her tighter in his embrace, careful not to put too much pressure on her injured arm.

Daniel had noticed the thick, pale scars on the boy's wrists the first day he'd met him. When he'd reached for his menu, and when he lifted his glass of iced tea. He was too young for carpal tunnel syndrome, that was for sure. But Reagan didn't appear ashamed of the disfigurement. Daniel didn't know if this was a good thing, or a bad one. He'd have to ask Ian about it. Anonymously, of course.

Why had the boy tried to take his own life? That was the rest of Mercy's story he had yet to hear. He didn't need to know until she was ready to share that with him.

When her sobbing subsided, she quickly pushed away from him. She swiped her hands down both cheeks and seemed embarrassed. Avoiding his gaze, she murmured, "I'm sorry. It's a big, heavy pile of dark dirt to heap on somebody. I'm just so tired of trying to breathe. I've been buried under it for so long."

Again, Daniel rested a hand on her knee and squeezed. "It's okay. I can't begin to imagine how the memory must haunt you. Now, it's your job to keep Reagan from ever reaching that jagged edge again." She met his eyes and his heart squeezed to see the deep furrows between her eyebrows. "It's both of our jobs."

She stared at him, blinking. He wasn't sure if what he saw in those misty eyes was disbelief, relief, or pure shock. They sat that way for a long moment, and Daniel could almost feel the connection between them strengthening. At first, like a weak electric current arcing between their bodies and souls, it was growing stronger by the minute. Daniel knew this was far from pure physical attraction. His heart ached for her pain and yearned to heal her hurt. He brushed her cheek with the back of his hand.

She came to him then, first wrapping her untethered arm around his neck, then gently drawing his mouth down to hers. Her lips were soft and warm, a little salty from the tears. Daniel kissed her chastely. Now was not the time to address the fire she'd just erupted down south of his belt buckle.

But when she parted his lips with her tongue, his fire raged out of control.

CHAPTER 11

*M*ercy wasn't sure when, exactly, her defenses came tumbling down. She knew they'd been weakening, tiny cracks appearing here and there over the past weeks with Daniel. His concern over her son had, of course, made the biggest dent. It didn't hurt that he was an incredibly good-looking man possessing what appeared to be a heart of gold.

Her loneliness, too, was a factor, she was certain. After all, she was a healthy adult woman with a normal libido. Just because her sexual drive, as well as her self-esteem, had taken a major hit not long ago didn't change that. At one time she thought her heart would never heal. This man was proving to her the healing process had begun.

Trust? It would take longer to redevelop the ability to trust a man. Any man. But after sharing her horrible tale about Reagan's attempted suicide with Daniel in the truck, in the dark, all alone, her instincts were screaming *to hell with caution. Take a chance.*

She was struck again by the newness of him. His scent, fresh and inviting, surrounded her like an intoxicating cloud. The brush of his bristly mustache along her lips sent shock waves of desire into her belly. But there was more here . . . more than just physical desire. She felt it in her heart, and from the way he'd looked at her, she felt sure he felt it too.

Tender, patient, unassuming—she wasn't used to that. Her ex had always been a demanding lover, quickly skimming past the more gentle, romantic foreplay. He'd never been one to spend too much time showing affection, with kisses and caresses. Luke always wanted to cut right to the chase, get her clothes off and get down to business. When she was young, she'd found his lovemaking style—the ravishing —exhilarating. He'd make her feel like a damsel in Victorian times who'd thrilled as the fabric of her bodice tore away.

Now, it would seem like an assault.

By the time he broke the kiss Mercy's heart was rat-a-tatting against her breastbone and her breath was coming fast. Daniel touched his forehead to hers and groaned, shifting in his seat.

"I'm trying to be a gentleman here, Mercy. I really am. But you're killing me. I can't seem to resist you."

She pressed her cheek against his and breathed in his warmth. Then she sighed. "I can't seem to resist you either, Daniel Gallagher. It's not a good idea. We both know that. I'm not even sure I'm ready. My heart is pretty badly damaged, and my ability to trust is shot to hell."

He pushed back and cupped her face in his hands. "I'm not asking anything of you, not until you're ready. If ever. Truth is, I could spend an entire evening just cuddling with you. Like this." His smile was so sincere, it washed over Mercy like a warm wave. "For right now, I'm simply enjoying your company, and that of your son.

She started, blinking back into the moment. "Oh. My son. What time is it?" She scrambled in her purse for her phone. "His night class ends at ten."

Daniel glanced at his watch. "No worries. It's only nine-thirty. You've got plenty of time to get to the high school." He chucked her under the chin. "Want me to go with you?"

Mercy thought for a moment, then nodded. "If you wouldn't mind.

But can you drive? My arm is starting to kill me, and I'd like to take one of those pills the doc gave me."

THE WEEK DRAGGED on so long, Mercy thought it would never end. She hated working in the office. Not only was it boring, but it gave her entirely too much time to think. To ruminate. To worry and wonder if this was the future Conner had planned for her. Her arm was improving, slowly, and when she went for her follow-up appointment at her doctor on Friday afternoon, he announced she was ready to begin some physical therapy.

"How long before I can get back to work, doc?" she asked. "My discharge papers from the E.R. said I'd be out of work for only two weeks."

Dr. Meineke's brows lifted and he blew out a breath. "That was a mighty optimistic prediction. Let's see how you do with the PT, and we'll reconsider in a week or so."

It was almost six o'clock by the time Mercy pulled into her driveway, weary and disheartened. She'd braced herself for one more week in the office, but now it was sounding like it could stretch out even longer than that. She'd have to call Conner Monday morning and give him the news. She was certain he wouldn't have a problem with it, seeing as his niece had given birth just a few days after she'd left. And there was no talk about either her returning to work, or of replacing her in any way.

Mercy would need to have a conversation with Conner about that. She'd have to tread carefully, since he'd been depositing her paychecks without disruption. He'd even told her it was okay for her to close up an hour early on Thursdays to get Reagan to his therapist. Now she'd have to hit him up for an hour for physical therapy every day. Maybe she could schedule them for her lunch hour.

The house was quiet, and Mercy remembered Reagan was

working tonight. And tomorrow night. She would have the house to herself both evenings. She was spending entirely too much time alone lately—all day in the office, and now for essentially the entire week-end. Loneliness engulfed her like a cloud of mosquitoes and sucked what little energy she had left right out of her. She found her mind wandering back to Daniel.

The last she'd seen him was on Wednesday, when he'd come to shoot hoops with Reagan. It was their new mid-week routine, but this time, when Mercy invited him to stay for dinner, he'd declined. He said he was headed to Kim's house to help Davin with some school project he was working on. She hadn't heard from him since.

Daniel was probably doing the right thing by backing off from her. She knew that. Best for both of them. After all, she really had played the tease with him, luring him into hot kisses and then claiming she wasn't interested in a relationship.

Mercy sighed. She reached for the bottle of wine she had stashed in the fridge and grabbed a tumbler from the cabinet. Guess she would be spending the evening drowning her sorrows in a few glasses of Barefoot Pino Grigio. Alone.

"Guess we share the same taste in wine."

Mercy jolted, sloshing wine over the rim of the glass. She spun around to find Daniel standing outside her screen door, a huge bouquet of pink roses clutched to his chest and a bottle of wine in his hand. Barefoot Pino Grigio.

He looked delectable standing there in his snug, crisply pressed jeans and a madras plaid shirt in shades of green and brown that matched his eyes. All the blood drained from her head, through her feeling-sorry-for-itself heart, straight down to her core.

"Well, are you going to ask me in? Or turn away a man bearing flowers and wine?" he asked, his grin fanning her already simmering body into full-blown flames.

"I'm sorry," she stammered. "I didn't expect you . . . didn't expect anybody tonight. I was just about ready to apply some alcohol to my aching self-pity. Instead, I applied it to my countertop, it seems."

He came in, handing her the wine. "It's cold already, but I guess we can keep it in the fridge until we finish the one you've got open." The cellophane containing the roses crackled as he laid it on counter. "Got a vase we can put these in?"

The impulse hit Mercy so fast, and so hard, she had no way of holding back the tide. She wanted attention. Affection. There was no denying it. She wanted this man, coworker or not.

The spilled wine could evaporate right there off the countertop. The roses could wilt in their plastic wrap. Wiping her hands dry on a dishtowel, she took two long strides and wrapped her arms around the big man's waist. Resting her forehead on his chest, she said, "I'm so glad you stopped by tonight. I've had a pretty rotten week, and I was just about to throw my own personal pity party."

He smoothed his hand down her hair. "I had a feeling. You must be bored to death in the office all day. Criminy, I have no idea why Conner even has an office. He could hire three bookkeepers and an answering service for what he pays in—"

Mercy cut him off with her hungry mouth, covering his with a lush, wet kiss. Tipping her head up, she looked deep into his eyes. "I don't want to talk about Conner. Or work. Or my son. Tonight, Mr. Gallagher, I want to talk about you and me."

DANIEL EXPECTED an appreciative reaction to the flowers and wine, but not this. Not that he was complaining. His attraction to Mercy had been growing stronger every day. That's why he'd made it a point to stay away for a couple days, distance himself from her. That tactic certainly hadn't worked out very well. He couldn't keep her out of his mind, his dreams. The guys at work were getting sick of him talking about her.

"Why don't you just go on over there and make your move on her,"

Conner told him. "You know it's no business of mine if you start banging a coworker. Just don't let it interfere with your job."

Such a classy guy, that Conner. He'd bristled at his boss's crudeness but said nothing. Daniel worked for the man, but it didn't mean he had to like him.

They stood in her kitchen for a long time, exploring each other's mouths with the passion growing between them at a frenzied pace. Breathless, he finally broke the kiss and studied her face. He ran his finger along her jawline to her now swollen lips.

"Are you sure this is what you want, Mercy? You made it pretty clear you didn't want to get involved with anyone just yet, let alone a coworker."

She nodded, her eyes never leaving his. "Yes, Daniel. I'm ready. You're . . . different from the man who broke my heart. Who destroyed our family. Who nearly killed my son. I'm willing to take a chance. If you are."

After locking the door, Mercy took him by the hand and led him up the narrow stairs to her bedroom. The house was quaint but small, with fading, flowered wallpaper lining the stairwell and upstairs hallway. When they passed what Daniel guessed must be Reagan's room, Mercy reached in and pulled the door closed. Even though he wasn't home, she obviously wanted to protect her son from the knowledge of this encounter.

A good mother. Daniel's respect for the woman hiked up another notch.

Her bedroom, like all the rooms in the house, was small. The queen-sized bed took up most of the floor space, leaving only a narrow walkway around. A compact chest of drawers was wedged beside the headboard on one side, with a tall, narrow nightstand flanking its other side. The single window overlooked the nearly nonexistent backyard, which sloped steeply down to the commuter train tracks.

"Man, I'll bet that takes some getting used to," he commented, pointing.

But Mercy acted as though she hadn't heard him. She led him to the side of the bed and pushed on his chest gently until he sat. She bent to kiss him again, her hair falling forward to tickle his cheek. His arousal burned hotter. Nuzzling his neck, she hummed as she breathed in his scent.

"You," she said, tapping his chest, "obviously got in a shower after work. I did not. Do you mind waiting?"

The bathroom door closed, and he heard the spray of the water. For a moment, he considered slipping in, stripping down, and joining her. But he decided against it. Not this first time. Let her make all the moves. Let her be in control. She apparently has been suffering from a lack of control in her life in the past months. He could wait. He would be patient.

Within minutes, she appeared in the doorway, a white terry robe wrapped discreetly around her body. Her hair was wet and twisted up into some sort of messy bun on top of her head. She wore no makeup —but then, did she ever? Daniel had never really noticed. She was a natural beauty, and at that moment looked to him like a goddess in white terry cloth and bare feet.

She undressed him methodically, unbuttoning his shirt and pushing it back off his shoulders. The whole time, her eyes stayed locked with his. Daniel kept watching for any sign of hesitation, of uncertainty. There was none. This was a woman who knew what she wanted and wasn't afraid to ask for it.

Yet there was no frenzy, no hurry, like some of the women he'd been with. It was as if Mercy was savoring every sensation, every taste, every touch. Her hands fluttered over his skin like attentive butterflies, and she made no sounds except for a small gasp when he finally lay there before her, nude.

They made love slowly on crisp white sheets that smelled fresh, as if they'd been dried outdoors. Fresh and new, just like this experience

—at least for Daniel. When at last their passion crested, together, Daniel felt as though he'd been reborn.

He was no virgin. He'd had relations with a number of women over the years. Yet afterwards, as they lay there, spooned on the now sweat-dampened sheets, Daniel was quite certain this was the first time he'd truly made love.

CHAPTER 12

The light was fading outside the window when Mercy finally lifted her cheek from Daniel's chest. She tangled her fingers in the curly red hair on his chest, then tugged on his beard. She grinned.

"You're a furry beast, aren't you?" she teased.

"Guess you could say that. Does that bother you?"

She snorted. "Did it appear as though it bothered me? It's a turn on. I feel like I've slept with a giant lion. A gentle giant."

Daniel yawned, stretching his arms over his head before encircling her once more. "You've certainly tired this lion out." He glanced toward the window, then turned to look at the clock on the miniscule nightstand. "What time does Reagan get off?"

Mercy sighed and closed her eyes. Hearing her son's name while lying here naked with Daniel seemed . . . strange. She shook the feeling off. She—as well as Reagan, when he eventually knew about them—would simply have to get used to the idea.

"The restaurant closes at ten, but he has to stay after to help clean up. I usually pick him up around ten-forty-five."

Daniel's brows drew together. "Reagan is plenty old enough to drive, isn't he?"

Mercy bobbed her head. "He'll be eighteen next month. His father had taken him to get his permit before . . . well, before our world came tumbling down around us. After what happened, and Reagan dropped out of school, I told him he couldn't apply for his license here in Mass until he earned his GED."

He pinched her chin. "Tough mama, aren't you?"

"I try to be. Trying to be mama and daddy both. For the past year or two, anyway." She stopped her explanation there. She'd share the sad story about her marriage's demise some other time. Not now. Not after such a splendid, romantic evening with this new and wonderful man.

Sensing her discomfort, Daniel stirred. "Well, we've still got, what? A couple of hours until he gets off. It's still light out there. Want to check out someplace really interesting with me?"

NOT SURE WHAT he had in mind, Mercy lifted her head. "Oh yeah? What?"

"There's a graveyard around the corner from the campus. Where they buried the patients who died there," Daniel said.

Mercy blinked in shock. "Really? Didn't the families come to claim their kin?"

"Sadly, most of the time, no," Daniel said. "It's a peaceful spot, up on a little hill. Let's take a drive down there."

It was dusk by the time Daniel pulled his truck up on the shoulder of Research Drive and killed the engine. Mercy stared at him, surprised.

"What are you doing?"

"I figured we'd park and neck for a while. You in?"

"Yeah, right." Mercy snorted, although a tiny voice in the back of her head was screaming *Hell yeah!* It hadn't been even an hour since they'd made love, and she was almost embarrassed to admit she was ready to go at it again.

She shook her head. "No, really. Where is this cemetery? No parking lot?"

"No parking lot. Up until a few years ago, no sign to even mark the spot. The Job Corps started mowing the plot about then. Before that, you'd never even have known there were graves here."

Daniel met Mercy on the passenger side of the truck as she stood on the edge of the ditch, looking around. She saw nothing except for a steep hill beside the road overgrown with weeds and wildflowers.

"Where are we going?" she asked through a chuckle.

He pointed to a small path a few feet up the road. "Up there. Come on," he said as he took her elbow.

Woods surrounded a cleared area of little more than a couple of acres, Mercy guessed. It encompassed the top of a small rise, sloping down at the rear toward another thick grove of woods. A painted, wooden sign, which looked fairly new, marked the spot as the "Corby State Hospital Cemetery."

"Locals call this Hillcrest Cemetery. I guess you can see why," Daniel said as they crested the last few steep feet of the path. "One thousand, forty-one patients ended up here."

"Holy cow," Mercy breathed, turning to survey the plot. To the right stood a stone structure that reminded Mercy of a turret on an old castle. Constructed of fieldstone, the tower stood forty or fifty feet high, and had an open doorway and a window about twenty feet up. It also appeared to be open at the top. "What on earth was that?"

"Water tower," Daniel said. "At least, that's what the state records say. Supposedly it was constructed just after the turn of the century, about three years after the hospital colony was established."

"Water tower . . . but it's got a door and a window—"

"Yeah, well, I guess there was a wooden tank mounted on top of it at one time. Since it's the highest point around, it made sense to store water here. Good pressure, steady supply."

Mercy wandered in that direction, peeking inside the narrow doorway. She found nothing inside except for a dirt floor strewn with a few of last autumn's old brown leaves.

"Looks like a prison cell, except without the bars." She stepped inside and a chill rose gooseflesh on her arms, though the evening air remained warm. Hugging herself, she turned back toward the doorway, where a wooden frame clearly showed evidence of long-gone hinges. "Who knows what kind of door hung here originally? Makes me think of Rapunzel's prison tower."

Daniel stepped into the opening and reached for her hand. "Come on. The light will be gone soon, and we don't want to have to stumble back down that steep path in the dark."

Together they walked toward what looked, to Mercy, like a patch of open land.

"Where are the graves?" she asked.

"You're walking on them."

A shiver racked Mercy's body as her eyes snapped to the ground beneath her feet. "What do you mean, we're walking on them?" She heard the quiver in her voice and wondered if Daniel did too.

He pointed to what looked like a small, surveyor's stone marker a foot or so ahead of them. "They're numbered. Just six-inches square, the concrete spikes had a number chiseled on top. They used to all stand up from the ground a foot or so. But over the years, most have sunken. Some clear down beneath the ground." He pointed to a scruffy patch of grass to their right, and another just beyond the visible marker. "You have to be really careful walking around up here. You could twist an ankle pretty badly stepping into one of those craters."

An overwhelming sense of sadness fell over Mercy like a dark blanket. "Just a number," she repeated. "How would one know what number corresponds to a loved one? An ancestor?"

"I doubt many people have any interest in finding out," Daniel said somberly. "You have to remember that mental illness was a source of family shame at one time. To this day, in some families still."

A flash of memory hit Mercy like a sucker punch to the solar plexus. Her son, sitting in his boxers in the bathtub. A razor blade sitting on the porcelain edge in a pool of crimson.

"Your son requires treatment, Mrs. Donohue. His attempt to take his own life may have been as a result of the recent tumult in your lives. But it also may stem from an underlying mental illness."

Reagan's therapist in Atlanta had broken the news to Mercy in a tiny, private room of the ICU unit. To her, alone. Her rat-bastard of a husband hadn't even bothered to attend the meeting.

Sudden tears blurred Mercy's vision, along with the fading light. An ache began in her chest that she couldn't quite identify. It was grief, but of a flavor more personal than it should have been. Her hands began to shake.

"Let's go. This place gives me the willies," she said as she turned toward the path.

Daniel held her hand more firmly as they made their way back toward the road. "Are you cold? Why are you shaking?" he asked.

"I don't know." By now, there were tears streaming down Mercy's face, though she couldn't say why. It was a depressing place, for sure. But the grief she was feeling was more profound, more palpable. Searing, clutching at her insides. It was as though the very soil under their feet was saturated with sadness, and it rose up around them like foul steam.

"It's so sad they didn't even provide them with gravestones," she mumbled.

She was glad the light had faded to the point where Daniel remained oblivious to her tears. When they reached the path, thankfully, the streetlamp below flickered on. But she didn't want Daniel to see her crying. Quickly, she turned to wipe her face on her sleeve.

When she looked up, she gasped.

The acres of graves beyond glowed with an otherworldly light. As the streetlamp had flickered to life, so had dozens . . . no, *hundreds* . . . of what looked like round Chinese lanterns. On the ground. Evenly spaced. Each one a little different from the next. Mercy blinked, trying to clear her vision. When the shapes came clearly into view, her heart stopped beating.

They were heads. Pale, illuminated heads with mournful faces. Painful grimaces. Some were frozen in a perpetual silent scream.

Headstones.

The world around Mercy went black.

The tug on Daniel's hand nearly pulled him off his feet. He'd felt Mercy's grip tighten before going slack. He turned just in time to throw an arm around her waist before her head hit the ground.

What the hell?

Had she stumbled on an exposed root? There were no graves up this close to the road, so she couldn't have stepped into one of those craters. But even as he dove to catch the falling woman, he had noticed an odd glow coming from behind them.

There was another road angling off from Research Drive and sandwiching the cemetery in the triangular space between. Must be headlights.

"Mercy? Mercy! Are you okay?"

Daniel quickly learned that it was no trip or stumble that had brought the woman down. As he laid her head on the cool, damp grass, he realized she'd fainted.

He felt for her pulse, which was rapid but weak. Patting her cold cheeks gently, he turned her head from side to side in an attempt to rouse her. Nothing. She was out cold.

Daniel was a strong man, but he knew there was no way he could lift and carry this woman down that steep embankment to his truck without incident. He needed help. Should he call 911? Momentarily at a loss, he crouched beside Mercy's prone body and scanned the space around them. He blinked.

The glow beyond was not coming from headlights. What he did see, dotting the graveyard in evenly spaced rows, were what looked like glowing globes. Fuzzy and insubstantial, they lit up the lot with an odd luminescence. What the holy hell?

He rubbed his eyes and shook his head. He'd seen solar grave markers in some of the cemeteries, a bizarre trend that, quite frankly, gave him the creeps. But he knew there were none of those in this graveyard.

This place sure did give off some weird vibes. He squinted in the waning light, struggling to make out what the shapes were. But when he blinked again, the globes were gone.

Mercy moaned beneath him, and he cupped her cheek in his hand. It was icy, clammy. It was a pretty warm evening. Did she have a medical condition she hadn't shared with him? What had caused this?

Bending close to her face, Daniel murmured, "Mercy? What happened? Are you ill?"

That's when she bolted upright so fast he didn't have time to move out of the way. Her forehead smacked his nose so hard he feared, for a moment, that *he* would pass out. The pain radiated up into his crown, and all the way into his jawbone. Falling back on his butt, he cupped his nose with one hand and felt it fill rapidly with warm liquid.

Blood, of course. Shit.

Mercy, in the meantime, had scrambled to her feet like a startled deer. How the hell had she recovered so fast? Grabbing his free hand, she jerked him to his feet with amazing strength.

"Come on, Daniel. We've got to get out of here," she barked. She sounded panicked. Terrified.

Together they stumbled down the steep pathway to the road, Daniel now holding the hem of his tee-shirt to his face to staunch the flow of blood. When they reached his truck, he dug in his pockets for the keys and tossed them to Mercy. She caught them, barely.

"Wha-what?"

Her eyes widened as Daniel stepped under the glow of the streetlight.

"Here. You're going to have to drive. I think you broke my nose."

A half-hour later, sitting in the emergency room of the Corby Hospital, Daniel could feel a hellacious headache coming on, and fast. The bleeding had about stopped, but already he could see the bridge of his nose swelling before his eyes. Mercy sat next to him, oddly quiet. She stared blankly at the floor in front of her.

"I'm so, so sorry, Daniel," she murmured. "I was so disoriented when I came to I didn't even know where I was."

"Hey. It's okay." His words were muffled behind the huge wad of gauze the nurse had given him for his bleeding nose. "But what the hell scared you so badly that you fainted in the first place?"

She pinched the bridge of her nose and shook her head. "If I tell you, you'll think I've lost my mind."

The door to the treatment rooms swung open and an older nurse in grey scrubs called out, "Daniel Gallagher?"

His nose, it turned out, was broken. A minor fracture with no displacement, so at least he wouldn't require surgery. The doctor warned him, however, that not only would he have a terrible headache for a day or two, but both of his eyes would be black by morning.

"Great," he grumbled. "I can't wait to tell the guys that our only female team member busted my nose and blackened both of my eyes."

Sitting in the chair in the small treatment cubicle, Mercy dropped her face into her hands. "I can't believe this happened. Seems like every time we get near each other, one of us gets hurt."

Daniel didn't say anything with the doctor still standing there, scribbling notes on a clipboard. He did wonder, though, if Mercy was referring to more than just physical injury. He hoped not.

With Daniel clutching a script for some pain meds, an ice pack, and wearing a strap of tape over the bridge of his nose, they left the hospital. Mercy checked the dashboard clock as they climbed into Daniel's truck.

"I'm sorry, Daniel, but I'm gonna have to swing by and pick up Reagan on our way back. He'll probably be waiting on me."

CHAPTER 13

"*D*ude! What the hell happened to you?" Reagan barked as he climbed into the back seat.

Mercy glanced at Daniel sheepishly. "Had a little . . . mishap. We took a hike up to the old graveyard. I slipped and fell on some loose stones, and when Daniel tried to help me up, I whacked him with my head."

"Geez, Mom. You've been mighty clumsy lately." He turned to Daniel. "Is it broke?"

Daniel nodded. "Yeah, but not too bad. Minor fracture."

"Are you hurt, Mom? How's the arm?"

"I'm good, Reagan. I think we'll both have a headache tonight, Daniel probably for a day or two. But nothing serious. How was work?" She was anxious to put the events of this evening behind them as quickly as possible. That would, she knew, be difficult, since every time she looked at Daniel for the next several weeks, she'd be reminded.

"It was good. Davin stopped in with a few of his buddies to grab a pie. He's got his license, you know. For like, almost a year." Reagan's tone was a bit more challenging than Mercy liked. She'd also about reached her limit this evening. What a freaking roller coaster.

"Yeah, well, Davin's also in school and earning his degree. As soon as you pass the test and have your GED, we'll revisit the driving subject," she snapped, having slid into full-on mom mode.

She felt Daniel's hand on her arm, but he said nothing.

Reagan, apparently ignoring his mother's retort, continued, "So, Davin wants to go to the mall tomorrow. You know, the one in Millbury? Can I go with him? He's borrowing his mom's car."

Mercy sighed. "Don't you have to work tomorrow too? And what are you going to do at the mall? Is there something you need?"

"We're just going to kick around, grab some lunch maybe. I don't have to work until three in the afternoon. He's going about eleven. Can't I go, Mom? It's the first time I've had a chance to hook up with any friends since we moved here."

She felt a twinge of guilt at his words, since they were true. Mercy had literally kept her son in a bubble, ever since almost losing him that horrible night.

"Davin's a good kid, Mercy." Daniel patted her arm and spoke quietly. "And he's a very careful driver, or Kim wouldn't lend him her car."

Mercy glanced at her son's reflection in the rearview mirror. He looked excited, happy. Normal. It had been quite a while since she'd seen that boyish twinkle in his eyes.

"Okay. But I want you home at least by two o'clock, so you can be ready for work on time."

When they got home, Reagan shook Daniel's hand as they stood in the driveway.

"Hope the nose heals fast." He wrinkled his own. "It looks . . . painful." Then he turned and raced up the steps and into the house.

Mercy came around the front of the truck and handed Daniel his keys. "Are you sure you're alright to drive home? I can drop you off and come back with your truck tomorrow."

"Renaissance"
by
Mildred W. Hilyard

I am a cousin to the winds.
Wind of October, nut-brown and apple-cheeked.
Trailing a smoky scarf into the endless sky.
Wind of December, crystal-clear,
Tossing bright sleigh-bells on the frozen pond.
Sly wind of March, pied harlequin with satyr feet.
Leap-frogging on the marsh to the first hyla's pipe.
Soft wind of June, gentle on the cheek.
Brushing new grass, tops with a baby rose.
Slow breath of August, honey-drunk,
Sprawled among the mad cricket's joy.
Dear kin, I hear you call outside my open door.

Earth is so good; so short a time
Have I sat here within the fire's glow.
Leave me a moment yet; Then I will come,
Young-limbed again and whole, and run with you,
Beyond the stars.

– Before her death, 1972 –

"I'm fine. I only took one of those pain pills they gave me at the hospital to hold me over until I can get the script filled tomorrow. Figured I'd need the other one to get through the night."

Mercy winced, cradling her own now-aching arm. She kicked at a loose stone on the pavement. "I can't tell you how sorry I am, Daniel. I feel like such a fool. I guess I let my imagination run away with me back there—"

"No. No, Mercy, I saw something too. Just before you came to and knocked my lights out. There *were* lights, though, out in the graveyard. Glowing patches over the graves. At first I thought they were head-lights from a car on Pine Street, but they weren't. I don't get it. It was really weird."

Weird doesn't begin to describe what I saw, Mercy thought, and a shudder ran through her.

Daniel rubbed his forehead gingerly. "But look, I'd better get home and take that other pill. Maybe chase it down with a beer. We can talk about this tomorrow, okay?"

Mercy gazed up into his eyes, which were darkening already beside a grossly swollen nose. She stepped into him, resting her fore-head on his chest.

"Before all of that drama," she murmured, "this evening was wonderful."

He tipped up her chin and leaned down to lightly brush his lips over hers. "It was for me too. Can I see you again this weekend? Do you have plans for tomorrow?"

"Nothing other than the usual. Laundry, grocery shopping, house-work. If you're feeling better, maybe I could stop by your house after Reagan goes to work?"

He pressed his lips to her forehead. "Sounds like a plan."

. . .

MERCY WAS MORE than a little surprised to see not one, but three young men in Kim's car when it pulled into her driveway the next morning.

"I thought it was just you and Davin going," she said as Reagan headed for the door.

He shrugged. "Maybe they're the guys who came into the pizza place with him yesterday." Then he pecked her on the cheek. "We'll be fine, Mom. It'll be fun."

Mercy's stomach twisted uneasily as she watched the car back out of her driveway. She stood at the screen door for a long time, chewing on one knuckle. She knew she had to let go sometime. After all, Reagan was practically a man. That didn't make the process any easier, especially after everything they'd been through.

Offering a feeble wave, she huffed out a breath and turned away. Gotta toughen up, Mercedes. Gotta give the boy a chance at returning to a normal life, even if both of theirs had been uprooted and torn apart as shockingly as a giant tree yanked up by a hurricane.

Her mind settled into a numb buzz while she tended to the boring routines. After three loads of laundry, stripping and remaking the beds, and half-heartedly going over the house with a feather duster, she was more than ready for a shower. If she ran to the grocery store in this condition, they might toss her out.

By two o'clock, she pretty much had it all done. She poured herself a glass of iced tea and carried it, ice cubes tinkling, to the porch stoop to sit. And wait. Reagan was supposed to be home by now.

By two-fifteen, her anxiety began. Or was it premonition? Mother's intuition?

When not Kim's car, but a police cruiser pulled up into her driveway, the glass of tea tumbled down the steps as her hand flew to her throat.

A mother's worst nightmare come true. Scrambling to her feet, she whooshed out a sigh of relief when she saw Reagan sitting in the back of the cruiser, his head down. He was the only boy in the car.

The cop, a sturdily built man in his thirties with a shaven head, came around the front of the cruiser.

"Mrs. Donohue?"

"It's *Ms.* Donohue. What happened, officer? Has there been an accident?" Her eyes flashed frantically from the blue eyes of the cop to her son in the back seat. Reagan averted his eyes and didn't get out. She wondered if his hands were cuffed.

"No accident, Mrs. . . . *Ms.* Donohue. I'm Officer Branson. Your son, though, well, he found himself in the wrong place at the wrong time today." His thin lips were pressed tight.

Mercy blinked fast, confused. "Wha-what happened? He was headed to the mall with a few friends. At least, that's what he told me."

"Why don't we go inside, Ms. Donohue. I'll let your son tell you what happened, from his point of view."

Reagan had not made eye contact since they'd arrived. He slunk in through the door, head down, ahead of the officer. When they were seated around the table, Officer Branson took out a notepad from his pocket and flipped it open. He turned toward Reagan.

"Reagan, why don't you tell your mother what you told me earlier?"

Over the next twenty minutes, Mercy learned that the boys' seemingly innocent trip to the mall had taken a somewhat more sinister turn. After an hour window shopping and, no doubt, checking out the girls, they had gotten bored. None of them, it seemed, had much money. At around one o'clock they all piled into Kim's car and were headed, Reagan thought, home.

He was mistaken.

"I had nothing to do with any of this, Mom," he said, his voice thick and quivering. "Davin pulled into the Shell station, and I thought he needed gas. But he parked off to the side of the building. All three of them got out without saying anything. I figured they had to pee. I had a creepy feeling about it, though, so I stayed in the car." Reagan's face crumpled and he turned away, embarrassed. "I had no idea they were going to try to buy beer—and cigarettes—with a phony ID."

Mercy's chin dropped to her chest and she exhaled. So, this is what both Kim and Daniel had been alluding to when they said Davin had gotten in with a "bad bunch." Why, oh why had she let Reagan go along with them today?

And why the hell hadn't Daniel warned her more explicitly about this bad bunch his nephew was hanging with?

"We didn't make any arrests, Ms. Donohue. Even if we had, your son obviously wasn't guilty of any wrongdoing. As I said, he was in the wrong place at the wrong time."

"With the wrong company," Mercy added bitterly, flashing a look at Reagan.

"My partner did take the other boys down to the station. More to scare some sense into them than anything else. I thought it best if I brought Reagan home directly, rather than having you pick him up at the station."

"Thank you for that, Officer. I guess Reagan—and I—will have to vet his new friends a little more carefully in the future. We're new to the area," Mercy said.

The officer nodded, rising. "Yes, well, Corby is a good community. But every town has its share of rambunctious youth."

After the officer left, Mercy stood glowering over her son. Reagan remained silent, sullen, staring at the placemat before him.

"So who were these two other boys, Reagan? Did you even get their names?"

He nodded but wouldn't look at her. "One's name is Alan, the other one Steve. I don't know their last names, but they live in Westboro. I guess they're seniors—a year ahead of Davin in school."

After a long moment, Mercy said, "Okay. I realize you haven't done anything wrong. But this could have turned out a lot worse, even if you hadn't known what the boys were up to. What if you'd gone into the store with them? You'd be down at the police station right now."

Reagan nodded again, but said nothing. Mercy couldn't help but feel sorry for him. He'd been so excited to have found some new friends. His new social circle had unraveled as quickly as it had formed. She glanced at the clock and sighed.

"Listen to me. You're not in trouble. But you aren't going to use this as an excuse to bail out of work. You've got exactly twenty minutes to clean up and get dressed. I'll drive you down to Anzio's. Then I'm headed over to have a little talk with Daniel. He should have warned us about those boys."

Reagan looked up, desperation written all over his face. "You're not going to blame Daniel for this, are you, Mom? I really look forward to playing ball with him on Wednesdays. And Davin . . . he's a good kid. I don't think he knew what Alan and Steve had planned either."

Mercy sincerely doubted that but couldn't help feeling the pang of pity stabbing her heart. *He misses his father*, is what he's saying. He misses his friends, and his old life. She shook her head.

"No, I'm not going to blame Daniel. I'm just going to have a talk with him. And before you spend any more time with Davin, I'm going to find out just what other kind of trouble the boy's gotten himself into."

Mercy barely got Reagan to the restaurant before he was due to start, at three o'clock. As he climbed out of the car, he looked back and mumbled, "Sorry again, Mom."

She headed straight for Daniel's house, trying to work out in her head exactly how she was going to approach this discussion. It *wasn't* Daniel's fault, she knew. But he obviously had more knowledge about his nephew's antics than he may have let on. She understood both Kim and Daniel wanting Reagan to act as a positive influence on *their* kid, but it wasn't going to happen at the expense of her son. Not on her watch.

She rang the bell, then stood there for several moments, waiting. His truck was in the driveway, so surely he was home. After the second ring and still no response, she was about to turn away and head home when she heard his heavy footfalls on the hardwood floor.

Mercy had completely forgotten about Daniel's broken nose until he pulled open the door. The poor guy looked like hell. Both eyes were swollen and purple, and she knew she'd woken him up. Bare-chested, he wore only a pair of faded grey sweat pants, which appeared to have been hastily pulled on—backwards. He squinted in the bright afternoon light spilling in behind her and winced.

"Hey. I woke you. I'm sorry," she said, feeling another pang of guilt and embarrassment at having caused this. Still, the stronger part of her wanted to air some of her thoughts about the events of this afternoon. About his nephew.

He waved off her apology. "It's pretty much all I've done for the past twelve hours or so. Come on in.

Daniel headed for his kitchen. "Wanna beer? I'm afraid to have one but I can live through you vicariously." He shot her an impish grin over his shoulder, then winced again. "Damn, it even hurts to smile."

"I'll take that beer. Daniel, something happened this afternoon that we need to talk about."

He froze and sobered, staring at her. "Something *else*? You didn't go back up to that graveyard, did you?" He twisted off the cap and handed her the bottle.

"No. Nothing like that." She kept her tone cool and distant.

The first long swallow of beer felt good—crisp, cold, and fortifying. The last thing Mercy wanted to do was to alienate this man: her coworker, her son's new role model, and now, her lover. But her son came first, and she needed to know more about Daniel's nephew before she allowed Reagan to get any chummier with him and his buddies.

Daniel raised his glass of ice water to clink against her bottle.

"Okay. Let's go sit on the back porch. It's still nice and shady there this time of day."

He settled into one of the rockers and rested his elbows on his knees. "So what's this all about? Are you sorry about what happened between us yesterday? Is that why you broke my nose?" His grin was followed by another grimace of pain.

Mercy kept her gaze level on his, her expression deadpan serious. "Daniel, Reagan went to the mall this morning with Davin. I had no idea he was bringing along two of his buddies. They both appeared to be older than either of our boys." She deliberately said, "our boys," since she knew Daniel took the raising of his nephew as seriously as would a father. She hoped that reminder would make him realize why she was so concerned.

He paused with his water glass halfway to his lips, staring at her. "I had no idea Davin would be bringing anybody else with him. I know Kim didn't either. She would never have allowed that. Who were they? Do you know?"

Mercy rubbed her arm, aching in its sling after all the housework she'd done earlier. She took another swallow of beer. "Reagan said they were seniors in Westboro. Alan and . . . Steve, I think? He didn't know their last names."

Daniel closed his eyes and dropped his head back. "Alan Powers and Steve Whiting. They both come from two of Westboro's richest families. Kids with a highly inflated sense of entitlement." He pressed the sweating water glass to his temple. "What did they get into this time?"

Mercy felt a flash of anger flare in her chest. "This time," she repeated. "*This time?* They've been in trouble before, obviously. Daniel, why didn't you warn me about Davin's pack of hoodlums?"

He leaned forward suddenly, slamming his glass down on the table and curling his strong fingers around her arm. "Hey, hey. For one thing, they're not hoodlums. They're mischievous kids. And besides, I had no idea anybody else would be going with Davin and Reagan today. I thought this was going to be a new start for Davin with a new friend. A decent young man."

She knew he was right, and her anger deflated as quickly as it had raged. She exhaled.

"Well, they tried to buy beer and smokes with a phony ID, and Reagan got his first ride in a cop car."

CHAPTER 14

aniel dreaded showing up at work Monday morning sporting what looked like the aftermath of a bar room brawl. He considered telling them that's how it happened—a much more macho way of suffering a broken nose than getting whacked in the face by a woman. He knew it was an accident, but the guys would rib him about it to no end, he was certain.

Studying his face in the mirror that morning, he determined that it didn't look nearly as bad as it had. His eyes were still black, and the bridge of his nose was twice as thick as it was usually. In the end, he decided to forego the bandage tape and not draw any more attention to himself than necessary.

"What the hell happened to you?" Conner smirked as Daniel climbed into the work van.

Daniel kept his head down and mumbled, "Long story. It was an accident. No big deal."

"Dude, that's gotta hurt. You okay to work? I mean, with all that dust and crap we're breathing in, can't be good for it." Jacob spoke from the back seat, meeting Daniel's eyes in the rearview.

"I said I'm fine. Just drive, Conner."

It wasn't fine. Daniel felt the blood pounding in his head every time he bent over to pick up a tool or roll of conduit. Climbing the ladder made him a little dizzy, and more than once he had to grab hold to keep from tumbling over backwards. The dust they kicked up made his irritated nostrils burn like hell. But he wasn't going to let this stupid incident cost him a day's work.

They were already a man short. Or, a woman. As if Conner had read his mind, he asked, "So how's Mercy's arm doing? Healing up?"

Daniel glared at him over his shoulder. "What makes you think I've seen her?"

Conner chuckled. "Just a hunch. Don't think I haven't noticed how you look at her."

Daniel let a long beat of silence tick by, breathing in slowly—albeit gently—in an effort to tamp down his irritation. Finally, he said, "She's supposed to start physical therapy this week. I think she's coming to talk to you sometime today."

It was just about lunchtime when Mercy's Camry pulled up to the job site. Daniel was about to hop into the van after the guys when he spotted her. She parked and walked up to the driver's side, where Conner's arm was perched on the window frame.

Mercy wasn't wearing overalls, or a baggy tee shirt over jeans. She was dressed up in a simple, dark blue dress made of some sort of stretchy material that hugged all her curves quite nicely. The hem fell a good couple inches above her knee, revealing very shapely legs. Enhanced by heels. Sexy, shiny red heels. Her voluminous dark waves fell about her shoulders in satiny sheets.

Oh yeah. She's working in the office. She has to dress the part.

Of course, Daniel wasn't the only one who noticed how attractive she looked. Both Conner and Jacob's whistles split the air. Mercy scowled, and Daniel had to tamp down a flare of jealousy that surprised even him.

"Alright, guys, keep your eyes above the sling," she growled. "Conner, I know you're headed for lunch, but can I speak with you a minute?" She tipped her head toward the building. "In private?"

Daniel watched as they walked a distance away to talk, into a spot shaded from the early afternoon sun by the hulking form of Gravely Hall. He crossed his arms and leaned on the van, wishing he could make out their words. He had a feeling Mercy wasn't going to like the answers she would get from his boss.

He was right. Within minutes, Mercy's posture stiffened, and her voice rose. She was gesticulating wildly in the air with her good hand. Conner crossed his arms and spat tobacco juice into the weeds beside him. Daniel saw him shaking his head, and Mercy threw up her hand and turned away from him. When Conner reached up to place a hand on her shoulder, she shrugged him off and stalked back toward her car.

"Hey Boss?" Daniel approached Conner as he headed for the driver's side of the van. "I think I'll skip lunch today." He tipped his head towards Mercy. "Maybe I can defuse some anger here."

Conner shrugged and climbed into the van. "Good luck with that, my man." Then he started the engine and peeled out of the driveway with a little more punch than necessary.

Daniel caught up with Mercy just as she was about to leave. He knocked on her window and she lurched. Then she closed her eyes and dropped her forehead to her steering wheel. Daniel opened her car door and crouched down beside her.

"What happened, Merce? Conner being a dick?" he asked softly. Reaching up, he tucked a strand of her hair behind her ear. It took him a moment to realize that she was crying. Silent tears of frustration and fury slid down her cheek.

"I'm an electrician, not a receptionist, Daniel. Conner has essentially degraded my status to nothing more than a . . . a Darcy clone." She met his eyes. "I've been knocked down enough these past two years. I'm not willing to take another kick in the ovaries."

Hmm, interesting twist on the male version of that particular slang, but he got her meaning. He took her hand from where it lay fisted on her thigh and rubbed it with his thumb.

"Why don't we go get some lunch, and you can tell me what's going on?" he asked.

Mercy drew a deep breath and nodded. "I don't know about lunch, but I sure could use a beer. Screw Conner's no-alcohol-on-the-clock rule." She glanced at him again and blinked, apparently really seeing him for the first time that day. "God, you look like hell."

"Gee, thanks," he said, and grinned.

They got takeout from a burger joint on Rte. 122 and took it to the small park that had recently opened on the corner of Bridge Street and Rte. 30. Mercy ordered the food while Daniel ran into the liquor store across the street and grabbed a six-pack of beer.

The park was small, but brand-new and quaint, encompassing an area that had been nothing more than clotted brush and untamed woods before. Now, an attractive iron railing sectioned it off from the road. There were only three picnic tables, but none were occupied. The sound of gushing water from the adjacent spill gate was soothing.

"This is so pretty," Mercy said as they settled at the table most obscured from the street.

Daniel twisted open two beers and placed them, discreetly, on the concrete pad supporting the table. He looked up at Mercy and shrugged. "No sense in taking chances."

She laughed, a sound that warmed him to his very core. God, he was becoming attached to this woman. Everything about her seemed . . . perfect. For him, anyway. Daniel was well aware of the unnatural and very unreal "high" that infatuation could incite. He'd experienced that high only a time or two since his fiancé's death all those years ago. But somehow what he felt happening between him and Mercy seemed different.

They unwrapped their greasy and completely unhealthy burgers and fries in silence. After taking his first wolfish bite of his own, he studied her. She was delicately disassembling her burger from its bun, using a plastic fork to fashion the lettuce and tomato on top of it.

"Don't tell me you're on some sort of diet," he said. "Lady, you don't need to do a damn thing to change that sexy body of yours."

She blinked up at him and narrowed her eyes. "I'm turning forty soon, Daniel Gallagher. A woman's metabolism takes a nose-dive about now. If I'm going to enjoy a few of these," she bent down and lifted her beer, "I have to cut back on carbs somewhere."

Daniel shook his head. "Whatever. Now, tell me what old boss man Conner said that's got you so riled up."

Over the next few minutes, Mercy retold her tale of woe. She was going to be taking Darcy's place in the office "for the foreseeable future." Daniel couldn't help the boil of rage he felt stirring in his own chest.

"That bastard," he muttered. "It's almost like he had this planned all along." He paused, then met her gaze. "But he's still paying you a technician's wage, right? So, you've got to be the highest paid receptionist-slash-bookkeeper in the state."

Mercy was licking mayonnaise from the burger off her fingertips, which Daniel found incredibly distracting. He cut his eyes away, then reached down for another slug of his beer. Stay focused, man. You can't jump her bones in a public park.

"Yes, he says he'll continue to pay me my agreed upon wage until my arm is healed. Or until the Grafton Hall renovation is complete. Whichever comes first." She glared at him, one eyebrow raised. "He doesn't want me in that building, Daniel. I'm not sure if I should be pissed off at him or grateful."

Daniel scrunched up the paper from his first burger and began unwrapping the second. "I think you should be grateful. There's something very sinister about that building. Some extremely negative energy. Did I tell you what happened the other day on the second floor, just as we were leaving for lunch?"

After he'd retold the story of the doors in the north hallway—all ten of them—slamming simultaneously, Mercy rubbed her arm.

"Yikes. You're right. There's negative energy there, alright. But how could there not be? It was a mental asylum, for god's sake. Who knows what horrors those poor patients suffered?"

"Speaking of," Daniel began, pointing a French fry at her, "what the hell scared you so bad in the graveyard the night you broke my nose?"

Mercy hunched her shoulders and looked away. "I . . . I'm sure I was just imagining it."

Daniel reached forward and closed his fingers around her wrist. "No. I need to hear what you saw. Because just before you came to and knocked my lights out, I saw something too."

Just then, a horn beeped from the road behind them. Conner's van sat at the traffic light, and he waved through his open window. He leaned out before spewing another disgusting stream of tobacco juice onto the pavement.

"Lunch break's over, kids."

CHAPTER 15

*M*ercy huffed and hugged herself. "Do you have to keep reminding me that I broke your nose? I feel bad enough as it is."

Daniel reached up and gently pressed on the bridge of his nose. "It's really not as sore today as I thought it would be. I heal fast." He lifted both arms, fists raised. "Me tough guy."

Mercy laughed and began gathering the trash from their lunch into one pile. "Okay, tough guy. I'm a tough chick too. But I don't think either of us wants to piss off the boss man by over-extending our lunch hour."

As Mercy drove Daniel back to the job site, she glanced at the dash clock and groaned.

"What the hell am I going to do for the next four hours? Unless somebody calls in for a quote, there's nothing—absolutely nothing —to do."

"Why don't you start researching your ancestry? You can do that all online now, you know." He shifted in his seat to face her. "Mercy, just what do you know about your roots up here? I mean, your real parents?"

She shrugged. "Not much. Just what I told you the night that Reagan asked. I do know my birth father's name. Where he is, or whether or not he'd be interested in hearing from me, I have no idea."

Daniel laid a hand on Mercy's arm. "You know, for your son's sake, you should try to find him. Ancestry records have come a long way since you were Reagan's age. Ancestry.com. You should go there and try to find out where your father is. Whether he's still alive. It can't hurt to try to contact him, if he is."

Mercy considered this for a long moment. She'd heard about the ancestry sites, and how people that had been separated decades ago were experiencing happy reunions. She was sure there were also a share of horror stories that never reached the public eye.

But for Reagan, she should. She probably should at least try, again. If the man was still alive and was at all open to reuniting, it would give her son a more stable base than he had now. Another man in his life.

Back at the office, she located the site easily enough and could even access some of the records on a trial basis for free. Mercy typed in her father's name—Devlin Doherty—and waited while the search engine did its thing.

Since she didn't have any identifying information on the man, like his social security number or even his birth date, she found herself drowning in an endless sea of information. There were Devlin Dohertys everywhere, it seemed. But okay, she knew where he was, at least where her mother was, when she was born. Boston. And she knew the date. Her birth date. She narrowed her search to the Boston area, 1972.

When the search engine completed its scan, Mercy's skin washed cold. Instead of looking at a long list of names, she saw only one. Sucking in a deep breath, she hovered her mouse over the "records available" column. A pop-up box flashed open.

Of course. In order to access any further information, she'd have to pay the introductory membership fee. It wasn't exorbitant, but Mercy hated putting her credit card information out into cyberspace.

After a few minutes of struggling, she made her decision. No. It wasn't worth it.

Even if she found her father and he was alive, he probably wouldn't be interested in hearing from her. He'd given her up for adoption willingly, hadn't he? Why would he want his now almost forty-year-old "baby" to come calling on his doorstep? He'd moved on. Probably had another family, a new wife, more children.

Just like Luke had.

She closed out the window and turned to clean up the atrocious breakroom area at the back of the office.

DECEMBER 25TH, 1970

God, how Devlin's head ached. He couldn't remember much of what happened after the midwife came out and told him he had a baby girl. All he could remember were the emotions. Elation followed quickly by the heart-rending news that he was now a widower.

How on God's green earth was he going to take care of a newborn babe? There simply was no way. And how could he possibly go on in this life, in this strange new land, without his beloved Breanna? It was impossible, it was. Devlin wanted it all to be over. He briefly considered taking himself down to the docks, tying some sandbags to his legs, and jumping in.

But he was a bit of a coward. There was no way he'd have the courage to take his own life. What he did do, as the midwife made arrangements for a wet-nurse to come feed the baby, is to go in search of his next drink.

Of course, there was none to be found. It was Christmas Day. His head pounding, his heart bleeding, Devlin stumbled out onto the snowy streets of Boston where the colorful lights and decorations only poked at his pain.

When Daniel got back to the job site, Conner and Jacob were unloading another large roll of conduit from the back of the van. He grabbed the crate holding dozens of outlet boxes and followed them inside.

"Where we headed with these, Conner?" Daniel asked.

"The third floor's about ready for the inspector. We move down to number two and get started there. I think the flooring contractor has all the old tile pulled, and they've cleaned it up some."

Daniel grunted as he climbed the stairs. The second floor, even worse than the tunnel, creeped him out the most. In his research of the building, he'd uncovered a sketch of the original floorplan. Patient rooms, which were more like prison cells, took up most of the second floor. Each door was three inches thick, and bore a tiny, round peephole, the glass reinforced with heavy wire. So, the caretakers could keep an eye on the patients without having to risk disturbing them.

Or getting hurt in the process.

The second floor was divided into two sections—nurse's quarters at one end, and treatment rooms at the other. They were starting in the treatment room, Conner had said, and would work their way to the south end of the building. The old floor tiles had been removed, leaving the wide board flooring exposed. Conner led the way but froze in the doorway of the treatment room.

"What the holy hell?"

Daniel ducked around him to see what the problem was. There, in the center of the room was a huge tarp covering something. The tiles in this room remained, their edges curling away from the wooden floor.

"Guess they didn't get to this room," Daniel muttered. He reached up and lifted one edge of the tarp. "Damn. What's this still doing here?"

A rusty, metal table held what Daniel at first thought was a hulking old radio of some kind. The box's face was dotted with numerous dials and knobs. There was a double-pinned cable hanging from one corner. He used a gloved hand to sweep the dust off the lower edge where some numbers and letters were barely visible.

"Liberson Brief Stimulus Therapy Apparatus. Offner Electronics Inc. – Chicago," he read aloud.

"What the hell is that?" Jacob asked.

Daniel felt a jolt run up his arm, as though the thing still had electricity running through it. "This, my man, was what they used to do electroshock therapy."

Conner picked up the other end of the cord dangling from the device. Two wooden handles with flat metal plates on the ends were attached to the cords. "What the hell?" he mumbled.

"Back then the medical community thought they could 'reset' a person's brain by giving it a good jolt. Sort of like jumping a battery on a car," Daniel said. "Except you don't have to worry about your car having convulsions or biting off its tongue."

Conner dropped the paddles like they were scorching hot, recoiling. They landed on top of the machine with a clatter. He wiped his grimy gloves on his overalls, his mouth twisting into a disgusted scowl. "When the hell are they going to get this old shit out of here? I'm gonna have to talk to the head man about it." He sent a stream of tobacco juice onto the old tiles. "Cover it up, guys. Let's get to work."

They set to work running conduit and installing outlet boxes. Daniel, whose taste in music differed drastically from the brothers, plugged his earbuds into his phone and tuned in to some coffeehouse jazz. Upbeat yet unobtrusive, it helped him concentrate on his work, unlike the boom-boom modern stuff Conner and Jacob preferred.

The work went quickly, and by an hour before quitting time, the guys were just finishing up in the big room on the south end of the building. Even over the music in his ears, Daniel heard what sounded like a scream. Ripping out his earbuds, he spun away from the wall. Had Conner or Jacob gotten hurt?

They had turned away from their work as well, and were frozen in place, wide-eyed.

"What the hell was that?" Jacob barked.

Conner reached down and switched off the radio, and they all stood there for a minute, listening. Silence. No sound except for the rustling of the tree branches outside the windows.

"That didn't come out of your radio?" Daniel asked.

"No way, man. It sounded like it was coming from—"

The scream sounded again, terrified and blood-curdling, from the other end of the hallway. High-pitched and screechy, it was impossible to tell whether it was male or female. The sound echoed, reverberating off the walls, and Daniel's stomach twisted in on itself. He was the first to set down his screwdriver and head in that direction.

He glanced into each of the rooms as he went, as all the doors were open. Nothing. Nobody. When he got to the far end, the old *treatment room*, he stopped short in the doorway. He stood there in shock, his mouth agape.

The tarp that had been covering the ancient shock machine had been ripped away and lay crumpled in a heap off in the corner. The paddles that Conner had dropped onto the box's top were on the floor. The electrical cords attaching them to the instrument were now stretched taut, as though someone had tried to pull them out.

Gooseflesh rose on Daniel's arms as his eyes flashed around the room. The scream, although it did not sound again, seemed to echo inside his head. His heart pounded in his chest as his mind conjured up just what had gone on in this room back when the asylum was in operation. It took him a long moment to regain his ability to speak.

"Hey guys? Either of you uncover this equipment?" he muttered, thinking the two men were right behind him. They were not. In the distance, he heard Conner's voice.

"Find anything, Daniel?"

Chicken-shits, they were. Both of them. He turned and stalked back down to where they stood, still in the doorway of the room where they'd been working.

"Somebody's ripped the cover off that shock machine and yanked on the paddles. The tarp is crumpled up in a far corner. Either of you do that?"

Silently, both of their heads oscillated from side to side. Conner pulled off his helmet and scratched his balding head.

"We gotta get this job done and done quick. I want outta this place," he grumbled. "Either of you got a problem working an extra hour for the next couple of days so we can get the hell out of here?"

"Fine with me," Jacob shot back.

"I can do that," Daniel said. He turned and stared back down the hallway. Thank God they'd finished the work they had to do in the treatment room today. He wasn't a chicken-shit, but he wasn't terribly anxious to hang around in that room any more either.

CHAPTER 16

The week dragged on for Mercy, but her arm, at least, was getting better. The physical therapy she did on her lunch hour seemed to be speeding along the healing process. The sling was gone, and her arm was nearly back to full mobility. By Thursday, she was thinking about stopping by the job site after dropping Reagan off for his therapist appointment. She might be able to convince Conner to put her back on the job next week.

That would leave the office, she knew, unmanned. But she had it all figured out, how she was going to try and sell the idea to Conner. Today was as good a day as any to lay it out for him.

On the way to Dr. McGuire's, Reagan seemed unusually sullen and quiet.

"What's wrong with you today, buddy? Not feeling well?"

He shook his head but continued to stare out the side window. She heard him heave a huge sigh. "Dad called me this morning. Wants to know if I can come down and spend some time with him when I finish my school and pass the test." He turned to her then, furrows between his brows. "Can I, Mom? I really miss him."

The pleading in his voice plucked at Mercy's heart. She knew how much Reagan missed his dad. But going to visit him meant thrusting him into Luke's new life. Mercy wasn't sure it would be good for Reagan at this point. She also secretly feared that Reagan would decide he wanted to stay in Atlanta and live with his father.

She thought about it for a moment before answering him. "We'll see, Reagan. You've got, what? Another few weeks of school left, right? You should be able to take your test by the first week of September." She glanced over at him and smiled. "Why don't you ask Dr. McGuire what he thinks about it?"

Reagan nodded. "I will. And Mom? Did you think any more about trying to find out where my grandfather is? If he's still alive? Maybe if he's local still, I could get to know him."

Jab. Twice in one afternoon. Mercy cringed.

"I did start a search, but got stuck and couldn't access any more information," she said, staring straight ahead at the road. It wasn't a lie, exactly . . . just not the whole truth.

"Maybe Daniel can help you. He's pretty good with researching stuff."

After delivering her son to the therapist, Mercy drove to the job site, where she knew the guys would be starting to wind down for the day. She was surprised when she stepped into the building and heard the whirring of electric screwdrivers still coming from the north end of the first floor. Conner's radio was blasting. When she stopped in the doorway to the big room, all three men were engrossed in their work. Daniel was on his knees, working along the baseboards. He was wearing earbuds.

Funny, she thought. When he and I work together, he never does that. Guess he doesn't care for Conner's taste in music.

"Hey guys!" she called over the din, then staggered back a step at their reaction. All three men spun around, wild-eyed. Jacob's tool clattered to the floor, and Daniel jumped to his feet, nearly falling when his boot got tangled under a length of conduit.

"Jesus, Mary, and Joseph, girl. You scared the shit out of us," Conner snapped.

Mercy raised her eyebrows and both hands. "Hey, I'm sorry. How else could I get your attention? And what's got you all so jumpy, anyway?"

Daniel pressed his fingers to the bridge of his nose. Gingerly. The bruising had faded from black to a greenish-yellow. It still looked swollen, and Mercy again felt a twinge of guilt.

"Just some creepy shit happens in this building, that's all. You should be glad you're not on this job," Daniel said.

Mercy stepped up to Conner and held out her injured arm. Then she raised it up over her head, lowered it, and flexed her bicep. "See boss? Almost healed. The doctor said I'll be good to come back to work—to my *real* job—by Monday."

Conner had started shaking his head the minute Mercy started speaking. "Now you know we can't do that, Mercy May. Who's going to man the office? Do the bookkeeping? Balance payroll?"

Mercy perched her fists on her hips and glared at him. "I'm not a receptionist or a bookkeeper, Conner. You hired me as an electrician and that's the job I want to do. If your niece isn't coming back then you're going to have to make other arrangements for that end of the business." She crossed her arms over her chest and narrowed her eyes. "And I have some suggestions as to how you might do that."

Conner rubbed the back of his neck and stared at the floor. "I know, I've been thinking about it. The rent I pay for that office would probably cover the cost of a bookkeeper." He met her gaze, scowling. "But rent's paid up until the end of this month. We should be done on this job by then. What's our next gig?"

Avoiding answering him, Mercy huffed. "Another two weeks, Conner? Seriously? What is it about this job? Don't you think I'm good enough—*manly* enough—to handle working in an old mental asylum?"

"Believe me, if I could do the bookkeeping, I'd trade places with you in a minute," Jacob mumbled.

Mercy glanced from Jacob, to Conner, to Daniel.

"What's been happening? More chalk scrawls on the wall?" Exasperated, she turned her back to the men and stared down the hallway. The place definitely did exude some bad energy. But Mercy thought if she had to spend another two weeks in the office, her brain would turn into oatmeal.

She felt Daniel's hand on her shoulder. "Look, Merce, the guys and I are working an extra hour every afternoon to get out of here. The place is not only creepy as hell, but it gives off some really bad vibes. It's not just you who got jumpy. As you just saw, we're all freaked out on this job."

But Mercy was only half-listening. She was angry and frustrated, and was afraid if she said anything, she'd jeopardize her job. She definitely couldn't afford to do that.

As she stared down the hallway, movement caught her eye. A shape began to appear, very slowly, emerging from within one of the rooms. It was blurry and dark, and for a moment, she thought it was a trick of the light. She squeezed her eyes shut and reopened them. No, there was definitely something coming out one of those doorways.

About three feet from the floor, a black arm reached out, then curled itself around the doorjamb. Daniel's hand tightened on her shoulder.

"Do you see that?" he whispered.

Following the arm, the black shape was followed by another shape, this one round, about the size of a human head. There were no features, just a silhouette, black and smudgy, as though it were made of smoke. Mercy felt tingles up her back and shrank closer to Daniel's body behind her.

"I see it."

"What are you guys looking at?" Conner barked, stepping up beside him.

The shadow figure remained for a fraction of a second longer, then withdrew out of sight, lightning fast.

"I don't see anything," Conner grumbled. "But you see why I don't want you on this job, Mercy?"

Daniel squeezed Mercy's shoulders and stepped around her, heading to where the figure had appeared. He strode boldly up to the open doorway, then stepped inside. After a few seconds, he called, "I don't see anything. But come in here, guys. This is really weird."

Mercy led the way, followed by Conner. As they approached the room Daniel had entered, she could feel it on her bare ankles before they even got to the doorway.

Cold, like stepping into a walk-in freezer. Chilled air, like from an air conditioner, poured out of the room in a forceful stream. Mercy's hair blew back from her face the minute she stepped inside. She rubbed her arms.

"You guys running portable air conditioners in here?" she asked.

The day was hot—it was late July, and without the ability to open any of the windows in the building, it was right steamy in there by this late in the day. She met Daniel's gaze and his one eyebrow was lifted. He shook his head slowly.

"No air conditioners. No power, Mercy."

Conner pushed past Mercy and turned a full circle in the center of the room. "Where the hell is that coming from?"

Abruptly, the airflow ceased. Mercy could feel the cold air sinking down her face, along her arms, and finally to around her ankles. A moment later, it was hot in the room again. This room faced the west and the glass-blocked window was magnifying the afternoon sun's rays. It had to be at least eight-five degrees in there.

"Fucking weird," Conner grumbled. "Let's call it a day, guys. I've had about enough of this place today."

· · ·

AFTER PACKING their gear in the back of the van, Daniel turned to Conner and said, "Maybe Mercy can give me a ride to pick up my truck later at the office. I'd like to talk to her for a few."

Conner slammed the van's rear doors and waved him off. "Fine by me. See you in the morning."

After the van pulled away, Daniel turned to Mercy. "You saw that, didn't you? That shadow figure in the doorway?"

Mercy visibly shuddered and hugged herself. "I did. I thought I was seeing things at first, but then it started looking more solid . . . more opaque. What did it look like to you?"

Daniel lifted his brows. "To me it looked like a person, sitting on the floor just inside the doorway. Holding onto the frame. Peeking out at us."

"A black ghost," Mercy said, and shuddered. "And that cold air. What did you think about that?"

"I think the place is fucking haunted up the wazoo, Mercy. I can't wait until we get this job done and get the hell out of here."

As they drove toward Dr. McGuire's office to pick up Reagan, Mercy turned to Daniel. "Didn't your sister say she had a psychic come in to her salon a couple evenings a month? Think it might be worth getting her into that building? I wonder how much she charges."

"You know, I always thought that psychic stuff was bullshit. Ghosts and spirits and poltergeists. Bullshit. All of it. Now, I'm not so sure." Daniel tugged on his beard. He couldn't believe he was actually starting to believe in this paranormal woo-woo stuff. "It might be worth a shot. For curiosity's sake, if nothing else. I'll pay for it. I'll call Kim later and get the psychic's contact info."

Reagan was waiting outside on the steps of Dr. McGuire's elegant old Victorian when Mercy pulled into the driveway. He hopped in the back and started talking before he'd even shut the door.

"Hey, Daniel. Good to see you, man. I didn't expect to see you for a week or two, what with your nose and all."

Daniel chuckled. "Well, I won't be shooting any hoops for at least another week. Not unless you're into watching me bleed all over your court. How are the sessions with Ian . . . Dr. McGuire going?"

"Really good," Reagan said. "I like the guy. He gets me, you know? And Mom?" Reagan leaned forward toward Mercy. "I asked him about going to stay with dad for a while. He thinks that by the fall, it would probably be a good idea."

Daniel shot a glance at Mercy and saw her shoulders droop. He'd have to find out exactly what happened down there in Atlanta, with Mercy's marriage. It wasn't natural—or healthy—for a mother to want to keep her son and his father apart.

Whatever the dad did, it must have been pretty horrendous.

"You mind dropping me off at the office to get my truck out of the lot?" he asked.

"No problem. Want to come over? Stay for dinner? I'm making chili."

REAGAN SHOT hoops in the driveway while Mercy cooked, Daniel sitting with a glass of iced tea at her tiny table.

"Reagan seems to be doing better," Daniel began. "He finishes his GED classes soon, huh?"

He watched Mercy's shoulders rise and fall as she stood at the stove, frying ground beef. "Yup. If all goes as planned, he'll be ready to take his test by early September. Once he passes, I promised I'd let him try for his driver's license." She sighed. "Now he wants to go stay with his dad for a while. I guess the bastard promised him that once he got his GED, he'd not only make sure he was ready for the driver's test but would buy him a car." Her throat was tight, and Daniel wasn't sure if she was holding back tears or a ranting rage.

Daniel cleared his throat. "Reagan is, what? Eighteen, or close, right? You can't hold him back forever, Mercy. I know he's had some problems. You both have. But he's a young man who needs to be trusted for a little bit of independence."

After a long moment of tense silence, Mercy spun to face him, gripping the edges of the stove with white-knuckled intensity. "Luke's got all the advantages, Daniel. Not only was he his son's best friend, but he's got the money to make all his wishes come true. I'm scared, Daniel. I'm terrified that once Luke gets him down there, he'll just absorb Reagan into his new family. I think that's exactly what he intends to do." Her voice broke around the last words.

Daniel was on his feet then, wrapping her in his arms. "I can't imagine how hard this must be for you, Mercy. He's all you've got now. I know that. But you really do have to consider what's best for the boy." He tried to make his voice soft, consoling. He knew this was not the advice Mercy wanted to hear.

He was right. She placed both palms flat on his chest and pushed him away from her, hard. Glaring up at him with glistening eyes, she hissed, "You have no freaking idea what I'm feeling. Or what's best for my boy."

Daniel's arms dropped to his sides. Helpless. What could he say? She was right. He'd never been a dad. He didn't know what she was going through, or what she'd been through. Either her or her son.

"Don't you think it's about time you spill all that toxic garbage and let me know what happened between you and your husband? How your marriage ended and why you had to run over a thousand miles to get away from him?"

CHAPTER 17

$\mathcal{M}$ercy waited until Reagan had climbed the stairs to escape to his video game world. Daniel helped her clean up the kitchen and put away the leftovers. He'd been especially quiet tonight, interacting only with Reagan who, Mercy noticed, really did enjoy Daniel's company.

There was that, anyway. If only Luke could have been more like Daniel . . .

But what the hell was she thinking? She hardly knew Daniel. She knew he was a hard and dedicated worker and was very concerned about his nephew's well-being. She also knew that her attraction to him went beyond the physical and wasn't sure if that was a blessing or an impending disaster.

It was time he knew the truth, though. Daniel had gone above and beyond to show attention and concern for her son. She'd been his lover, for heaven's sake. It was time for her to spill the toxic tale.

Daniel retrieved the unopened bottle of Pinot Grigio out the fridge after Reagan disappeared upstairs, the one he'd brought that night last week. He held it up and asked, "Share a glass with me?"

Mercy nodded and flopped down on the sofa. She was staring out the window at the makeshift basketball court in their driveway when Daniel came in and handed her a chilled glass. He clinked with hers, then settled himself in the recliner opposite. After a long moment of silence, she heard his soft, rumbling voice.

"Don't you think it's about time you tell me what happened, Mercy?"

She took a long swallow of the wine and squeezed her eyes shut. "It is. It's not pretty. It's proof that my ex is selfish asshole. Still, I can't help but blame myself for what happened."

Daniel settled back in the chair, his wine glass resting on his chest. "Why don't you let me be the judge of that?"

"Okay." She set her glass down on the coffee table and leaned forward, elbows on knees. Her eyes shifted to the stairwell, where the echoes of Reagan's video game reverberated. "If that stops at any point, stop me."

Daniel nodded.

"So, Luke and I met shortly after I earned my journeyman's license down in Atlanta. Don't ask me why the field fascinated me so, but it did. I have a love-hate relationship with electricity. I'm awed by it, but it terrifies me too. Regardless, Luke was a year older than me, and his dad had already set him up with his own company. The minute I got certified, he hired me. I was only twenty-one. By the time I was twenty-two, I was ready to give birth to my son."

Daniel nodded, showing no judgement or other expression. "Did he at least marry you first?"

"Yeah, about two weeks before Reagan was born. Said he wanted to be sure the boy bore his name. That I couldn't ever take him away from him." Mercy took another long swig of the wine and dropped back against the cushions. "We were happy. I mean, I guess we were. For almost fifteen years, anyway. We worked together, raised Reagan together. For all I knew, we were a perfectly normal, All-American family."

Daniel drained his wine glass and set it down on the table. "Obviously, something changed."

Mercy snorted. "I'll say. At first, Luke started working a lot after hours. Doing what he called 'site visits' for future jobs. The business was booming—still is. I never questioned his whereabouts. Until the night I did." She locked eyes with him. "You know, when a little bird lands on your shoulder and whispers into your ear—*something isn't right here.*"

Daniel shifted his gaze over his shoulder toward the stairwell. There'd been a brief pause in the booming and crashing of Reagan's video game. They sat silently for a moment until Mercy heard the flush of the upstairs toilet. The soundtrack for the game resumed.

"So," she continued, "I followed him. Reagan was over at a friend's for the evening. I did my own reconnaissance thing and followed his truck through downtown Atlanta, in Friday evening traffic. All the way across town to a posh, bedroom community on the west side. Had to make a couple of quick turns onto side streets once we were the only two on the road." She lifted her eyebrows.

Mercy folded her arms across her chest and stared out the window. Struggle as she did, she couldn't help the tightness in her chest, her throat, from bubbling up into tears. Taking deep breaths until she could again speak without sobbing, she continued.

"Sharon's house was nicer than ours ever was. Brand-new. Hell, I think our team even did the wiring on the place—including me! She was having a birthday party for her two-year-old daughter. I slipped around the side of the house and caught them all there, in her backyard. A big, family celebration."

Daniel squeezed his eyes shut and rested his face in his hands. "Don't tell me it was—"

"Yes," she snapped. "It was Luke's daughter. Shit, the kid looks just like him. He'd been living a double life, with two completely separate families, on the opposite ends of the city for almost three years."

"Did she know about you? Reagan?"

"Hell yeah, she did. Didn't care. As long as he kept her comfortable —her house and bills paid, stopped by to fuck her a couple times a week during his off hours, and gave the kid his name—*his name*. Donohue. Paisley Donohue. Do you believe that?"

She was talking through choked sobs now but had no power to stop them. After first glancing at the stairwell, where the soundtrack of the video game echoed on, Daniel rose and knelt before her. Swiping her tears off her cheeks with his thumbs, he cupped her face and sought her eyes.

"You are absolutely right. He's an asshole. Scum of the earth. I don't blame you for not wanting Reagan to have anything to do with him. But you do realize—"

"Yeah, yeah, I know. I can't ever forgive him, but Reagan already has. Reagan is jealous of his half baby sister and wants back into his father's good graces. I'm just so afraid, Daniel. So afraid that once he goes down there that I'll lose my son forever."

Drained, Mercy melted into Daniel's arms and wanted for the moment to never end. It felt so good to spill her demons on someone who wouldn't judge her for the hatred she felt for her ex. She sobbed into the crook of his neck.

"I always felt . . . still do, feel as though it was because I wasn't . . . enough. Pretty enough. Sexy enough. I mean, Luke looked at me like I was one of the guys. Yeah, we had a sex life, although it was mostly an only-for-his-pleasure kind of thing. And then, for those last three years, he almost never touched me." Coughing, she leaned back and gazed into his eyes. "Probably only came to me when she had her period or something."

Daniel caught her chin between his fingers and locked eyes with hers. "This had nothing—absolutely nothing—to do with you. It had to do with this selfish bastard's wandering eye. Mark my words, in a few months, maybe a year, he'll leave this . . . this Sharon woman for another, younger version. When he finds himself having trouble being the man he always thought he was in the bedroom. Fresh meat. I know a lot of guys like that."

Mercy froze when the noise from the stairwell ceased. A moment later, Reagan's rumbling footsteps drifted to them. Daniel cleared his throat and stood, hands in his pockets. When Reagan came around the corner, he stopped short, his gaze wandering from one of them to the other.

"What? What's going on?" he asked.

Mercy wiped her face on her sleeve and stood. "Nothing. Daniel was just getting ready to leave. It's been a long day, for both of us."

Reagan nodded and rambled on without skipping a beat. "Do you think you could drop me off at Davin's . . . Kim's house? There's a tournament going on tonight. We want to enter it as a team." He glanced at his mother. "That okay with you, Mom? I'll be home by eleven, I promise."

Mercy looked at Daniel, then at her son. "How will you get home? In all likelihood, I'll be crashed on the couch by then."

"I'll take him," Daniel said. "And pick him up too." With his back to Reagan, he winked at Mercy. "That okay, Mama Bear?"

A half-hour later, Mercy wasn't surprised to see Daniel's truck pull back into her driveway as she stepped out of the shower. Nor was she disappointed. She'd hoped that wink was significant. After spilling her vulnerable guts out to him earlier, Mercy was in dire need of some coddling.

He didn't even knock, just slipped in through the screen door as she came down the stairs. Daniel blinked when he saw her, as though seeing her for the first time.

"What?" she asked through a chuckle.

"You." He said, his voice low and grumbling. "You are the sexiest thing I've ever put my eyes on. Or hands."

She stepped forward and wrapped herself around him, covering his mouth with hers. Deftly, Daniel used one booted foot to slam the door behind him. He pressed his body to hers, his already hard and ready.

How could this be, Mercy thought? How could I possibly have this kind of effect on a man, when the last one betrayed me with a blonde Barbie clone? Did Luke pay for those big, fake boobs Sharon sported too? Her blood simmered at the thought.

No. I'm not going to think about the evil ex tonight. I'm going to enjoy the moment. Enjoy the affection and attention this very sexy man wants to bestow upon me. No matter what the cost.

All she wore was an oversized Atlanta Braves jersey and teeny little panties. That's what she'd intended to sleep in. She didn't realize— although she had hoped—she'd be stripping them off before she closed her eyes to sleep tonight.

In one smooth movement, Daniel grabbed the hem of the jersey and had it up and over her head. Then he paused with the blue and red cloth dangling from two fingers as if it had been skunked. He glanced at her, his lip curling.

"Right colors, wrong team," he muttered, and tossed the jersey onto the chair. Then he stepped back and scanned her body, from her tangled, wet hair to her feet. "You," he purred, "are a goddess."

Self-conscious, Mercy crossed her arms over her naked breasts. "A matriarchal goddess, with these sagging, nearly-forty boobs and an I've-had-a-kid belly paunch." She patted her slightly rounded belly.

Daniel's face softened and he stepped into her space. Taking her hand, he pressed it to the hard mound in his jeans. "I must have a thing for matriarchal goddesses, then."

Slow, gentle, attentive. Those were the three words that kept echoing in Mercy's brain as Daniel took her into his arms and worshipped her body with his hands, his lips, and his tongue. When he'd kissed her silly and managed to get her near orgasm without ever removing her now damp panties, he swept her off her feet. She giggled as he carried her up the narrow staircase. It took some maneuvering to make it to the top without her toes catching in the railing.

"Nice work, Rhett Butler," she breathed on his neck as he ducked into her bedroom.

Mercy could not ever remember enjoying the sex act as much as she did with this wonderful, furry-faced, quick-witted man. She loved his taste, his smell, the way his beard tickled and scratched erotically in all the places he explored. And yes, she could see how she aroused him. With Luke, she'd always had doubts. Wondered if when he coupled with her, his eyes always closed, if he were imagining he was with someone else.

When Daniel made love to her, lowered his big, strong, muscular body over her, his eyes remained locked on hers.

CHAPTER 18

*a*n hour later, Mercy lay snuggled up to Daniel's side, his big arm encircling her. Her cheek pressed to his furry chest, she drew tiny circles on his skin with her finger, reveling in the scent of this incredibly sexy man. He was a little musky now with the sweat of their lovemaking, which did nothing but delight her. A big, hunky, sexy man with a heart. At least, he seemed to have one. Mercy could never remember feeling this content.

He broke the peaceful silence with a question.

"How'd you do with the ancestry search? Any luck?"

She stiffened ever so slightly, and he must have felt it. He squeezed her closer. "What are you afraid of, Mercy? The worst thing that could happen is you find out your father passed, right?"

"No. Not the worst thing. The worst thing would be if he rejects me. Again." She couldn't help feeling that way. Not when the man had given her up for adoption as an infant, never looking back.

Daniel stroked her hair and ran his fingers up and down her back. "Well, it's not like you'd meet him in a coffee shop, and then he'd stand up and walk out on you. If you find him, you send him an email. If he doesn't respond, you find his address. Send him a note. If he doesn't reply, then you'll have your answer."

Mercy sighed. "I think I did find him. I think it's him. He's still in the Boston area. But I couldn't access any more information without putting in a credit card number. I'm not comfortable doing that."

Daniel shifted to look down at her. "You're kidding, right? Don't you have a Paypal account?"

She shook her head and buried her face closer to his chest. "I don't want to know, Daniel. I really don't want to know."

"For Reagan's sake—"

"I know, I know. If his grandfather is still around, it would certainly be nice if he got to know him. Especially with Luke vying for him right now, threatening to scoop him out of my life with an emotional backhoe. It might anchor Reagan up here, with me."

"Do you need help setting up a Paypal account? I have one you could use. Or you can use my credit card, if you want."

Another tiny corner of Mercy's heart melted. This was a truly kind, caring man. Is it possible that she got this lucky? That she and Reagan would get a chance to start over?

Start over at almost thirty-nine, though? Which raised another question in her mind. She had no idea how old Daniel was. She assumed he was younger than she was, but by how much?

"How old are you?" she blurted.

His quick chuckle reverberated in her ear. "Where did that come from?"

"I'm thirty-eight. Gonna be thirty-nine next month. Am I now a cougar because I'm sleeping with you?" she asked through a grin.

He snorted. "Yeah, right. I wish. I just turned thirty-five, though, so I am younger than you are."

Her grin widened. "Wouldn't big, bad daddy Luke be surprised that I landed a hunky, young stud," she growled.

"That, milady, sounds like a challenge."

Daniel moved so fast Mercy gasped. In a lightning-bolt flash, he rolled her to her back and was balanced over her. He paused then, his gaze flashing to the alarm clock.

"We still have almost an hour until we have to go pick up Reagan. I'm up for it. How about you?"

We. Mercy's heart squeezed at the tiny, simple word. Daniel considered the two of them a *we*.

AS THEY DROVE to Kim's house, Daniel said, "Going to the library again on Tuesday night. Tiffany thinks she might have found a list of those names I was after. Wanna go?"

Mercy cocked her head. "What names?"

He shot her a glance as he drove. "You don't remember? The one-thousand-forty-one names. Of the people buried in that graveyard. You know, the one where you broke my nose?"

Mercy slapped both hands over her face. "Why do you keep reminding me of that? Not only do I feel horrible for doing that to you all over again, but I get flashbacks of what I saw there that night."

Daniel narrowed his eyes. Oh yeah. They never did discuss that further. "What exactly did you see that night, Merce?"

"I still wonder if I imagined it. It was horrible." She hugged herself, hunching her shoulders up around her ears. "Heads. I saw heads, Daniel. Faces hovering over each and every one of those blasted numbered markers."

A chill washed over Daniel's shoulders as she spoke. "Yikes. I saw something . . . glowing, but I wasn't really sure what I was looking at. Just before you busted my nose."

She slapped him playfully on the arm. "You think I was seeing things, don't you? You think I'm a hysterical woman with an overactive imagination."

He sobered and put his hand on her thigh. "No, my dear, I do not. Like I've said before, I've never been one to believe in the paranormal.

But with the shit that's been happening at the job site, I'm starting to think maybe I'm wrong."

Mercy slid closer to him and laid her head on his shoulder. "That shadow figure was creepy, wasn't it?"

"Sure was. I told you about the screams we heard, didn't I? The day that somebody—or some*thing*—pulled the tarp off that old shock machine?"

He could feel a full body tremor roll through her. "You did. And we have to drive right past that place tonight. It's dark and spooky and you're freaking me out. I don't want to talk about this anymore."

He patted her leg. "Okay. But that reminds me. When we get to Kim's, I need to get the contact info for that psychic she knows."

The boys were still in Davin's room battling it out in virtual cyber-space when they arrived. Kim was tucked in an oversized recliner, a paperback in her lap. She grinned as she looked up over half-sized readers. Her bright red hair was still perfectly styled, makeup artfully applied. Quite a contrast with the tattered plush bathrobe with pictures of kittens all over it, along with giant, fuzzy slippers. Daniel couldn't help thinking his sister looked like a very sexy, little old lady. He smiled.

"Hey, Sis. Love the outfit. You look like Grandma Moses, reinvented."

"Ha." Kim dropped the book on the table beside her and jumped up to hug her brother's neck. "Reinvention. That's my business, Bro." She turned to Mercy. "And hey, you. Good to see you again. When are you coming to the shop so we can start on your rein-vention?"

Daniel wrapped his arm around Mercy's shoulder and pulled her to him. "Back off, baby sister. This woman needs no reinvention. I don't want one tiny thing changed about her." He smiled down at Mercy.

Kim's eyebrows rose. "Oh, so I see how it is." Then she whacked Daniel's arm so hard he winced. "Good for you, big brother. And good for you too, Mercy." She winked. "I'll call the boys. Or do you want a nightcap? Cuppa?"

Daniel shook his head. "We both have to get up early. So, unless Mercy wants something, I'd just as soon grab the kid and run."

While they were waiting for Reagan to come down, Daniel asked, "Hey Kim. That psychic that comes to your shop. She any good?"

Kim blinked and took a step back. "You? Asking about a psychic?" She pressed a hand to her throat. "What brought this on, oh-so-skeptical one?"

Daniel shoved his hands in his pockets and stared at the floor. "It's this building we're working in, Sis. Some really crazy shit goes on in there. I'm not the only one who sees or hears stuff, either. I wondered if she might be willing to do a little after-hours tour. You know, kinda on the sly. It's not exactly the kind of inspection the contractor would approve."

"What kind of shit?" she asked, crossing her arms.

Mercy lifted her shoulders. "A bunch of stuff, Kim. From voices to rattling chains to shadow figures."

Kim brought a hand to her mouth. "Wow. Okay. I'll get you Cierce's number." She started for her phone, which was lying on the countertop. Then she stopped and held up a finger. "Wait. On one condition. Can I come along?"

Daniel looked at Mercy and back to Kim. "Cierce? Seriously?"

Kim laughed. "Say 'Psychic Cierce three times fast, Bro, and I'll give you her number. As long as I can come with on the night of the *inspection*."

As Daniel drove Mercy and Reagan home, he dialed the number for the psychic. Yeah, it was late. Almost eleven o'clock. But they had barely two weeks left on this job site. If he couldn't get an appointment to have her come in before that, it wasn't going to happen.

He figured he'd get her voicemail. Daniel was genuinely surprised when a soft, lilting voice answered.

"Hi, there. Hey, I'm sorry I'm calling so late, but my sister gave me your number. Cierce, right? You do readings at my sister Kim's shop a couple times a month."

"I do," she said enthusiastically. "Those nights are the highlights of my month. And you can call me Cici, by the way."

"Well, Cici, I'm going to put your abilities to the test. My team and I—I work for Progressive Electrical—we're working on this old asylum building."

The woman paused on the other end of the line. "You're not working on that creepy monstrosity up there at the Technical Institute, are you? I've heard some things about that place. Some bad energy trapped there."

Daniel glanced over at Mercy, then back at the road. "Do you make house calls? Or I guess it would be a site visit?"

"I do," the woman replied. "What time frame were you looking at?"

"It would have to be soon, Cici. Our team is only on the site until the end of the month. Is it possible you could schedule a visit before then?" Daniel asked. "Oh, and it would have to be after hours. I'd have to, uh, well, sort of sneak you in."

"No problem . . . Mr.—"

"Daniel. Daniel Gallagher. And Kim wants to know if she can come along. My girlfriend, too. She's one of our electricians."

THE MINUTE DANIEL'S truck backed out of her driveway, Reagan spun to face Mercy, elbows drawn back. Even in the dim porch light, she could see his face was an angry mask.

"Girlfriend, huh? So, what? Now you're not only working with this guy, but you're playing with him too?" he snapped.

Mercy had cringed when she heard the word come out of Daniel's mouth. For herself, it warmed her heart to hear him refer to her that way. But not in front of her son. Not yet, anyway.

She sighed as she unlocked the door. "I thought you liked Daniel, Reagan. Why should it upset you so much that I do as well?"

Reagan stomped in behind her and slammed the door, heading for the stairs. Sullen Reagan, Mercy thought. I'll get the silent treatment while he sulks off to his room.

She was surprised when he stopped at the foot of the stairs, hands shoved in his pockets. Without turning to face her, he huffed out a breath. "I don't know, it's just . . . weird, that's all, Mom. It's hard for me to think about you with anybody but Dad. It almost feels as though you're cheating on him."

Mercy perched her fists on her hips. "Oh really. How can you possibly even *think* those words, let alone say them after what your father did to me? To us?"

"I know. You're right. I just miss Dad. First I lost him, and now I'm going to lose you, too."

The tremor in his voice slashed Mercy's heart. She crossed the room and wrapped her arms around him, laying her head on his shoulder. "Don't say that, Reagan. You will never lose me. I promise you that." His shoulders shook, and he sobbed, ripping another jagged rent in Mercy's heart. "I'm sorry, Reagan. I know you miss your father."

"Don't you understand, Mom? We have nobody up here. No family, no friends. Well, now I guess *you* have somebody. I just feel so . . . alone."

Mercy squeezed his shoulders and turned him to face her. "We might," she said quietly. "I'm not sure yet, but I think I may have found your grandfather."

The minute the words left her lips she knew it had been a mistake. What if she did find her father and he didn't want anything to do with either of them? What if he was dead? Another disappointment for Reagan. But in that moment she needed to give him *something*. Some small hope to anchor him.

He lifted shocked eyes to hers. "Really? You did that ancestry search thing? I typed in his name after you told me what it was, but there's, like, a bazillion of them in New England."

"I did. And I was able to narrow it down by date. There's no guarantee that he's the right Devlin Doherty, but . . ." She cupped his chin. "Hey, I'm not sure if he'll even answer if I try to contact him. He gave me up for adoption, remember? But I'm . . . I'm going to try."

DANIEL WAS THRILLED when the psychic called him the next morning to say she could come to the job site that very night. His initial exhilaration was quickly replaced by jitters when he thought about the chance he was taking by sneaking an outsider into Gravely Hall. Not just one outsider, but two, if his sister came along.

How in hell was he going to pull this off? There was security on the campus, around the clock. Plus, they locked the building after hours. How would they even get in?

He'd have to level with Conner, that's all. He'd have to explain to him what he wanted to do, and risk either getting laughed at, or fired. But both Conner and Jacob had heard and seen the same weird things that he had.

He waited until they were eating lunch, what had become their Friday ritual—a pizza they'd picked up at Anzio's and brought back to the site. There was a picnic table out behind the building under a huge old maple. After taking his first huge bite of pepperoni heaven, he said, "So, hey. You guys are both creeped out by the stuff that goes on in there, right?" He pointed a thumb over his shoulder at the building.

"Hell, yeah," Jacob said. "Why do you think we're working overtime to get the hell out of here?"

Daniel turned to Conner. "Well, I'm curious. I don't believe in the paranormal stuff, but I am interested in history. This place has a sinister history. My sister, she knows this psychic. I thought I might ask her to come in and see if she picks up on anything."

Conner's head snapped up and he stopped chewing. After staring at Daniel for one long, tense moment, he burst out laughing. "You're kidding, right?"

Jacob had put down his pizza crust and was staring at Daniel, too. He wasn't laughing. "You're not kidding, are you? You think some of them crazies' spirits are trapped in there, don't you?"

Daniel shrugged. "Like I said, I've never been one to take stock in anything supernatural. But you have to admit—"

"Hell yeah!" Jacob said. "I wouldn't mind hearing what a psychic had to say about the place."

Conner helped himself to another slice of pizza, shaking his head. "It's fine by me. Gotta be after hours, though." He pointed at Daniel. "And on your nickel."

Daniel nodded and took a long pull on his water bottle. "If it's okay, she can come out tonight. She can't be here until about eight-thirty, though. Can you tell security to let us in?"

Jacob's eyebrows shot up. "Eight-thirty? Starts getting dark by then. You mean to tell me you're going through that place after dark?" He hunched his shoulders up to his ears. "I'll be anxious to hear what your psychic lady has to say. But don't be expecting me to come along."

CHAPTER 19

Friday morning at the office, Mercy made sure all the paperwork for the next job was in order. Conner signed a contract for the rewiring of a cute old Victorian where the Historical Society was housed. After she'd answered phone messages and emails and gone through the mail, there was really nothing left to do. She stared at her computer screen and sighed.

Then she pulled her credit card out of her wallet and logged in to Ancestry.com.

December 31st, 1970

When Devlin awoke, his head was pounding, and his mouth tasted sour. He was huddled in an alleyway under a threadbare blanket, shivering. The fire in the barrel that a few other homeless guys had started had long gone cold. Looking around, Devlin realized the other men were gone, as well.

He'd spent the last week squandering every last penny he had on whiskey. It was the only way he could cope with the pain. He thought losing his Breanna had broken him beyond repair. Watching the men in pale blue scrubs load his beloved on a gurney, then cover her face with a sheet . . . But when the social service people came later that day, and took the babe away, Devlin's whole world came crashing down around him.

He couldn't stay in the flat. The midwife had stripped the bed and tossed the sheets in the trash bin, but the mattress was soaked with Breanna's blood. Her scent, mingled with that unmistakable, coppery tang, permeated the air in every room.

Besides, he'd have no rent money come the first of the month, anyway.

There was no way he could work. What for? He had nothing left, nobody who needed his support anymore. He really wished he was brave enough to slash his wrists or jump off the docks. But he wasn't. He'd heard of alcohol poisoning, though. Maybe he'd just try to drink himself to death.

He'd drifted back off when a sharp jab in his ribs woke him.

"On your feet, buddy," a gruff voice shouted before delivering another kick.

Devlin squinted up at the uniformed police officer, quickly realizing why the other homeless bums had moved on so quickly. Staying in one place for more than a few hours would get you caught and thrown in the drunk tank.

And after that? Who knew what would happen to him?

MERCY STARED at her computer screen in shock. Disbelief tried to convince her that her discovery was wrong. That she was looking at the record for the wrong man. The faded image of a death certificate, almost forty years old, filled her screen.

THE COMMONWEALTH *of Massachusetts*
   Standard Certificate of Death
   Full Name: *Devlin R. Doherty*Sex: *Male*Color: *White*
   Marital Status: *Widower*Usual Occupation: *Dockworker*

Permanent Residence: *Corby State Mental Asylum*
Date of Death: *January 9ᵗʰ, 1973*Cause of Death: *Unknown*
Place of Burial: *Hillcrest Cemetery, State Hospital Grounds*

THAT NIGHT, when Daniel arrived at Mercy's house, he knew she would be alone. It was Friday, and Reagan was working. He was glad, because he'd hoped for some time alone with her before they met with Cierce at the job site. Kim was going to meet them there as well.

But Mercy met him at the door looking shell-shocked. She stepped back as he came through the door, and instinctively, he knew not to try to embrace her. In her trembling hands she held a paper, which she silently held out to him.

"What's this?" he asked, then instantly knew the answer. His heart ached for her. "Your father. You . . . found him."

"I haven't told Reagan yet. The last thing he needs to hear right now is news like this." Mercy paced the kitchen, wringing her hands. "He's bugging me to go back to Atlanta, to live with his father. I thought, if I could just find one good reason why he should stay here with me . . ."

Daniel stepped in front of her and wrapped his arms around her. She wilted against him, sobbing into his chest.

"I'm so sorry, Mercy. You're sure it's him? The right Devlin Doherty?"

She nodded and hiccupped. "The dates match. And he was a widower. *And* he was a dock worker. Too many coincidences for it *not* to be him." She stilled for a long moment, and he held her, waiting. He knew she was trying to work through this new information. "I would have been about two years old by then. Two years old and living in the same town where my birth father was locked up in an insane asylum." Mercy raised tear-filled eyes to his. "It was him. That night, in the basement. When I went back for my phone. Calling out to me."

"You don't know that, Mercy." Daniel stroked her hair and shushed her. Then, he blurted, "No, it couldn't have been. Didn't your adoptive parents tell you they got you as an infant? Didn't they name you?"

"That's right," she said, pushing away to commence pacing. "They did. Devlin Doherty probably never knew my name." She raked her hand through her hair, then stopped to point a finger at him. "But that number scratched in chalk on the tunnel wall? 1033? How much do you want to bet that number—*that number*—is the one carved into the pillar marking his grave?"

Daniel tugged at his beard, thinking. "You might be right. We may be able to get some answers on Tuesday night. I told you, Tiffany says she thinks she found some more asylum records. Or maybe," he hesitated, locking eyes on hers, "maybe we'll know something more later tonight. The psychic is meeting us at Gravely Hall at eight-thirty."

SUNSET this late in August was just after seven thirty p.m., and sure enough, twilight was upon them as Daniel pulled his truck up in front of the building. Kim was already there, chatting animatedly with the young security guard, who stood with his arms crossed, looking bored. He and Mercy climbed out just as a very nice, late-model Audi pulled up behind his vehicle.

Guess psychics make pretty good money, he thought absently, then remembered he'd never asked how much this gig was going to cost him.

An attractive blonde about his and Mercy's age climbed out. She was casually dressed in slacks and a sleeveless blouse—all black, of course. One lock, braided with black and purple ribbon, peeked out from under her shoulder length tresses, fluttering in the breeze.

She certainly looks the part, he thought. *Hope she's not just some kook with a good tagline.*

"Hi there. You must be Daniel." She extended her hand and Daniel shook it, taking in the long, manicured talons painted bright purple. "I'm Cici."

"Nice to meet you. This is my coworker, Mercedes." He ducked to look around the psychic toward her vehicle. "Do you have any . . . equipment I can help you unload?"

Cici threw back her head and laughed. "I'm a psychic, Daniel. Not a ghost hunter. No. No equipment. Just what I've got right in here." She placed her fingers on her temples. Glancing at the uniformed security guard, she lowered her voice. "You said you would have to sneak me in. Have we been busted already?"

He shook his head. "No. I managed to get permission to bring you in. All of us. The guard will unlock the building, and then lock up after we're through. How long do you think this will take?"

She scanned the monstrous three-story structure. "I don't know. It's a big place. Are there certain hot spots? Places you've experienced more activity than others?"

Mercy stepped forward, hugging herself. "The tunnel. There's a tunnel that connects the buildings. And the basement, for sure."

Cici narrowed her eyes as she studied Mercy for a very long, tense moment. "You," she began, "you have a special connection to this building. Don't you?"

Daniel felt the hairs stand up on his arms. *Hell, I guess maybe this chick is for real after all.*

Mercy's gaze slid away, and she murmured, "I may."

Cici glanced up at the darkening sky. "Well, we'd better get started, then. Everybody bring flashlights?"

CHAPTER 20

"How much do you know about this place?" Mercy asked the psychic as they waited for the guard to unlock the door.

"Well, I grew up here, in Corby. So, before the Technical Institute bought it, I know it was a state hospital. This particular building, I was told, was for the most disturbed patients." Cici rubbed her arms as if she were cold. "They did some of the *procedures* here as well, I believe." She put air quotes around the word.

"Lobotomies, shock treatments, hydrotherapy. Am I right?" Daniel asked.

She nodded. "Lots of bad energy here. I've been feeling it for years, just driving by the place. Never thought I'd have an opportunity to go inside."

Kim, who hadn't said much since they'd arrived, studied the psychic with rounded eyes. "Aren't you afraid? I mean, do you ever get afraid?"

Kim looked scared to death, and Mercy wasn't even sure if she'd follow them inside. She hung back near the security guard on the porch landing.

Cici was shaking her head. "Nothing to be afraid of, really. Most of the time, the spirits are just residual energy. Like imprints from the past, flickering like old black-and-white movie film."

The guard stepped aside, and the psychic led the way in. She carried a lantern very much like the one Daniel carried, identical to the one Mercy had been using down in the tunnel. The light was already gone inside the building, and her lantern's glow flashed eerily off the floor and glass-block windows on the far wall.

Mercy's guess was right. Kim stayed behind, standing close beside the handsome, young security guard. "I guess I'll just wait for you guys out here," she said with an embarrassed smile.

Mercy attached herself to Daniel's arm with no intention of letting go. The psychic may not be afraid, but she had to admit, she was.

"I'd say we should start in the tunnel and work our way up," Cici said, after turning in a circle in the center of the large room. "I'm not getting anything much in this area. Where's the access?"

Daniel showed her where the entrance to the stairwell was located. The narrow, pantry-size door that had originally hidden it from view had been replaced by a wooden interior door of normal dimensions. There was no way the renovation would pass inspection if that hadn't been done, even though Mercy didn't believe the tech school intended to use the tunnel for anything more than storage.

The trio made their way down the narrow staircase. Cici boldly led the way, even though Daniel offered to take the lead. Mercy wasn't sure if she respected the woman's boldness or thought her a complete idiot.

"There are light bulbs hanging from the ceiling, but the power's been shut off. So, the lanterns will have to do," Daniel said.

"That's fine. Mercy, you said you sensed activity down here?" The psychic stood at the bottom of the steps looking first one way, then the other. "Which direction?"

"To the right," Mercy said. "I heard noises—"

"Shh," Cici cut in, holding up a hand. "I'm hearing something now myself."

It was faint, not nearly as loud as the day Mercy had been working in the tunnel by herself. The day she fell and hurt her arm. But she could hear it again, the same sound, like chains being dragged along the concrete floor.

Unlike the day she got hurt, there were no piles of broken concrete and stone. The tunnel floor had been broken up and re-poured. The walls had been sealed and painted—covering the bizarre display of chalk numbers. The green slime had been cleaned off the few glass blocks near the ceiling. Cici's lantern glinted off them as she headed off at a rapid pace, disappearing around the bend in the tunnel.

Daniel glanced down at Mercy with one eyebrow raised. "She's a brave one, I'll give her that. Is that the same sound you heard the day you fell?"

Mercy nodded. "Yes. It's just not nearly as loud now as it was then."

After a brief moment, the psychic's light reappeared. "That's because it's residual energy," she said, looking at Mercy. "There's really no spirit here. Not now, anyway. It's just energy that's trapped down here. It will play over and over again in a loop, until it finally fades completely away."

Mercy shook her head. "No, I saw something that day as well. A shape, like a figure made of fog. It moved from one side of the tunnel to the other."

"And something snatched the chalk from Mercy's toolbelt and wrote on the wall," Daniel added. "A number, dozens of times all over the stones."

Cici tipped her head. "Really? You know, spirits—intelligent hauntings, they're called, as opposed to residual—they require a great deal of energy to manifest. Did you have any equipment running down here that day? Was there an electrical storm in the area?"

Mercy shook her head. "No, it was sunny. Some of the light was coming through those glass blocks." She pointed to the narrow row near the ceiling. "And my battery-powered lantern and screwdriver were the only power tools I had."

The psychic pursed her lips. "Not usually enough to cause a true manifestation. Unless this particular spirit was highly motivated to make contact." She paused and shot Mercy a meaningful look. "I told you—I can sense you have a particularly strong connection with this place. Do you have any idea what that might be?"

"No. No clue," Mercy lied.

Shrugging, Cici headed toward the stairwell. "Well, if there was an intelligent spirit here then, it isn't here now. Just the echoes of horrors past." She sounded sad and pinched the bridge of her nose. "I can't imagine what they put those poor people through back in the day. Okay, on to the basement."

Mercy had watched the demo team struggle the huge, porcelain bathtubs up the stairs two months ago. Yet she still expected to hear the sloshing water, and the pathetic voice calling for mercy—not her name, she now realized, just a plea for compassion. Gooseflesh rose on her arms as they followed the psychic down the basement steps.

She nearly plowed into the woman when she stopped short on the bottom step.

Cici set the lantern down at her feet and rubbed both of her temples, as if she had a terrible headache. "Ooh, there's a lot of residual pain down here. It's so thick I can hardly breathe."

The sound of sloshing water came to them then, again, not as loud as the night Mercy came back for her phone. And no voice this time. She huddled in closer to Daniel. "Do you hear that?" she whispered.

"Yes, I do. But there is no plumbing down here anymore. The tubs, sinks, toilets—all gone and capped off. There's nowhere water could be running—"

"Again, residual haunting," Cici interrupted. She sucked in a deep breath and picked up her lantern, moving into the center of what was now a wide-open, empty space. "But nothing more." Again, she turned small circles in the center of the room, then shook her head. "It's gone now. Every time it happens, it will lose strength. Just like the poor, sick patients who got buttoned up in those tubs for hours, sometimes days." She shook her head and headed back toward them. "Daniel, didn't you say there was activity on the upper levels as well? Was it the second floor?"

Daniel led the way this time, Mercy scurrying along beside him, still not letting loose of his arm. When they reached the large central room on the second floor, Daniel pointed down the corridor to the right. "Treatment room down that way. There was still an old ECT box there when we first started."

Not so bold now, Cici inched her way toward the corridor, still lined by what were once patient rooms. Now refurbished, they would be offices once the renovation was complete. Mercy hung back, clinging to Daniel. She was starting to hyperventilate, remembering the day she and Daniel had seen the shadow figure. Daniel squeezed her hand.

"Let's just wait here," he said.

When they heard the psychic speaking, Mercy thought at first she was addressing them. Then her words came through more clearly. It became obvious she was not.

"Why are you still here? What do you need to move on? How can I help you?" The psychic's voice echoed from the other end of the hall.

Mercy glanced up at Daniel, who looked as spooked as she felt. "She's found some . . . thing. Some*one*."

Cici's voice continued to echo down the corridor to them, fading slightly as she moved farther toward the treatment room. "Your suffering is over. You are free to leave this place. Communicate with me. Tell me how I can help you to cross over."

Then, silence. Seconds ticked by, then minutes. Daniel said, "I don't know what to do. I don't want to interrupt her, whatever she's doing. But this is making me very nervous. If she gets hurt on the premises, Conner will have my—"

Mercy nearly leapt out of her skin when a spine-tingling scream split the silence. It was followed by a sickening thump.

CHAPTER 21

*D*aniel pulled away from Mercy's grasp and ran down the corridor, his lantern swinging wildly. This was not the same scream he'd heard on the job that day. This was a very real, very human, very female scream. The psychic's scream.

"Cici? Cici, are you alright?" he called. No response.

He found her sprawled in the center of the treatment room, her lantern extinguished and lying on its side. There was nothing in this big, empty space for her to have tripped over, he thought frantically. The creepy electric shock machine with all its wires and paddles and tarp had been hauled out weeks ago. The room now sported a new tile floor and was completely empty.

Kneeling beside her, he picked up her hand and patted it.

"Cici. Cierce, can you hear me?"

Again, no response. She had either been knocked out cold, or fainted dead away.

"Mercy," he called, not realizing she was right behind him.

"What happened?" she asked.

"I don't know. But we need to get her out of here. Can you take the lanterns while I carry her?"

The security guard met him at the foot of the stairs, blinding him with his damned flashlight.

"Step aside," Daniel barked. "She fainted. The lady needs some fresh air. Mercy, can you grab the blanket out of the back seat of my truck?"

It took only about five minutes for the psychic to regain consciousness once Daniel and the guard arranged her on the blanket in the grass. The guard retrieved a bottle of water from his cruiser and handed it to him. Daniel unscrewed the cap, took a long pull from it, then recapped it and held the cold bottle to the side of Cici's face.

Kim stood over the psychic, wringing her hands. "Do you know what happened? What she saw?" she asked.

Daniel shook his head. "She was talking to . . . someone, somebody, some*thing*. Right before she screamed."

"Probably the same thing we saw, Daniel. The shadow figure," Mercy said.

When Cici's eyes fluttered open, she started, struggling to sit upright. Daniel held her down with a firm hand on her shoulder.

"You're okay, okay, Cici. Just lay back here a minute. Get your bearings."

He felt her relax under his grip. She closed her eyes and started wagging her head side to side. "I'm . . . sorry. That's never happened to me before."

"Do you want some water?" Daniel tipped his chin toward the guard, who hurried off to fetch another bottle. "Are you feeling strong enough to sit up? Here. Let me help you."

With Daniel's supporting arm behind her, Cici sat up, then took the water bottle from the guard. After a good long drink, she lowered the bottle and raised her eyes. But she wasn't looking at Daniel. Her gaze drifted past him to Mercy, who stood just behind him.

"You," she said, again, "you have a strong connection with this place."

Mercy came around beside Daniel and knelt in the grass. She reached out a hand and took the psychic's in both of hers. "I may. I think I do. What did you see?" she asked.

Cici held the water bottle to her temple and closed her eyes.

"There is, or was, an intelligent haunting on that floor. I didn't see it, but I sure as hell could feel its presence." She shuddered. "A tortured, agonized entity."

Mercy waited a beat, letting the woman regain her composure. Then she pressed further.

"What did you feel? Why did you scream?"

The psychic raised haunted eyes to Mercy. "Nothing I would want anyone, ever, to go through. Ever again." She drank again and exhaled. "I think I experienced exactly what some poor patient did, God knows how many years ago. Electro-shock therapy. I actually felt the paddles on my temples. The next thing I knew, my brain felt as though it was exploding inside my skull."

"Oh my God," Kim muttered in the background.

"But I think," Cici continued, holding up one finger, "I believe the entity used me—my life energy—to finally get past its misery. I think it's gone now. It's free."

As they drove back toward home, neither Mercy nor Daniel had much to say. Mercy, for one, was in a sort of shock. At the last minute, just as they came up on Anzio's, she blinked back into the present.

"Reagan. I have to pick up Reagan. What time is it?" she asked.

"A little past nine-thirty. You've got another hour before he gets off, right?"

She nodded.

"Let's go get a beer and talk this thing through."

He pulled into the parking lot of the Post Office Pub, and they managed to snag a corner high-top in the bar. The place was busy, it being Friday night, with a US Open Tennis match dominating the majority of the dozen or more television screens. Mercy climbed onto the barstool and rested her face in her hands.

She felt Daniel's strong grip on her wrist. "You okay? I know, that was pretty scary. I nearly pissed my pants when Cici let out that scream."

Mercy folded her arms on the table and looked off out the window. "Tell me. You know, at first I was angry at Conner for locking me out of this job." She met his gaze. "Now, I'm kind of glad he did."

"You should be."

They ordered beers and that first, cold swallow felt heavenly. Mercy took deep breaths, trying to calm her racing heart. She kept glancing up at the clock above the bar.

"I don't want to be late getting Reagan. I hate to think of him standing outside the restaurant, once it's closed, in the dark, only a half-mile down the road from that place. And from the graveyard." A shudder racked her body.

Daniel reached forward and took both her hands in his. Even his strong, usually warm hands felt cold and clammy. "The psychic did say there was nothing to fear from the residual hauntings. They're just echoes of the past."

Mercy snorted. "Do you think it was residual energy that zapped the psychic's brain tonight? No, even she made it clear that there was an active entity on the second floor. A potentially dangerous one."

Daniel quirked an eyebrow. "But she said she thinks she *freed* it," Daniel scoffed.

Mercy narrowed her eyes. "Daniel, it could very well have been the spirit of my father trapped in that building. Cici didn't say as much, but what she did say doesn't rule out that possibility."

Daniel raked a hand through his hair. "This is really tough for me to swallow. I don't believe in supernatural bullshit. Never have. You die, you're dead. But here I forked over five hundred big ones to a woman who may just be a really good actress." He scowled. "At least she claims she's *freed* him, then." His voice dripped with sarcasm.

Irritation and impatience bubbled up in Mercy's chest. She couldn't believe that after Daniel had been the one to initiate tonight's visit, now he was backpedaling. She'd shown him the death certificate. They both knew her father had lived—and died—at that facility. And who knew what *Cause of Death: Unknown* really meant? Mercy wondered just how many of those "unknown causes" resulted from an over-application of electricity to the brains of those poor souls.

"Well, then, thank you very much for your investment. I'll cut you a check for my portion of it. Subject closed." She glared at him. "But for the next two weeks, I don't want to hear about one more single *strange thing* that happens while you're on the job site. If you don't believe it's happening, you should just be able to ignore it."

January 8, 1973 – Gravely Hall, Corby State Mental Hospital

Devlin Doherty pushed the grungy mop back and forth methodically over the tile floor. This was his life now, had been ever since the officer picked him up in the drafty alleyway two years ago. It only took two days in the drunk tank—without a drink—for the delirium tremors to begin. The dreaded DTs he'd heard his homeless acquaintances talk about.

"Don't ever let them catch you and lock you up," they'd warned. "You know what happens to people like us. A few days without the drink and, well, we start acting crazy. And you know what they do with crazy people."

Devlin had no memory of the first seizure. When he came to, though, two of the guards were holding him down, and his mouth was stuffed full of bloody cloth. A wrapped spoon, he discovered afterward. To keep him from biting off his own tongue during the seizure, the guards had forced a hand-kerchief-wrapped spoon into his mouth.

That was an eternity ago. His withdrawal symptoms had lasted less than a month. Since then—and since being admitted as a patient into Gravely Hall—his mind had sunken just about as low as one could go. He wanted to die. Life wasn't worth living anymore, and certainly not in this place.

The doctor in charge diagnosed Devlin with "extreme melancholia." Deep depression. There was a treatment, he'd told Devlin. It was experimental, but it might cure him. Then he could get out of this place.

"There are some risks, however," the doctor warned. "The convulsions this treatment causes can get violent. We take every precaution to avoid injury. But some patients have experienced broken bones from the seizures. In rare cases," the doctor folded his hands on his desk, "the procedure can be fatal."

Devlin stared at his hands. "I'm no stranger to convulsions. And I have no fear of dyin'."

THE DRIVE back to pick up Reagan was silent and uncomfortable. Reagan, of course, had no idea what they'd been through tonight, nor did Mercy have any intentions of telling him. And until she could definitively locate her father's grave—his number—she wasn't going to share that information either.

"Hey, Mom. Any luck with the ancestry search?" They were the first words out of his mouth after climbing into the truck.

Mercy closed her eyes and sighed. "No luck, Reagan. I'll have to do a little deeper digging to verify that I'm looking at the records for the right man."

Reagan fell silent for the rest of the short drive home. He climbed out and sprinted to the door, but Mercy held back. She turned to face Daniel.

"Look, I'm sorry," Daniel began. "I know you feel you have a personal investment in this whole deal. But it got a little too strange for me tonight. I'm not sure I believe a thing the psychic said." He laid a hand on her thigh. "I'm sorry, Mercy."

Mercy straightened and squared her shoulders. "So, I guess I'll see next week."

Daniel blinked as though she'd slapped him. "Soo . . . I won't see you again until then?" he asked.

"No. I've got a lot to catch up on this weekend." She forced a smile. "Enjoy your weekend, Daniel."

CHAPTER 22

*R*eagan came rumbling down the stairs about a half-hour before he had to leave for work. Mercy was folding towels on the sofa. He plopped down in the recliner and leaned forward. She noticed he was gripping the arms of the chair so tightly, his knuckles were white.

"Mom? Can I talk to you for a minute?"

She laid the last folded towel into the basket and sat beside it. "Sure, Reagan. What's up?"

Mercy wasn't sure what her son wanted to talk about, but he seldom sounded this serious. This mature. It worried her and made her uneasy. In fact, it frightened her.

"I just got off the phone with Dad," he began. "I finish up my GED classes on Tuesday, and I've registered to take the test at the library on Thursday. After that, I'd like to go to Atlanta."

How had the time gone by so quickly? He was right, though. His last class was Tuesday. His test, as well as his last appointment with Dr. McGuire, was on Thursday. On Friday, he turned eighteen years old. At which time he'd probably have achieved his GED.

Mercy exhaled and closed her eyes. "For how long?"

Reagan hopped up and began pacing the length of the room, hands stuffed in his pockets. "I'm not sure. Dad said he'll help me get my driver's license—in Georgia, while I'm down there. If I decide to stay with him and Sharon—who has no problem taking me in, by the way —well, Dad said he'd buy me a car. He said he'd put me on as an apprentice with his electrical team. See if that's something I'd like to do for a living."

So there it was. Mercy had known this was coming but had tried to bury the possibility in the cellar of her mind. Now, here it was, rising up from the depths of her worst fears like dank air.

She knew she had no right to try to change her son's mind. He would be eighteen in just a few days. But she had so hoped to be able to give him a new start—both of them, a fresh, clean start—miles away from the influence of his father. A man whose moral standards were, in Mercy's opinion, questionable at best.

"Dad said the minute I call him with the news that I've passed, he'll buy me a ticket," Reagan continued, his voice softer now. "I hate to leave you, Mom, but you're all I've got here now. All of my friends are in Atlanta. My Dad. My half-sister."

Ouch. Those last words stung the worst. Mercy sucked in a breath and let it whoosh out, hoping some of the pain in her heart would follow.

"A one-way ticket, then."

Reagan nodded. "You've got Daniel now, Mom. It's not like I'm leaving you all alone up here. Besides, you still may find your own father."

Mercy swallowed the sudden rush of bile that clogged her throat. She wasn't so sure about Daniel now, who had obviously backpedaled on helping her to unravel the mystery behind her father's death. But had he, really? He was still researching the history of the building. She felt certain he would continue to help her find the list holding the names of the 1041 anonymous patients.

Yeah, she might have Daniel, if she wanted him. And she could always hang around in the cemetery down the street and talk to a man who'd been dead for almost forty years. If she could ever locate him in those three-acres dotted with numbered pillars.

Mercy lifted her chin and put on her big-girl panties, saying the words she knew she had to say.

"Okay, Reagan. If that's what you want to do, you have my blessing."

MUCH AS SHE would have liked to stay angry with Daniel, by Saturday night, she was missing him. After she dropped Reagan off at work, she couldn't face going back to her empty, clean house. One that would very soon be much emptier than it was now.

Mercy decided to go back to the cemetery while it was still daylight. Part of her was terrified to return to the place. But now she knew it was the final resting place for her birth father. She'd never met the man in her life, didn't know a thing about him except that he'd lost his wife the day Mercy was born. Somehow, the man had ended up in a mental asylum.

What had been his problem? Had he gone off the deep end when her birth mother died? Mercy knew, from what Daniel had shared, that back in those days, all sorts of illnesses could get you locked up in an asylum. Diabetes, epilepsy, even alcoholism. Maybe he'd attempted suicide, and that's what brought about the diagnosis of insanity.

She shuddered to think that her son had possibly inherited this mental weakness—a tendency toward suicide—from a grandfather he never knew. Did things like pass through in the genes?

It was half-past four when Mercy pulled up alongside the road and parked near the path leading to Hillcrest Cemetery. A very warm, humid September day, she was glad she'd dressed as though it were still summer. Even so, by the time she hiked up the steep hill, her skin was slicked with sweat. She was grateful for the still, fully-fleshed out trees that shaded the cemetery. Only a few had started to change color from green to yellow or red. Dappled sunshine danced across the grass, which waved in the slight breeze.

It looked like the Job Corps hadn't mowed the plot in a while. She'd have to watch her step, so as not to turn an ankle in a hole obscuring one of the many sunken markers. Mercy wondered how she would ever be able to locate the concrete pillar, which she was assuming held the number "1033," in this sea of over a thousand graves.

After crouching to sweep the dirt away from the first dozen or so markers, Mercy's heart sank. The numbers didn't appear to be in any order, at least from what she could tell. And the numerals were worn and fading from time and weather, some so badly they were difficult to decipher.

Finally, discouraged and lonely and feeling very sorry for herself, she plopped down in the grass next to a hole where a marker had sunken completely beneath the earth. It was obscured by thick grass. How would one ever identify these markers? At least, without partially disinterring the graves?

She sat there for a long time, hugging her knees, allowing an occasional tear to leak down her face and soak into her pants. Traffic on the road below was light, but she could clearly hear every car or truck that passed by. She lifted her head when she heard a rumbling engine approach, then suddenly cease.

Daniel, she thought. He'd seen her car and was coming to see her. In that moment, Mercy's feelings were torn. Loneliness made her affection for the man seem stronger. But she felt doubt now. He'd been so sarcastic, doing a complete about-face on his opinion of the psychic that night. A sense of betrayal had slashed through her positive feelings toward him, and the wound was still bleeding.

She waited, watching expectantly. Several minutes passed, but Daniel did not appear from over the crest of the hill. Then, to Mercy's surprise, a figure did emerge. Slowly, a small, hunched, elderly man leaning heavily on a cane came into view.

Hmm, Mercy thought. Maybe I'm not the only one who comes to visit deceased family on this dismal site.

She stood and approached the man, who didn't acknowledge her presence at first. All she could think about was the danger of a man this old, who had trouble walking to begin with, poking around in a field full of holes hidden in the grass. She would offer to assist him, she thought.

He had to be in his late seventies, eighties maybe. His hair was pure white and wild, swirling about his balding scalp in disarray. He kept his eyes to the ground until Mercy got to within ten feet of him. When he looked up, his watery eyes squinted at her.

"Afternoon," he croaked in a whiny voice. "Got me a task this afternoon, I do. Gotta locate a marker for a young lady down in Florida."

Mercy tipped her head, not understanding what he was talking about. "Excuse me? Is there something I can help you with?"

She knew the minute the words left her lips how lame they were. She knew nothing about this cemetery and had no better a chance at locating a particular numbered marker than this old man did.

Or maybe he *did*.

Mercy stuck out her hand and introduced herself. The man took it in his cool, gnarled one, studying her face with knitted brows. "You got kin buried here, I reckon?" he asked.

"I think I do. My father's buried here. At least, I think he's my father." Mercy cringed at how uncertain and confused she must sound. "You?" she asked.

The old man tipped up his chin. "Nope. I'm on the committee for the Historical Society, though. I got a letter from a lady down in Florida who says her grandfather is buried here. She sent me money, too. Wants me to have a headstone—a real one—made up and set in to replace the blasted numbered pillars the state put in." He shook his head. "Sad business, all this. Imagine, living your life, then ending it a place like this, only to be buried as namelessly as you lived."

Exactly my opinion, Mercy thought. Then a spark of hope lit in her chest. "So, you have access to the list of names? You know what number to look for?"

He scratched the scruff on his face. "I do. This lady's granddad is a low number, though. I think we might have trouble finding it, since the pillars set early on sank pretty bad. Doubt I'd even be able to read the number if I can find it."

"Let me help you," Mercy said. "It's dangerous for you to walk through here anyway. The holes are deep, and some of them are totally obscured by the grass."

Nodding, the man dipped into the pocket of his plaid shirt. He scowled, fishing around in the obviously empty space. Then he reached into his trouser pockets, first one, then the other, shifting his cane. His mouth twisted.

"Damn it all to hell," he growled. "Must have left the paper in my car." He held up a finger. "I'll be right back."

Mercy cringed to think about this decrepit old soul climbing first back down, then back up the path, leaning heavily on a cane the whole time.

"Can I go get it for you?" she asked. "I mean, I know you don't know me, but I promise, I won't steal anything."

But he was shaking his head. "No, no. Not even really sure it's in the car. I might have left it on my desk back at the historical society. That's where the list is, you see. Only copy there is, that I know of. That's why I keep it locked up in my office."

He turned back toward the path, and Mercy stepped up beside him. "Here. Let me help you back down that steep hill. It's easy to lose your footing. I've done it myself."

His hand waved angrily in the air beside him. "No, no need for that. I'm perfectly capable. I don't like to take anybody's help I don't need until I need it," he snapped. "If I'd started letting people help me get around ten years ago, I'd be in a wheelchair by now."

At a loss for what to do, Mercy stopped, watching him hobble along until he reached the path, then slowly sank out of sight. She would wait, and if she heard his engine start, she would follow him back to the Historical Society. He has access to the list. The key. The only way she would ever, once and for all, locate the numbered grave where her father was buried.

Seconds later, she was shocked to see Daniel's tall form appear from over the hill. He strode toward her purposefully, his eyes never leaving hers. He looked delicious in snugly fitting, faded denim jeans and a Red Sox tee straining over his sculpted biceps.

And then there was that. The lust factor. Silently, Mercy cursed her body's reaction to him.

"Saw your car parked down there. Thought I'd come up and make sure you were okay," he said when he reached her.

Mercy wondered what happened to the old man from the Historical Society. Had she missed hearing his car start? Maybe he'd found the paper he was looking for in the car and was on his way back up here right now.

"Did you see the old man? An elderly, hunched man with a cane. He just headed back to his car to find a slip of paper he needed to locate a grave," Mercy sputtered. She moved past Daniel toward the path. "He works for the Historical Society, Daniel. He has the list with the names that match these numbers."

Daniel caught up to her and grabbed her arm. "Where are you going, Mercy? There's no old man down there. Yours is the only car parked alongside the road. I didn't see anyone—"

Mercy spun around and stared at Daniel in disbelief. "You . . . you had to see him. You probably passed him on the path. He disappeared just seconds before you crested the hill."

But Daniel was shaking his head, studying her face with concern. "Nobody, Mercy. Nobody came over the hill. There was no car parked other than yours."

She had to see for herself. He must be wrong. Either that or the old geezer could move faster than she thought. Running to top of the path, Mercy stared down at the road. Daniel's truck was parked behind her car. There was no trace of another vehicle anywhere in sight.

Mercy dropped her face into her hands and burst into tears. "I'm losing my mind. I'm just like my father—bat-shit crazy. And Reagan .. ." Her words garbled with sobs as Daniel took her into his arms.

"You're not crazy, and neither is Reagan. You've both been on a slow-moving train through hell for the past couple of years, that's all." He smoothed her hair and she melted against him, allowing her tears to soak front of his soft, fresh-smelling shirt.

Through hiccups, Mercy mumbled into Daniel's chest. "Reagan's leaving, Daniel. After his test next weekend, his father is flying him to Atlanta. A one-way ticket." Her heart ached in her chest as though a knife were twisting into it.

Daniel said nothing, just continued to hold her and shush her tears. Didn't he get it? Didn't he get that her whole world was coming apart around her?

After wallowing in a few minutes of self-pity, Mercy pushed away and looked into Daniel's eyes. "The man, or . . . whoever, *what*ever he was. He said he had the list. It's at the Historical Society. Locked in his office. The *only* copy, he said."

Daniel tugged on his beard. "The Historical Society. Why the hell didn't I think of that sooner?" He held out his hand, and she took it. "Come on. Maybe we can catch the speedy old bastard."

A half-hour later, Mercy and Daniel stood on the steps of the Corby Historical Society. The door was locked, and there were no lights on inside. The sign on the door said they were open only two days a week: Tuesdays from one to four p.m., and Sunday during the same hours.

"I spoke with him. Just a few minutes ago," Mercy blurted. "He said he was coming back here to get the paper he needed. I wonder what happened?"

She knew, though, by the way Daniel was looking at her, that he thought she'd imagined the entire episode. He was humoring her, which infuriated her. He had approached the door, cupping his hands around his eyes and peering through the thick glass.

"Isn't this the building we're working on next? I thought Conner said something about an old Victorian. This one sure is old."

"Yes, it is. In fact, they're supposed to be moving all of their artifacts out of here this week. They'll be stored on the lower level of the library while the renovation is done," Mercy said. "Does it look like they've started packing up? Conner will be pissed if the site's not ready on the first of the month."

Daniel drew back and shoved his hands into his pockets, his mouth grim. "I don't think your old man was coming back here to retrieve anything, Merce," he said. "Take a look."

Mercy pressed her forehead to the cool glass and shaded her eyes. The interior was dim in the early evening light, but one thing was for certain. The building was nearly empty. Not a single display case, bookshelf, or cabinet remained. A few boxes were piled in one corner. There was, however, a doorway leading off into a small room, its interior hidden from view.

"That could be his office," Mercy said. "Maybe they haven't cleaned out his office yet."

Daniel shrugged. "Possible."

But Mercy could tell by Daniel's tone that, again, he was humoring her. She gritted her teeth.

"Then maybe his office has been moved to the library already," she snarled.

"The library closes at three o'clock on Saturday, Mercy," he said through a sigh.

Mercy glared up at him. "Don't talk to me like I'm some kind of imbecile." Then she spun to stomp back down the steps toward her car. She raked her hand through her hair as tears stung the backs of her eyes. "Or maybe I am just as screwed up in the head as my father was."

He caught up to her just as she was opening her car door.

"Babe, please. You've had a pretty traumatic week. You've been under an unbelievable amount of stress lately." He pulled her against him, but her body remained stiff, hands fisted at her sides.

He stepped back and lifted her chin, forcing her to meet his gaze.

"Look. The sign indicates this place is open on Sunday. If they're still in the process of packing up, maybe we can catch somebody here then. I'll come with you. We'll see if we can get some answers."

Mercy felt her shoulders relax and she blinked, causing one hot tear to streak down her cheek. She swiped at it angrily. But he was trying. She had to give him that.

"Okay."

"Tomorrow, then," Daniel said. "We'll come back tomorrow afternoon and see what we can find out."

CHAPTER 23

*D*aniel watched Mercy drive away from the old Victorian, standing there until her car disappeared around the turn. He blew out a breath. He had kind of hoped they could spend the evening together. With Reagan working, she would be all alone. In her state of mind, he hated to think of her sitting by herself in an empty house, thinking. Plotting. Planning. Ruminating over this whole crazy quest she was on to find her father's grave.

Okay, it wasn't crazy, but it wasn't life threatening, either. True, he'd started this whole ancestry search thing. He'd even had to work hard to convince her to start it. But once she dove in, she did so with both feet. Daniel understood her not wanting to lose her son to his father over a thousand miles away. There'd been a chance, if the boy's grandfather was still alive, she might have been able to convince him to stay in New England.

But it appeared all that was left of her family lay buried deep under the ground. Surely, once Reagan turned eighteen and got his degree, he'd fly south. A secret, selfish part of Daniel was glad Reagan wanted to move away. That would leave nothing, or nobody, in the way for the Daniel and Mercy to grow closer. He felt guilty about it, but he couldn't help it either.

He'd sensed Mercy pulling away from him, ever since the night with the psychic. True, that was his idea too, but it was more curiosity than anything else driving him to hire her. Once he'd experienced her vague and inconclusive diagnosis about the hauntings, he truly wondered about whether her "gift" was real or an acting job.

And what happened to sensible, grounded, I-don't-believe-in-ghosts Mercy? She certainly had done a turnaround, and so fast it made Daniel's head spin.

She was an exasperating woman, of that there was no doubt. Once she made up her mind to something, there was no swaying her. If he had to compare her with anyone, it would be to himself, or to any other man he'd ever known. Stubborn, pig-headed, righteous.

Come to think of it, his deceased fiancé had also fit that description perfectly.

How could he have let this happen to him again? He swore he would never lower his guard and expose his tender underbelly to another woman like Keelin again. And what had he done now? Exactly that.

Keelin's stubborn streak had cost his fiancé her life.

It was Thanksgiving Eve, and Keelin always—*always*—spent the holiday with her Mom in Back Bay. They'd cook together, drink wine, and invite the whole family. Of course, her entire family lived within walking distance of their quaint Boston Victorian. She'd come from money. Her father had done well, following in her grandfather's footsteps to take over the import-export business he'd established shortly after immigrating from Ireland.

By that time, Keelin was living with Daniel in the new home he'd bought for her in the Corby woods. One of the worst Noreasters to hit New England blew in mid-afternoon on Wednesday. At least two, possibly three feet of snow was expected to fall, and fall fast, at a ridiculous rate of two to three inches per hour. Wet snow, high winds. Travel conditions impossible.

Daniel refused to risk either of their lives by driving into Boston, where snow removal was difficult at best on the narrow and convoluted streets. He tried to talk her into taking the train. But the storm was so bad, even the commuter line had suspended many of their scheduled runs. By the time they'd called, the last train to Back Bay was already gone. With the holiday, and not knowing how long the storm would last, the train schedule for Thanksgiving Day was sketchy at best.

She feigned heartbreak but recovered quickly with an idea. Looking back now, Daniel realized her tears had dried *too* quickly. Keelin asked if it were possible for him, being he had a four-wheel drive truck, to drive the two miles to the grocery store before the roads got too bad.

"I'll just cook a turkey here," she'd said. "It will be our first Thanksgiving together." Then she'd wrapped her arms around his neck and kissed him stupid. "Be careful," she said, patting his butt as he stomped out the door into the swirling snow.

Keelin tricked him. By the time he'd returned with a fresh, ten-pound hen turkey under one arm and a bottle of wine under the other, her car was gone. This was before the age of cell phones. For four frantic hours, Daniel paced and worried. When his landline finally rang, he prayed it would be Keelin's voice he would hear, announcing she'd made it safely to Mom's house.

It was not. Through choking sobs, Keelin's mother told Daniel the horrific news: his fiancé's car had slid across the Mass Pike just a few miles from home. After slamming into the guardrail, the car flipped and tumbled off the bridge into the water—water still not frozen because it was so early in the season. Unable to free herself from the sinking vehicle, Keelin had drowned.

By the time the rescue team reached her in the near impossible weather conditions, Keelin was as cold and stiff as Daniel's heart.

If only she'd listened to him. If only she hadn't been the kind of woman who made up her mind to do something, then went ahead and did it, regardless of the risk.

The same kind of woman, he feared, that Mercedes Donohue was trying very hard to be.

Sunday dawned grey and dismal, threatening rain. Mercy stared out her kitchen window at the makeshift court where Reagan and Daniel had played weekly, only two months ago. She didn't want to admit it, but a deep depression was settling over her. She'd had to be the tough one, the sturdy beam to keep her son's life from crumbling out from under him—a task she'd nearly failed at.

Now, she realized, her own world was crumbling out from beneath her. But honestly, what had she been hoping for? Yes, Daniel was great with Reagan, really good to her, and sexy as hell. There was no denying the chemistry between them. Had she really believed they could start over as a brand-new family, as if hers and Reagan's lives hadn't been turned upside down two years ago? What a freaking fantasy.

Mercy could see cracks in Daniel's shiny suit of armor now, too. How he'd completely turned around on his belief in the haunting of the old asylum. How he'd accused Cierce of being nothing more than a money-driven actress. Not to her face, but still.

It bothered her, too, that Daniel hadn't seemed at all upset by the news that Reagan wanted to move back south. In fact, she thought, looking back, he'd almost seemed glad. Happy he could have her all to himself? Should that make her feel cherished or did that just brand him a selfish bastard?

How long, she wondered, had she turned a blind eye to the cracks in Luke's armor?

And what, exactly, was finding her father's exact grave marker going to accomplish? Mercy guessed it would give her a sense of closure, if nothing else. Maybe she'd even do like the woman from

Florida the old man told her about. Maybe she'd go ahead and order a gravestone, a real one, to mark her father's final resting place.

Daniel came by to pick her up just before one o'clock to head to the Historical Society. She'd dropped Reagan off at Anzio's for his noon-to-five shift, and was waiting, keys in hand, on the porch steps when Daniel pulled in. She didn't wait for him to get out, just hopped up and climbed into the passenger's side.

"How are you?" he asked cautiously. She noticed he kept his hands on the wheel, not reaching for her as he usually did. Part of her was relieved. Another part, right in the vicinity of her heart, died a tiny death.

"I'm good. Think we'll find anyone there?" she asked, fiddling with the straps on her purse and avoiding his gaze.

"We might. They've got to have all their stuff out a week from Monday, and they're obviously not finished yet." Daniel backed out of the driveway, then turned to look at her. "You'll be coming back to work with the team when we start on this next job, right?"

Mercy hesitated, unsure if she should share with him the thought that had been floating around in the back of her brain since last night. "I think so. Probably."

"Conner's on board with it. Didn't you find him a bookkeeper to take over that end of the business? He said you set up an answering service, too—"

"I'm not sure what I'm going to do, Daniel. Life is changing for me. Fast. Too fast. I was thinking maybe I should move closer to Boston and look for work on another team out that way."

His head snapped around and he stared at her in shock. "Why? Why the hell would you do something like that, Mercy? You've just gotten yourself established on Conner's team. Why would you want to start all over? Again?"

Mercy shrugged, picking at a hangnail on her workman's hands. "Money's better, I've heard. Plus, what will I have holding me here? A hole in the ground with my father's number attached to it? A father I never knew, by the way."

She jumped and shrieked a little when Daniel braked hard and pulled his truck into a church parking lot, wheels squealing. He threw it into park and spun around in the seat to face her.

"Mercy. I know we've had a few differences of opinion in the past few days, but I have to ask, girl. What about us? I thought we might have the beginning of a good thing started. I was hoping we could explore our relationship a little more."

Mercy's heart clutched at the desperation she heard in his voice. He really was a nice guy, she reminded herself. But working alongside the same man she slept with didn't exactly work out for her before. What made her think the chances would be any better this time?

She laid a hand on his thigh and met his gaze. "I'm not sure about anything yet. Right now, I'm in reactive mode. I'm in the midst of a lot of new discoveries and more information than I know how to process. And I do like you, Daniel. Very much. Our chemistry is amazing. But we seemed to have switched places in the past few weeks. I was the skeptic and didn't believe in ghosts. Then you opened Pandora's box and brought Cierce in. Once I was convinced the building was haunted, you changed your mind and practically called the woman a charlatan."

Daniel huffed and pinched the bridge of his nose, then jerked his head back and moaned. "Shit. I wonder how long before this damn thing isn't so tender."

Great. The guilt card again. Yet Mercy always fell for it. She slid across the bench seat and laid her head on his shoulder. "I'm sorry, Daniel. We've been through an awful lot in an incredibly short period of time. I guess it wouldn't hurt to wait until things calm down some. Give us some time."

He turned to face her, and she planted a gentle kiss on his oh-so-sexy, whiskery lips. When his lips parted to stroke her mouth with his tongue, her defenses evaporated. She took the kiss deep and combed her fingers into his hair. It was a long minute, maybe two, before they broke the kiss, panting.

Looking up in shock, Mercy realized they were sitting directly in front of the First Congregational Church, and the noon service was, apparently, just getting out. A gawking line of worshippers of all ages streamed past the hood of Daniel's truck, all wearing the same judgmental scowl. One young mother snatched her little boy's hand and jerked him, barking, *Don't stare at that. Shameful.*

"Oops," Daniel muttered, quickly firing up the truck and pulling back out onto the street.

They snickered like children all the way to the Historical Society.

CHAPTER 24

To Daniel's surprise, they arrived at the old Historical Society building to find it bustling with life. Both the front and side doors were propped open. Two teenage boys were carrying boxes to load into a van parked out front.

"Good," he said. "There might be somebody here with some information."

"Good afternoon," Daniel greeted one of the boys. "Is there someone here in charge?"

The tall, lanky boy with a sunny, blond buzz-cut bobbed his head and pointed to the front door. "Ms. Terrian is just inside. She's the President."

Daniel snatched up Mercy's hand and they mounted the steps, dodging another young fellow headed out with a box that seemed a bit too heavy for him. Daniel paused, then held out his arms. "Why don't you let me carry that one, young man? Looks pretty heavy." Eagerly, the boy complied.

After settling the box into the back of the van, Daniel returned to find Mercy deep in conversation with a tall, distinguished looking woman with a dark bob and black-rimmed glasses. They were standing in the doorway of the room he and Mercy had speculated was an office. Their assumption appeared to have been correct.

All that remained in the room now, though, was an old oak book-case, a few shelves, and an assortment of wires hanging out of various electrical outlets on the wall. Whatever desk that might have been there was gone.

The woman was listening to what Mercy was saying but continued to shake her head very slightly side to side as she spoke.

"He was a very old man, hunched and walking with the aid of a cane. He said he worked here, at the Historical Society," Mercy explained.

"I'm sorry, Miss. But I've been on the Board of Directors here for over eight years. We've not had anyone working here that fits that description. Nor anyone on the Board of Directors."

A short, matronly woman stepped in from the back door and came around the corner. Her puff of silver hair framed a round face with kind eyes. The dark-haired woman looked past Mercy to her and asked, "Collette, you've worked here longer than I have. Do you remember any short, elderly man working here? This lady seems to have met someone at the Hillcrest Cemetery who says he has some of the old asylum records."

The elder woman blinked, thinking. After a moment, she said, "Not for a very, very long time."

Daniel could see Mercy's frustration mounting. She shifted from one foot to the other and raked her long hair back from her face. He could see her skin glistening with sweat in this hot, humid room.

"You don't understand. I saw him. I talked to him, just yesterday. He was coming to find the grave of some lady's grandfather. She sent him money from Florida to put in a real headstone. You know, in place of the numbered pillar."

The silver-haired woman's eyes went wide, and she swayed. Daniel stepped forward and grasped her upper arm. "Are you alright, ma'am?

Here, let me get you a seat." With his free hand he grabbed a spindle-backed chair and pulled it up, settling her into it.

"Collette, what's wrong? Are you having one of your spells again? Do you need me to get you a nitro tablet?" the tall woman asked, concerned.

Collette's gaze drifted off out the window, and for a long moment, she said nothing. Then she raised watery, pale eyes to Mercy.

"I remember that story. The woman—she lived in Miami, I think. She sent Kevin a letter and enclosed a check. She wanted him to order a headstone for her grandpa. Kevin said he knew where the list was, you know. The one with the names and numbers of those poor souls buried up there," she said. Her voice was weak and cracked, and Daniel feared the woman was about to faint.

Spotting an ice chest in the corner, he lifted the lid and pulled out a bottle of water. He twisted off the cap and handed it to Collette. It took several seconds before she even acknowledged his offering. Her mind had drifted off, far away from the here and now.

Finally, she blinked and focused on the bottle. "Oh. Thank you, young man." She took two dainty sips and blotted her lips with a crumpled tissue she drew out of the sleeve of her blouse.

Mercy knelt before the woman and spoke softly. "Collette, so, you do know this . . . Kevin person, then? The one who says he has the list of names?"

Collette nodded. "I *knew* him. Knew him pretty well, as a matter of fact. He served as the president of the Historical Society for almost ten years. An odd bird, he was, for sure."

"Why do you say that?" Mercy asked.

"Well, he had the list, you know. Guess he'd known the last super-intendent in charge of records of the old hospital. That man, I don't remember his name . . ." Collette wiped her watery eyes with the tissue, "that man told him to keep the list private. So that none of those government agencies would get stuck paying to put in real gravestones." She stared into Mercy's eyes. "Those things are expensive, you know."

"So, where is this Kevin now? Do you know how I can get in touch with him?" Mercy pressed.

The old woman wagged her head from side to side and stared at her lap. "You can find him at Fairview Cemetery. I can even show you where he's buried. I watched them put him in the ground." She sighed, a tired, sad sound. "He never did get the headstone put up for that lady. We ended up sending the check back. None of us knew where Kevin kept the list." She stared at Mercy with haunted eyes.

Daniel felt a chill wash over him, even though the air in the old Victorian was thick and humid. This just couldn't be. He had been certain Mercy had imagined the old man. Surely, she couldn't have come up with details this specific out of thin air.

Mercy placed a hand over Collette's. "You don't understand, ma'am. I saw Kevin, just yesterday. I spoke to him. He said he was coming back here to get the list so he could locate the man's grave—"

Collette's eyes grew sharp, and she spoke her next words with conviction. "I don't know who you saw, or what you might think somebody told you. But Kevin O'Rourke has been dead now for over ten years. We found him slumped in his office chair with that lady's check lying on the floor beside him. Massive heart attack. We never did find any list."

As they left the Historical Society, Mercy turned to Daniel. "Do you still think I'm imagining things?"

Daniel raised his eyebrows and exhaled. "No way to explain it now," he said, "except for one."

Hate to admit it though he did, there was no other logical explanation for Mercy's story. There was no way she could have known about that request, the check. Hell, she even knew where the granddaughter's letter came from. He tugged on his beard.

"I spoke to a ghost, didn't I?" Mercy said quietly, then wrapped her arms around herself. Or . . . or a . . . what did Cierce call them? Residual haunting. I wonder how many times that old man has made the trek up the hill to the graveyard to try and fulfill the Florida woman's request? Over and over again, in a never-ending loop. Until he'll just fade away."

"Or, he's not just an echo from the past. His spirit is stuck here, having never fulfilled his last task on this earth." Daniel glanced at her, raising an eyebrow. "That would be the theory, if I was one to believe in such things."

Mercy shot him a look. "Are you making fun of me? This isn't funny, Daniel. This whole thing is creeping me out."

He reached over and tucked a strand of hair behind her ear. "I'm not making fun of you. I believe what you said you saw was real."

"A ghost. You're saying you believe I spoke with a ghost," Mercy challenged.

Daniel pinched the bridge of his nose, more gingerly this time. "I'm not sure what you saw, Mercy. But I believe that *you* believe you did. Speak with the ghost of Kevin O'Rourke."

It was only three o'clock when they arrived back at Mercy's, and Daniel was relieved when Mercy invited him in.

So, he might be wrong about this. He was man enough to admit that. Yes, Mercy was stubborn and once she got her teeth around a bone, she didn't let go until she got what she was after. He could accept that about her. As long as it didn't jeopardize her safety, or she didn't lie to him.

Mercy headed straight for the fridge and pulled out two cold beers. "Could sure use this right about now," she said, handing him the bottle. "This mystery keeps getting stranger and stranger, doesn't it?"

Daniel drained half his bottle in three swallows, then wiped the foam off his beard with two fingers. "You got that right. But you've got your answer now. The list, wherever the old man kept it, is pretty much lost forever. The search ends here."

She spun to face him. "No, it doesn't end here. Not by a long shot. The list has to exist somewhere, Daniel. Somebody must have found it in that man's office. He said he kept it locked up. Surely it wouldn't have been discarded as trash."

Daniel lifted a shoulder.

Truly, he was done with this. It just kept getting weirder by the hour. The day's events, he had to admit, had spooked him. Made him question what he believed, and what he thought was just woo-woo bullshit. But still, he couldn't allow Mercy to keep traveling down this path. If nothing else, it would surely threaten whatever emotional stability she'd managed to accomplish.

She needed to get a grip. For herself, as well as for her son's welfare.

"Mercy, I know you want to find the exact location of your father's remains. I get that. But really, now, after all these years, does it matter? You know where he's buried. He's somewhere within that three-acre plot. Can't we just take flowers and plant them somewhere on the site? To honor him?"

He saw her shoulders slump and knew immediately: *wrong thing to say*. Shit, though, he was a guy. Weren't guys always really good at saying the exactly wrong thing at the exactly wrong time? Daniel wasn't going to let this get between him and the woman he loved. He—

Wait. What? Loved? Where the hell had that come from?

Daniel slammed his bottle down on the counter and closed the distance between them in two strides. She didn't resist him. He snatched the beer out of her hand and set it on the counter, taking her into his arms.

"Look. I'm not saying I know all the right answers. Everybody has to grieve, or remember, or honor . . . hell, I don't know. We all have our own ways to cope with losing a loved one." He cupped her cheek in his hand and grabbed her gaze. "Mercy, damn it all to hell, I'm falling in love with you. At this point I really don't give a flying rat's ass what happened forty years ago, or forty days. Or forty hours. I just know that I love you, and I want us to have a chance at a life together."

Mercy ducked her head against his chest, and he could feel her chuckle. Chuckle? That had to be a positive sign. When she raised her eyes to meet his, she was smiling.

"Are there really such things as flying rats?" she asked, smirking.

He grinned. "Yup. They're called bats. But let's not go there right now. We've got enough vampire-like lure taunting our lives at the moment."

THEIR LOVEMAKING WAS DIFFERENT, somehow, Mercy thought as they rolled and laughed and kissed on her bed that afternoon. Something inside her had let loose. Maybe it was for better, maybe for worse. But it sure felt damn good in the moment. *Their* moment.

Lovemaking. Okay, there it was. The difference. She had suddenly begun internally referring to their sexual encounters as more than just sex.

He was a deliciously exciting lover. Lean and strong but bulging and cut in all the right places. His abs were reminiscent of a Greek statue. Big, muscular thighs and biceps held him effortlessly over her, when he chose to be on top. But he had no problem when she took over, swinging a leg over his lean hips to settle down on him in indescribable pleasure.

Was this love? Or just lust? Hard to tell, no pun intended. Luke had been the only lover she'd ever known, so who was she to say? She wondered if what she and Luke had shared had ever been more than lust. When they'd gotten together, she was a young, innocent girl infatuated with a man she'd been certain was her true soulmate.

Daniel's scent, the taste of his kiss and of his skin, the tenderness of his touch—all these things delighted Mercy to her core. She'd accepted Daniel wasn't perfect. No man was. Neither was she. Yet she couldn't help hoping that this man was, perhaps, the perfect man for her.

As they lay spooned under slightly sweaty sheets that afternoon, the rumble of thunder in the distance punctuated their joining. Electricity. That's what they shared. Both as a vocation and between their two hearts. Mercy dropped her guard and decided: she was ready to risk her heart again. She wasn't ready to give up on Daniel Gallagher just yet.

CHAPTER 25

*A*s boring as sitting in the blasted office was for Mercy, it was somehow easier knowing she had only one week left. Next week she'd be back on the job, working—ironically—at the old Victorian that housed the Historical Society. It wasn't a big job. They should be able to knock it out in less than two weeks. After that they were headed to an investor's duplex on the other side of town.

Concentrating on the work ahead kept Mercy from ruminating over Reagan's impending departure. He was finishing his classes this week and was scheduled to take his test this Friday at the Worcester Adult Learning Center. If he passed, his father promised to book a ticket for him to fly out as soon as possible. Possibly by this weekend, her only child would be living over a thousand miles away. Maybe permanently.

A knot of raw emotion, the size of a tennis ball, lodged in Mercy's throat every time she thought about it. But there was nothing she could do. Reagan would turn eighteen on Friday.

Daniel had been especially attentive, sensing her pain. He'd call her on his lunch break every day, and even stopped by one night to shoot hoops with Reagan. The boy had to be coaxed into joining Daniel on the court, though. Things just hadn't been the same between them since the *girlfriend* comment.

She and Daniel were still set to go to the library on Tuesday to see what Tiffany had dug up in the way of asylum records. But Mercy's enthusiasm for the quest had waned. Daniel was right. What good would it do for her to find the list of names? He promised that once Reagan had left, he would go with her as often as she liked to bring flowers to the cemetery.

Daniel came and had dinner with them on Tuesday. Mercy bought some steaks, and the man proved to be an excellent grill master.

"Man, those smell awesome," Reagan said as he laid a napkin across his lap. "Whenever Mom grills, she usually burns them."

Mercy scowled at her son. "I haven't seen you stepping up to take over grill duty. I always thought that was a man-thing."

Reagan shot a sidelong glance in Daniel's direction before mumbling, "I'll have Dad teach me. He's an awesome grill master too."

Another jab to her heart. Another passive-aggressive shot at Daniel. Mercy sighed. This is how it had been ever since the night Reagan realized they were a couple. She wondered if he'd told his father about them.

She wondered why she should care.

"Hey, anymore spooky stuff go on up there at the haunted building?" Reagan asked. He cut a huge forkful of the sizzling meat and stuck it in his mouth. Then he gave Daniel a thumbs up.

"Nah. We're about finished up there. Building inspector comes tomorrow. If all is good, I might even get a few days off before the next job," Daniel said, seasoning his steak. "Hey, isn't your birthday on Friday? Wanna do something?"

But Reagan was shaking his head even as Daniel spoke. "I'll be packing. I take the GED this Friday. Once I pass it, I'll be flying South." Reagan fashioned a bird with both hands and waved them up and away.

Another jab.

Why was he being so mean about this? Didn't he realize how hard it would be for me once he's gone?

Daniel cleared his throat. "Aren't you going to miss your Mom?"

Reagan was quiet for a moment, chewing. Then he lifted a shoulder. "Sure, I'll miss her. But she's got you, now, Daniel. Just think how much better it will be for the two of you once I'm out of the way."

There it was, plain and simple. Mercy hated to think of the situation in that light. In some warped, twisted way, it made Daniel the reason her son was leaving.

She knew it wasn't true. Reagan had been making noises about leaving even before she and Daniel got together. Still, a selfish little worm buried in Mercy's heart found it easier to blame Daniel for her son's decision instead of herself.

"When's he flying out?" They'd dropped Reagan off at class and were headed to the library.

Mercy stared out the window, her arms crossed on her chest. "Not sure. Luke promised him as soon as he got the test results, he'd book him a ticket. Could be as soon as this weekend."

Daniel ran gentle fingertips down her arm. "I know this is going to be really hard on you, Merce. I'm here, whenever you want to talk."

She nodded but said nothing. Daniel knew enough to back off, at least for now. A mother with empty nest syndrome, he'd heard, could be a mighty nasty raptor.

Tiffany smiled brightly at them as they entered the Reference Room.

"I was wondering if you two would be in tonight. I think you might be interested in what I've found." She lifted a manila envelope out from under the counter bearing a yellow sticky note that said, "Corby Asylum Records."

"Where'd you luck into these?" Daniel asked, taking the envelope. "I thought you'd already located everything the library had."

Tiffany leaned both elbows on the counter. "I'd forgotten there were some boxes and things in the basement that came from the Historical Society. They had to move all their stuff down there because of the renovation."

"I know," Daniel said, grinning. "We're doing the re-wire."

Mercy perked up, reaching for the envelope. "Is this all of it? I mean, everything out of all the desks and cabinets?"

"Pretty sure," Tiffany said. "But if what you're looking for isn't in there, maybe I can sneak you down to the storage room to rummage around a little more." She winked at Daniel.

After ten minutes of rifling through the thin stack that slid out of the envelope, Daniel realized the list of names was not there. His shoulders slumped.

"Guess this was a waste of time," he murmured to Mercy. She simply shrugged, her indifference palpable.

Time to let go of this investigation, Daniel thought. It doesn't matter to her anymore. Why the hell should it matter to me?

He brought the packet back to the desk and slid it across to Tiffany. "Sorry, Tiff, but I guess we wasted your time. There's nothing in here but some financial reports. We're looking for a list of names."

Tiffany took the envelope and frowned. "That's too bad, Dan." She leaned toward him, shooting a glance toward the open door. "If you come back around closing, I might could sneak you into the basement storage locker."

Daniel noticed Mercy was leaning on the doorjamb, arms crossed, looking bored.

"Nah, that's okay, Tiff. I guess it really doesn't matter that much anyway."

But somehow, it did. After he dropped Mercy off—sullen and distant—he was driving home. He couldn't stop thinking about those poor patients who'd been buried without so much as a name. There was something morally wrong about it. There had to be records *somewhere*. Surely, you couldn't bury a body in Massachusetts without there being a record of it in some public records office.

His dash clock showed the time as seven-forty-three p.m. The library closed at eight. Screeching into a random driveway, he turned his truck around and headed back toward the library. If he was lucky, he could catch Tiffany before she left.

When he approached the building, he could see Tiffany and Agnes chatting and laughing about something as Agnes locked the front door. He pulled his truck into the restaurant parking lot across the street and waited. Once Agnes had fired up her ancient Cadillac and pulled out—in an obvious hurry—he threw his truck into drive and met Tiffany just as her car reached the street.

He leaned out and waved, and she stopped, rolling down her window.

"You change your mind?" she asked, grinning.

"I did. You sure you won't get into any trouble for this?"

Tiffany scoffed. "No way. Agnes can't wait to get home and shake up one of those pretty pink martinis she drinks. There's no way she'll be back tonight."

Daniel raised his eyebrows. Pretty pink martinis on a Tuesday night. Now that's something he would never have guessed of the strait-laced, classic librarian, Agnes Pincher.

Tiffany led Daniel to a door at the rear of the building that was metal and rusted around the edges. As she fumbled the keys out of her purse, he asked, "No alarm system?"

She shook her head. "Nope. Not activated, anyway. Ever since the Historical Society has been hauling their stuff down here at all hours, we've had to give them a key and leave the security system disarmed. Besides, who in Corby is going to come in and steal a bunch of library books?"

The door screeched and squealed as Tiffany pulled it open, making Daniel wince and glance around. "You sure nobody is going to bust us for this? I mean, you could lose your job, couldn't you?"

Tiffany eyes scanned the parking lot and up and down the street. "You know what? If you wouldn't mind, I'll let you go in and poke around for a few. I'll wait out here and in case anybody comes by, I'll talk really loudly. Tell them I opened up for the Historical Society. That'll be your signal to wrap it up."

Daniel nodded and ducked through the low basement door. He found a light switch on the wall, and four, dust-covered bulbs flickered to life overhead. Then he sighed. The place was crammed full of everything from glass-fronted display cases to bookshelves. There were boxes piled everywhere, each bearing huge letters in black marker labeling their contents. He could barely fit as he tried to move through the stacks, and god forbid he caused one to come crashing to the floor.

He was never going to find anything in this mess.

It was just as he'd turned to leave when he spotted the desk in one corner. A few boxes littered its surface. But it looked antique, and just about the right size for that tiny office in the old Victorian. There were several drawers, including a narrow pencil drawer. Only one on the right side bore a keyhole.

Could this be the desk that came out of the office at the Historical Society?

He started with the unsecured drawers, wiggling them out of their cocoons with difficulty. The dampness down here wasn't doing this piece of furniture any good. He couldn't imagine it was preserving any of these other artifacts very well either. He'd have to suggest to Tiffany to run a dehumidifier during the course of the renovation.

Of course, none of the unsecured drawers held anything except a dead moth and the stub of an old, yellow pencil. And—of course—the locked drawer was locked. Daniel felt along the sides of the desk and along the bottom of the pencil drawer, but there was no key taped anywhere.

He was just about to pull out his pocket knife and potentially break some law when a voice behind him caused him to jolt, slicing his thumb in the process.

"You're not going to find what you're looking for in there, young man," a whiny voice informed him.

He spun around to find himself face-to-face with an old man. One with straggly white hair, stooped and bent, leaning on a cane. An attendant? Daniel thought. Tiffany didn't say anything about an attendant working down here.

"How . . . how do you know what I'm looking for?" he asked, sticking his bleeding thumb into his mouth.

The old man's thin lips twisted into a crooked smile. "We both know, don't we? I wasn't able to complete my task. Maybe you can finish it for me." He pointed the end of his cane at him, and that's when Daniel realized he could read the black marker labeling one of the boxes.

Victorian Tea Set – Fragile!

Except that the box stood directly behind the rapidly fading image of the old man.

The elder spoke again, this time his voice fading away to an eerie echo as his manifestation became more and more translucent.

"I need someone to finish the task. The task. For me . . . for me . . . for me."

The initial blast of ice that flushed through Daniel's veins slowed him only a moment. Logic kicked in. He knew once the apparition disappeared he might never get the information he needed.

"Old man . . . *Kevin* . . . please. Where is the list? The list of names of those buried in Hillcrest Cemetery?"

"Like I told your lady friend. Locked in my office. Was then, still is."

In the next instant, the ghost had evaporated.

CHAPTER 26

*E*ven though every day in the office had dragged for Mercy until now, the last week flew by. Like a cart rolling downhill with no brakes to slow it, time sped up. Reagan's test was Friday morning, eight a.m. Mercy dropped him off before going in to open the office, knowing she would be late.

It didn't really matter anyway. All week she'd been packing up what little contents the office held. This would be the last day Progressive Electrical would have to occupy the space. Friday was August 29th, and the lease ran out on Monday. Conner had hired a moving van to come Monday morning to load up the office furniture and bring it home to store in his basement.

The test ran about two hours, Mercy knew. By ten a.m. she should know whether or not her son had earned his GED. As well as his ticket to freedom. Ironic he should be taking it on his eighteenth birthday, she thought. Bittersweet irony.

Her cell phone rang at exactly ten minutes past ten. The caller I.D. said *Reagan*.

The building inspector had come and passed the tech school building's electrical components on Wednesday afternoon. After

Thursday cleanup day, Daniel would have Friday off. He'd suggested that he pick Reagan up from the testing center, and then pick up Mercy.

"We can go have a nice lunch to celebrate," he'd said. "Conner said since the rest of the team has Friday off, so should you, Mercy."

Mercy stood at the windows of the nearly empty office, waiting for Daniel's truck to pull into the parking lot. She felt as empty and hollow inside as the room around her. Another ending, another transition in her life. After Reagan called, she'd cried tears of joy, then of sorrow.

They pulled up to the door at a little past eleven. Mercy gathered her purse and the one file folder of her personal paperwork and met Daniel at the door. Looking past him, she saw Reagan sitting in the truck, cell phone to his ear. She raised an eyebrow.

"He's got a phone already?" she asked.

"I let him use mine. He couldn't wait to call his father," Daniel said, stepping inside and pulling Mercy away from the window and glass-fronted door. Then he wrapped his arms around her, pulling her head down to his shoulder. "It's okay, Mama. You can cry."

She didn't want to. She didn't want to spill all her tattered emotions, let down her guard. But his body was so strong and hard against hers. Resisting for only a moment, she finally let it go.

Maybe he does understand. Maybe he does really care about me, *for me*, and not just for his own selfish reasons. Maybe he really is as good a guy as I'd like to believe.

When they climbed into the truck a few minutes later, Reagan was vibrating off the back seat with excitement.

"Sunday, Mom. Dad's got me a ticket out of Logan on Sunday. Can you believe it? I was afraid to hope it would happen so soon."

Mercy leaned back and fist-bumped her son, forcing a watery smile. "Congratulations, Son. You passed, first shot. I'm proud of you. You have an amazingly bright future before you."

Too bad it's a future halfway down the east coast, away from me.

Reagan's flight was at eleven Sunday morning. Daniel offered to drive them, in his truck.

"More room for your stuff," he'd said.

Mercy was glad, knowing she'd be too jittery to make the drive into Boston, and too much of a mess to drive home alone. Goodbyes at the gate were, Mercy thought, more painful than the labor pains she'd suffered the day he was born. At least after that torment, she'd had a warm bundle to hold in her arms. This time, she was losing him. Probably forever.

"Will you come home for Thanksgiving?" she asked through tears as she hugged him one last time.

Reagan hesitated a beat too long, giving Mercy her answer. "That's kind of soon, Mom. I was thinking Christmas. Would that be okay?"

As he disappeared down the corridor past security, Reagan turned and waved, and Mercy felt her heart fracture. Daniel, beside her with an arm around her waist, folded her to him. Again, she cried.

On the way back from Boston, few words were spoken. Mercy sat staring out the passenger window, watching the traffic and the billboards and the train stations whiz by. She felt completely empty, brittle, gouged out, like an avocado skin after its innards were scooped out.

Finally, Daniel turned to her, laying a hand on her knee. "Why don't you come stay with me for a few days? This way you won't have to go back to an empty house."

Silently, she nodded.

"CONNER WANTS us still to meet and park at the strip mall, then ride to the job site in the van," Daniel said as they neared Corby center.

Mercy nodded. "Would you mind if I stopped by my house and packed some work clothes and toiletries? Otherwise we'll have to get up at the butt crack of dawn."

Daniel waited in the truck. He figured it would be easier for her to go in and grab what she needed without him getting in the way. He was surprised at the volume of "a few days' worth" Mercy lugged out the door.

A tiny spark of warmth ignited in his chest. Maybe he could convince her to stay for longer than a few days. He certainly intended to do his best to try.

Work began on the old Victorian without delay, first thing Monday morning. Just as with the asylum building, they first had to rip out all the old wiring and outlet boxes. This time, Conner double —then tripled checked every fuse panel in the place to be sure there was no power coming in from the main.

Stealthily, Daniel went behind him for a final check. The last thing he wanted to happen now was for Mercy—or any of them—to get hurt on their first day.

Mercy was back on the job just like before. Her hair tucked neatly under the safety helmet, her Carhartts hanging baggy from her frame, Daniel still thought she was the most beautiful woman he'd ever seen. Something, though, was missing.

It was her spark. The enthusiasm and good humor she'd exhibited when she first joined the team seemed to have vanished. She was quiet and made little conversation, with either Daniel or the other men, all day. At lunchtime, as they sat in Subway, she picked at her salad as though she were looking for bugs hidden within the leaves.

Depression, obviously, had settled its heavy blanket over Mercedes Donohue's life. Daniel found himself deeply saddened, but also frustrated. He knew there was little he could do to change her state of mind.

He hadn't told her about seeing the little old man in the basement of the library Tuesday night. Her psyche was a little too unstable, a bit too tender at the moment. Plus, she appeared to have completely lost interest in finding out anything more about her father's burial site.

To be honest, Mercy had lost interest in just about everything. Including him.

He gave it a few days before he tried to hold her after they'd climbed under the sheets at night. She always snuggled up to his side, sometimes crying softly into his chest when she thought he was already asleep. After three days, he began softly stroking her back, moving around to cup her breast as they lay side by side. She didn't turn him down.

But by the same token, she wasn't the same woman he'd made love to just a week or so ago. Mercy went through the motions. She moaned at all the right times. Daniel was convinced, though, she was acting. A good actress, but acting all the same.

A good actress. Just like Keelin. Once that thought buried itself into Daniel's brain, it lingered there, pricking like a thorn sunken beneath the skin.

CHAPTER 27

"I figured we'd be out of here in a month," Conner growled, spewing tobacco juice out an open window of the Historical Society's building. "This is looking more and more like a two-to-three-month job."

Daniel said nothing but had to agree.

They'd spent the past two weeks ripping out all the old wiring and outlet boxes from the Victorian building, but it was more like a demolition than a renovation. The rooms were small which made working conditions difficult. Most of the wiring was hidden behind plastered walls, so considerable damage to the original surfaces was unavoidable. Conner had made two calls already to the head contractor to let him know the cost was going to be higher than originally quoted.

Daniel and Mercy worked side by side, just like before, but Daniel could sense her drifting farther and farther away from him. Her son was gone, apparently quite happy to be back in Atlanta. But it had been a month since Reagan left, for god's sake. She needed to start getting over this.

In those first weeks, he'd ignored the nearly daily calls she made to

Reagan. He could tell by what he heard on his end that Reagan didn't really have much to say to her. She was clinging, and they both knew it. Mercy was still staying at Daniel's place, only occasionally spending an afternoon at her own house to tidy up and do some laundry.

In the beginning, he'd been all for suggesting she give up the little rental. He'd wanted her to move in with him. Now, he wasn't so sure that was a good idea.

Exactly one month after they'd driven the kid to the airport, they were sitting at his dinner table, eating the excellent shepherd's pie that Daniel had made. It was another bone of contention gnawing at Daniel's gut. Mercy was an excellent cook, yet had made no effort to contribute to meal preparation since she moved in. She hardly ate anything anymore and had lost at least ten pounds. They ate in silence, until halfway through the meal, she shoved the plate away from her. She reached for her cell phone.

"I'm going out to the porch to call Reagan," she mumbled.

Daniel's fist came down on the table so hard every piece of porcelain and flatware became airborne before clattering back to the wooden surface. Mercy jumped back, staring at him.

"What the hell is wrong with you?" she snapped.

"You've got to stop this, Mercedes. All you're doing is driving that kid farther and farther away from you. Don't you see it? You're obsessed. It's time to move on before you lose your son completely."

Mercy glared at him for a long, stunned moment. Then she scrambled to her feet. Without saying a word, she spun on one heel and headed for the back porch, phone in hand. Before she'd reached the door, Daniel muttered, "You'll lose Reagan, and you'll lose me too."

She froze, one hand on the door handle. When her chin lowered to her chest and he saw her shoulders shaking, he stood and went to her. Coming up behind her, he gently wrapped his arms around her. He rocked her, whispering words of comfort into her ear, until the worst of her sobs began to subside.

"I know . . ." she blubbered, "I know I'm screwing this all up. I can't help it. I can't stand the thought of Reagan living with . . . *them*. Calling that bitch *Mom* and accepting her as though it was okay what she did. What his father did. To me. To us."

Daniel turned her to face him, lifting her face to meet his eyes. "Mercedes, maybe you ought to go see Dr. McGuire. Ian knows Reagan. He knows this whole situation. He helped him through a tough time, right? Reagan learned to accept life the way it is now, and to move on. Maybe he can do the same for you."

He'd spoken softly and meant nothing by his suggestion except to help Mercy out of this terrible depression she had fallen into. Her reaction both shocked and appalled him.

Pushing him back so hard he stumbled, she fisted her hands at her sides, so hard he heard the case on her cell phone crack.

"You're thinking, *oh, poor little Mercy May is a nut-case*, just like her daddy was. Aren't you? Aren't you?"

Daniel raked a hand through his hair and lifted both hands. "Mercy, no. But I do see what's happening to you. You're depressed. Clinically depressed. I don't want you to suffer through this any more than you already have." He reached out and took her hand, though she struggled to snatch it away.

"Look at me. Look. At. Me."

When she finally raised her gaze to his, he wasn't sure what—or who—he saw in those eyes. Surely, not the woman he'd come to know and love. This woman was wild, feral. Distrust and fear were written all over her face.

It bewildered him, and it scared him. He swallowed hard and pushed on.

"Mercy, I love you. I want to make a life with you. Here. Working together. Living life together." He lifted her hand and placed a soft kiss there. "Loving together."

For an instant—an infinitesimal fraction of a second, he saw the old Mercy flash across her eyes. Just as quickly, it was gone. She yanked her hand free.

"I'm packing my stuff. I want you to take me home. To *my* home. My. Home," she spat. She turned and headed for the bedroom.

CHAPTER 28

The beauty of fall turned the little town of Corby into a colorful postcard. This was usually Mercy's favorite time of year, when the crisp, cool days hinted that the holidays would soon be upon them. By now, she usually had a pumpkin and colorful pots of mums on her front porch.

Not this year. She was back home, living in the cute rental she and her son had shared. But Reagan wasn't living there anymore.

There were three weeks until Thanksgiving, and Mercy sank lower and lower into her self-inflicted pit of despair. At times she paced through the empty house, ranting aloud to herself. To the world. To God.

"What? What the holy hell have I done in this life to deserve this fate, oh masterful creator? Okay, I lost my virginity before my wedding vows, yeah. I admit it! But hey, am I the only one? And you couldn't have been *too* pissed. You gave me a beautiful, smart, handsome boy who loves his mother."

That's where she'd stop, choke up, and amend her rant.

"He *used* to love his mother. Now he's paying homage to the woman who stole his father away from me. How can she deserve him more than I do?"

Mercy's mind, poisoned with self-doubt and guilt, then progressed to the next stage of her rant.

"And what was Daniel? Was he my consolation prize? Oh, I get it. He was the guy who lured me into another relationship—another hook-up—one that cost me my son. *Lead us not into temptation*." Her bitter laugh made her sick to her stomach.

These nights usually ended up with Mercy on the couch, unconscious, with an empty wine bottle on the table.

Her work began to suffer, and she knew all the guys saw it. Most mornings she stumbled out of her car in the parking lot, still half-drunk from the night before. Pasting on a fake smile, she'd climb into the van and spurt, "Hey, team. How's it hanging?"

Neither Conner nor Jacob had ever seen her act this way. Daniel cringed in his seat and averted his eyes.

Conner pulled her aside the Friday afternoon before Thanksgiving to have a talk.

"Look, Merce. We all know you've been through a rough patch. It's okay. I understand. But again, lady, you're a hazard on the job if you don't get your shit together." He gripped her shoulder and riveted her eyes. "Look. Next week is three work days only. Turkey day is Thursday and you know I always give the team Friday off. I'm giving you the entire week off. Because I'm the boss." He hesitated when she raised a hand to resist. "On my nickel. Our secret. Take a mental health week. I think you need it."

Mercy pulled into her driveway that afternoon, killed the engine, and rested her head on the steering wheel. *A mental health week*. Damn, she really *was* losing it. Maybe Daniel was right. Maybe she needed to call Dr. Ian McGuire.

.   .   .

THE WEEKS LEADING up to Thanksgiving were always the hardest for Daniel. And now, with Mercy gone, they would be even worse. His own family had been retired in Florida for years now, and that was the last place he wanted to be anyway. Too much well-intentioned sympathy. And Keelin's family in Back Bay was no better. Their grief still tainted the air there, oozing up from the floor like spilled oil.

No. There was no way he was spending turkey day with Keelin's family.

Sometimes, he went to Kim's. But this year, Kim had found herself another man who she'd been dating for a month or so. She'd called to invite him, and said she was cooking a full-blown turkey dinner. But Daniel declined.

So, what was left? A turkey sandwich, that's what. An excellent, Boar's Head, sliced turkey sandwich and a six-pack of Sam Adams in front of the football game. That would be Thanksgiving for Daniel.

Thanksgiving Day, 2008, dawned sunny but cold, the expected high temperature only thirty-five degrees. Daniel threw another log into his woodstove after stumbling out of bed around ten o'clock. He was grateful he'd picked up his Thanksgiving dinner the night before. Hell, it was only a turkey sandwich and a six-pack of Sam, but he had it already in. No need to climb out of his warm flannel pajama pants and Patriots sweatshirt to go anywhere.

Anywhere.

He couldn't help but wonder how Mercy was spending the holiday. He knew Reagan wasn't coming home. She'd taken the whole week off, so he hadn't seen her. Had she decided to fly to Atlanta and crash her ex's party? He hoped not. It would only mean more heartbreak for her, he was certain.

Daniel had enough heartbreak of his own to deal with, every year, on this holiday. Yeah, it had been twelve years since he got the horrific news. News that would haunt his heart until the day he died. The day his beloved Keelin had drowned, then turned into a frozen corpse in a drainage ditch off the Mass Pike before anyone could save her.

Because she was stubborn. Because she'd done what she wanted, no matter the danger. Because she'd deceived him.

Despite his better judgment, Daniel was just popping the top off his second beer at two p.m. when a knock came on his door. *Who the holy hell could this be?* he wondered. Lifting aside the living room curtain, he saw Mercy's car sitting beside his truck.

He hadn't showered, hadn't shaved, had just barely mustered up the energy to brush his teeth. Raking his fingers through his hair, he grabbed a paper towel to wipe the beer foam off his mustache. Then he answered the door.

She stood on his porch looking like a goddess. Her long, dark hair flowed wildly over and around her shoulders. He blinked in shock to see she was wearing a dress—Mercedes, in another dress? But there she was, all five-toot-ten of her glorious goddess beauty, pale green fabric draping over her curvy form, ending way too short. Beneath, her shapely legs were wrapped in grey tights, and matching suede boots capped her knees. The outfit brought out the green in her eyes, which glowed like icy fire in the pale November light.

"Mercy," Daniel sputtered. "What the—"

In her arms she carried an aluminum foil pan, supported underneath by a cookie sheet. A dome of more of the silvery stuff hid something that smelled like heaven. A hell of a lot more appetizing than a cold, day-old turkey sandwich.

"Turkey. I brought us turkey. For dinner. You know, Thanksgiving?" She tipped her head and winked. "For you, *turkey*."

Then she hit him with a smile that nearly melted his knees out from under him.

The turkey ended up having to be reheated. Surprising, since the heat in Daniel's cabin definitely hiked up a notch once Mercy arrived. They didn't waste time talking, making excuses, explaining to each other what had kept them apart for the past weeks. The minute Mercy stepped through the door, Daniel took the pan from her, set it on a wooden sideboard, and attacked her mouth with his.

No hot pad to protect the wood. Okay, so the sideboard would need refinishing. Things can be replaced. Repaired. Human hearts are harder to mend.

With the cold, wintery sky outside his bedroom window, Daniel proceeded to show Mercy just how much she meant to him. He undressed her slowly, peeling off the fluffy cardigan sweater first, then unfastening the celery green dress one button at a time. She stared into his eyes the whole time.

Mercy.

She was back. It was Mercy this time in those eyes. *His* Mercy. Not some frightened, injured feral animal. Oh yeah, there was a sort of feral quality to her gaze. But only the good kind.

MERCY WASN'T sure if she was doing the right thing. She'd seen Dr. McGuire twice a week since that last day she'd been with Daniel. It helped he was already familiar with her situation through his meetings with Reagan. She'd finally opened up, pouring out all the grief and guilt and toxic hatred she'd been bottling up for two years.

He warned her to take it slow, especially with Daniel. Give herself time to get her bearings. Time for her heart to heal.

But Mercy was done waiting. Her heart had been down and bleeding and helpless these past two years since she'd caught Luke with his *other* family, joyously throwing his *other* child in the air, celebrating her birthday. Luke had moved on. Now, Reagan had too. It was time for Mercedes to take action to secure her own future.

A future with Daniel Gallagher. A man who had fallen into her life like a four-leaf clover atop a pile of lawn clippings. No, she wasn't letting this chance get by her.

In her heart, she knew she loved this man. He'd already said he loved her too.

Mercy had remembered, just the day before the holiday, what Daniel told her happened on Thanksgiving twelve years ago. How hard the holiday was for him. She thought there was no more perfect time to help him lift the black cloud hanging over this day of thanks.

She knew the memory would never stop haunting him. But maybe, just maybe, she could reset the holiday. Mercy made it to the grocery store just before closing Wednesday evening and grabbed the last, fresh bird, along with fixings for stuffing. She rose at dawn and took comfort in a ritual she hadn't indulged in for quite a while. She cooked.

A tiny spark of fear pricked her as she stood on his porch, holding the pan. Would he turn her away? After all, she'd walked out on him weeks ago and they hadn't spoken a meaningful word on the job since. Well, she'd just have to take that risk. Daniel Gallagher was definitely worth risking her heart again.

Mercy trembled as Daniel undressed her—with anticipation, with desire, with need. His eyes never left hers until she stood before him, nude. She felt no embarrassment under this man's scrutiny. It was easy to see his appreciation for her body as he scanned her, then licked his lips.

"I've missed you," he said, his voice thick.

"I've missed you too."

They made love all afternoon, taking a break only once to move the turkey pan into the oven.

"We don't want to end this day with food poisoning," she'd said, grabbing his sweatshirt to pull over her as she made her way out into the kitchen. She returned, moments later, frowning. "Sideboard's ruined."

"Who cares?" Daniel said as he grabbed her hand and pulled her back onto the bed. "I have a feeling, after we get finished this afternoon, my sheets will have scorch marks on them too."

Mercy could never remember experiencing this kind of passion, these intense emotions along with physical sensations that literally blew her mind. Daniel worshipped her body with lips and tongue and gentle fingers, bringing her to heights of pleasure she'd never known. Again, and again and again.

The light outside the windows was fading by the time they were sated—at least temporarily. She dozed lazily in the crook of his strong, sculpted arm, his scratchy beard tickling her cheek. Mercy knew she'd never been this content in all her life.

She jolted when he blurted out, "I'm fucking starving." Then she burst out laughing.

"Yeah, that about nails it. Do you mind cold turkey?" she asked.

He did that lightning-fast pin move again, flipping her onto her back. Resting his weight on his elbows, he hovered over her, pure possession burning his gaze into hers.

"Not when it comes to you, Mercy May. I never, ever want to go cold turkey from you again. Ever. I love you, you crazy, stubborn bitch." He kissed her, not so gentle this time. His mouth moved over hers frantically, demanding, exploring, almost desperate. When he finally let her come up for air, she cupped his cheek and stared into his eyes.

"I love you too, Daniel Gallagher. You may be too good to be true, but I'm willing to hang around to find out."

CHAPTER 29

"So, is your boy coming home for Christmas?" Conner asked as he and Jacob struggled to snake a length of conduit behind the plaster wall of the old Victorian. Daniel could barely hear him, since he was sequestered in the tiny office, installing outlet boxes. The job was getting pretty near to done, and Daniel was glad. He was tired of the small, cramped spaces and all the damned plaster dust he carried around in his beard all day.

Mercy was sitting on the floor of the main room, doing the preparatory assembly. "He is. Flies in next Wednesday. I was going to ask if you minded if I cut out a little early to get him at Logan," she said.

"No problem. How early?"

"His flight lands at five, so I was thinking I'd only need to leave an hour before quitting time. You can dock me. That okay with you?"

Conner used to be a hard-ass about hours, Daniel thought, but he certainly had lightened up about it. The whole team seemed to have been a lot more upbeat, ever since Thanksgiving. Ever since the tension between he and Mercy had dissipated over the best damn turkey dinner he'd ever eaten.

Conner grunted as he finally, after a good five minutes of struggling, yanked the conduit through the hole in the plaster wall. "Fine by me." He turned, dusting off his hands. "Let's just call it an early Christmas present."

"I'm ready for the next outlet assembly, Merce," Daniel called.

"Sure thing. Got the next two ready to go."

She stepped into the small space and handed him the boxes, then glanced quickly over her shoulder. Conner and Jacob couldn't see into the office from where they were working. She leaned in and gave him a quick kiss, then sputtered.

"You taste like plaster," she said, grinning.

"Tell me about it. The next job is a new construction, right? Drywall instead of plaster, I hope?" he asked.

Mercy bobbed her head before kissing him again. *Love you*, she mouthed silently.

Love you too.

God, how he did. The past few weeks with Mercy had been absolute heaven. She'd more or less moved in with him but decided to keep her rental until after Christmas. It might be too weird, his first trip home, to ask Reagan to stay at Daniel's with her. Daniel understood completely. She could give up the little house at the end of January, when her lease ran out anyway.

By then, Daniel planned to have a ring on that hard-working finger of hers. Maybe if Reagan was there, witnessing her opening her Christmas present, the young man would accept that he and Mercy were now a permanent thing. At least, he hoped he would.

Mercy perched her hands on her hips and scanned the walls of the office. "You've about got this beat," she said. "Nice job running the lines along the baseboard. Once they're painted, you'll hardly notice them."

Daniel frowned. "Yeah, there's just this one spot I'm a little worried about. I'm wondering if we should ask the plastering crew to check on it. It's behind where a desk would go, but it feels spongy. I'm afraid to set a box too close to it that I'll punch right through the wall."

"Where?" Mercy asked, getting down on her knees beside him. He pointed to a patch about the size of his hand where the plaster was cracked in an almost rectangular shape. As though someone had cut it out, and then replaced it.

Mercy pushed on the edge of the small, irregularly shaped panel. It gave underneath her fingertips. "This will definitely need a patch, Daniel."

Daniel sat back on his feet and studied the spot, thinking. A memory drifted back into his mind, one he'd discounted and buried as a stress-related imagining. But the words echoed inside his head.

Locked in my office. Was then, still is.

Maybe *locked* didn't necessarily mean *under key*. Maybe it just meant well-hidden.

Pulling a rubber hammer from his tool belt, Daniel held up a hand to Mercy. "Step back. I don't want you get splattered with plaster chips."

"What are you doing, Dan—"

With one swift wallop, Daniel landed his mallet along the bottom edge of the loose area. The top edge popped out easily, almost as though it was hinged from the inside. Working his gloved hand into the opening, he discovered that it was, in fact, hinged along the bottom inside edge.

"Holy shit," he muttered. He lifted his eyes to Mercy, who was looking at him as if he'd lost his mind.

"It's probably a patch they put in to cover an old rat hole," she said. "No doubt they'll have to rework that part of the wall now." As Daniel reached into the black space, Mercy said, "Good thing you've got leather gloves."

The boom from Daniel's mallet had brought both Conner and Jacob to stand in the doorway. "What you doing, dude? We're past the demo stage. We're supposed to be fixing the place up, not breaking it down," Conner barked.

But Daniel ignored the boss man when his fingers closed around a square box lying on the floor inside the hole. His heart sped up to pound against his chest. Carefully, he worked the box, which appeared to be metal, out of the hole. It took some maneuvering, since the ancient container barely fit.

"What the hell? Looks like you found yourself some hidden treasure. Is there a finder's-keeper's clause in our contract, Conner?" Jacob asked.

Daniel sought Mercy's gaze and held it, wide-eyed. "The list. The old man told me it was here. He said it was locked up, in his office. I just assumed it was in a cabinet or desk drawer."

Mercy squinted and tipped her head. "What old man? What *list*? What are you talking about, Daniel?"

But Daniel had already started examining the box for some sort of latch, or hinges. There were none. Like an old metal cookie tin, the box's lid simply fit down over the base. It was rimmed by rust, so it was, indeed, sealed shut.

He brought a screwdriver out of his tool belt and began working the flat end underneath the lid's seam, scraping the rust and jimmying the edge loose. It took only a minute before a satisfying *pop* sounded, and the lid was free.

Inside, nestled on a bed of yellowed, crumbling newspaper, was a clear plastic envelope with a snap closure. The waterproof folder held an ordinary, white envelope. On the outside, inscribed in a shaky hand in smudged pencil, were the words *Hillcrest Cemetery*.

"DON'T you even want to scan the list for your father's name? At least, check who number 1033 is?"

Daniel was driving them home from work, the plastic folder lying on the truck seat between them. Mercy's entire demeanor had changed that afternoon after he'd discovered the document. It wasn't a subject she wanted revisited, that was obvious. Daniel wasn't even sure if the envelope held the list—he hadn't wanted to open such a precious piece of history with grimy hands on the job site.

Still, the packet lay between them, and Daniel could feel it represented more than simply a physical divider between them.

Mercy said nothing for a long while, staring out of the window. Finally, she covered her face with both hands.

"Why now, Daniel? Why did this have to come up again now? Reagan is coming home next week. What am I going to say to him? 'Gee, it's great to see you, Son. By the way, I found your grandfather. He died in a nut house and is buried right up the street. Wanna go visit his grave?"

Daniel reached over and squeezed her knee. "We don't have to say a word to Reagan about any of this, Mercy, if you don't want to. I think, at some point, it might be information he needs to know. But only when you're ready to share it with him."

She studied his eyes, biting her lip. "What are you going to do with this? If it is the long-lost list of the nameless?"

Daniel tipped up his chin and pulled on his beard. "What should have been done decades ago. I'm going to contact the state and get them to erect proper headstones. I know I've probably got a huge, uphill battle in front of me, but I'm up for it."

Later that night, after making slow and gentle love to Mercy, Daniel waited until he was sure she was fast asleep. Creeping out of bed as stealthily as he could, he made his way into his office, where he'd slid the plastic envelope into his desk drawer. He closed the door behind him and flicked on the lamp.

CHAPTER 30

"*When the Corby State Mental Hospital closed its doors in 1973, 641 patients remained. Eight patients died that year. Approximately 543 patients were successfully relocated to other facilities. It is estimated that fourteen percent of the remaining (ninety-eight) were given a $20 stipend and turned out into society, homeless.*"

Personal account from former employee Judy Thompson in a 1995 interview.

Daniel stared at the records before him for a long time, documents he'd asked Tiffany to re-locate for him the following Tuesday night when he went to the library, alone. The envelope hidden in the wall of the Historical Society had, in fact, held the list of the patients who had died during their stay at the Corby facility. Death dates and causes of death were noted, when known.

The number of "unknown" causes of death made Daniel wonder just how many died from the experimental "treatments" inflicted upon them. It made him shudder to think about it.

Mercy had not asked about the envelope he'd found, and said she refused to talk about it until after Reagan returned to Atlanta after the first of the year. So, she didn't know that patient number 1033 did, in fact, correspond to a man named Devlin Doherty. Her father. His cause of death was, as was stated on the death certificate she'd found on Ancestry.com, "unknown." He'd also been the first of the eight patients to die in the last year of the hospital's operation, on January 9th, 1973.

Daniel made some calls to a number of state agencies but was shunted from one to another, gaining little ground. Nobody, it seemed, cared much about 1041 people whose graves remained anonymous. He also felt certain that it would be difficult to find any agency willing to foot the bill for making this right. It would take thousands of dollars to remove over a thousand stone pillars to replace them with proper headstones.

Finally, he locked the list in his own desk drawer and decided, like Mercy, it was probably best to let this lie until after the holidays.

Wednesday dawned overcast and uncharacteristically warm. A cold front was headed their way from out west but wasn't expected to affect temperatures until late Wednesday night. Daniel was relieved. He hated to see Mercy driving to the airport in snow or worse, freezing rain.

It did pinch his heart to find Mercy's luggage, a duffel bag, and her cosmetic case set just inside his front door when he got home from the library Tuesday night. He knew it was only temporary, but it stung just the same.

"It's only for a few weeks," she purred into his ear when she greeted him at the door. "We'll have Christmas together, and New Year's, the three of us at my house. Then I'll be back. This time," she tugged on his beard, "for good."

But by late Wednesday morning, the wind kicked up and it had started to rain. The team was starting their cleanup in preparation for the electrical inspection later that afternoon, their work at the Historical Society almost complete. They all lurched and looked at each other when the sound of thunder rumbled in the distance.

256

"A thunderstorm? In December? Who the hell ordered that?" Conner joked. He shook his head. "Damn crazy weather here in New England lately. Can't ever tell what's going to happen."

Daniel saw the concern on Mercy's face. "I hope Reagan's flight isn't delayed."

Conner scoffed. "Wouldn't worry about that. This is probably an isolated cell. Sounds like it's west of here. Logan's due East. Should be all over by the time your boy's plane lands."

The rains came, and they came down hard. A few flashes of lightning had the whole team jumpy by the time the inspector arrived about half past three. Daniel pulled Mercy aside while the man looked over the blueprints with Conner.

"I hate to see you driving to Boston in this. But there's no way Conner's going to let me go early, too. Are you sure Reagan can't just take the train in?" he murmured.

Mercy's head shot back, and he could see the hurt in her eyes. "The train? I haven't seen my boy in almost three months, and you want me to put him on a train to come home?"

Daniel tried not to let his own hurt get in the way of his worry. He had to understand—a mother's concern for her son would always, *always*, come before him. A hard pill to swallow, but she was worth it.

Just as Mercy was donning her slicker to leave, she heard the inspector say something about the cold front.

"She's moving in faster than anybody expected. Already dropped about ten degrees out there." He eyed Mercy. "If you're heading far, young lady, I'd keep an eye on the temperature. Watch the bridges especially. They're the first to turn into skating rinks."

Daniel's stomach dropped. He grabbed Mercy's arm. "Why don't you wait? Another half-hour and I can drive you, in my truck. The inspector should be done by then, and Conner won't mind if I leave—"

Mercy snatched her arm away and tossed her head like an angry bull. "Daniel Gallagher. I was born and raised a New Englander. I'm perfectly capable of driving in the rain. Besides, the longer I wait to leave, the higher chance I'll have of dealing with ice or snow instead of just rain." Her eyes softened then, and she cupped his cheek. "Don't worry, love. We'll be fine," she whispered.

THE RAIN CONTINUED to pound down, and by the time Mercy got onto the Mass Pike, the winds had started kicking up too. She jumped every time lightning flashed. How bizarre, she thought. Such a violent thunderstorm in the middle of December.

Storms like this, she knew, demarcated two areas of pressure. The high-pressure system that had been keeping the temperatures in the mid to upper fifties all week was about to get kicked off the coast. By morning, she guessed, she'd awaken to a world covered in white.

Alone. She wasn't looking forward to sleeping alone for the next few weeks. But getting to reconnect with her son would be worth the sacrifice.

Reagan's flight was delayed. By the time Mercy got to the airport, the display board showed that many of the incoming flights were delayed, and some outbound ones cancelled altogether. How can this be? she wondered. Surely, Boston's pilots were among the most skilled in the world. Why would they be afraid of a little old thunderstorm?

It wasn't until she perched at a table in the Dunkin Donuts kiosk and saw all the people around her staring at the television monitor overhead that she learned the reason.

"This unseasonal weather we're having is bizarre, but not without explanation," the forecaster was saying. She pointed to an illuminated map of the Boston area. "The cold front we've been expecting to hit us by midnight decided to catch the express train. As you can see, it's moving fast in our direction—very fast. It's already turning the rain into sleet over the Springfield area. We're expecting sleet and freezing rain to start falling over Worcester in the next hour. Road conditions will become hazardous, even impassable, by as early as seven p.m."

The latte Mercy had ordered suddenly turned sour in her mouth. Driving in snow was one thing. But she'd always been dicey about ice. Even if they had come in Daniel's truck, four-wheel drive helped little on ice. It just meant that instead of two wheels locking up and turning into skates, all four did at the same time.

She made her way back over to the display board and was relieved to see that no further delay had been posted. Instead of landing at the scheduled five-past-five, his flight should be on the ground by six-fifteen. Mercy proceeded to do what she was best at when faced with a worrying problem. She paced.

DANIEL WAS NOT DEALING with the worry very well, at all. By the time the inspection was finished, and the guys called it a day, the rain had begun to turn to sleet. The rat-a-tat of frozen little balls bounced off the truck windshield as he drove home. The radio forecaster was warning that within the next several hours, most of New England would be covered with a clear, candy apple coating of ice. His stomach churned and nausea threatened to turn it inside out.

He waited until after five o'clock to try Mercy's cell phone. The last thing he wanted to do was distract her while she was driving in what was already turning into hazardous road conditions. When he got home and turned on the Weather Channel, he breathed a small sigh of relief. Because of their proximity to the water, the weather in Boston was still rain.

"Mercy. Hey, did you make it there alright? Did Reagan's flight land?"

"Yeah, I'm here. But the flight was delayed. Now it's scheduled to land in about," she paused to check the time, "about forty-five minutes."

Daniel dragged in a breath. "Listen to me, Mercy. It's already getting pretty bad here. Freezing rain. The roads are okay still, because it's been warm the past few days. But with these winds, and the temperature dropping so fast, I'm not sure what it will be like in a couple of hours."

Mercy grunted. "Yeah, well, just as soon as we get Reagan's luggage, we'll be on our way. I'll call you when we're leaving."

CHAPTER 31

By the time Reagan's flight landed, Logan Airport was beginning to look like it must every morning at three a.m. Nearly deserted. The difference was that the entire display board was red, with all flights cancelled. Mercy honestly believed Reagan's plane was the last one to hit the runway before they shut the terminal down.

When he came striding up the corridor from the gate, Mercy started waving like an idiot through the glass doors. He finally looked up and saw her, and his smile warmed her to her soul. She swore, as she hugged him, that he'd grown two inches since she saw him last. He'd also grown a scruff of a beard, which surprised her. Luke hated facial hair on a man. A little voice in the back of her brain whispered, "I wonder if he's emulating Daniel?"

"Man, hairy flight," he grumbled, shaking his head as they waited for his luggage. "We had to circle the airport three times to avoid the storm cells. Really bad turbulence. And the lightning . . ." he blew out a breath, "I really wondered for a few if I was going to make it home alive."

Home. There was a word Mercy loved hearing. She hugged his neck, as she'd done for about the twentieth time since he arrived.

"I'm glad you're home, too, Reagan. I've missed you so much."

"Missed you too, Mom." Reagan delicately unwound his mother's arms from around his neck and looked around, embarrassed. "How's Daniel?"

"He's good. Good to me, too."

Reagan bobbed his head. "Good for you, Mom. Dad's pretty happy too. His new wife is a piece of work, but my baby sister," he paused for a huge grin, "now she's a delightful little sprite."

Mercy deflated. The last thing she wanted to do was talk about Luke and his new family. But she knew she had no choice. Especially now that Reagan had become part of *the other* family.

"Does Sharon treat you okay?" she asked.

"Yeah, she's great. She's not much older than I am, which is weird. But she's really good to Dad."

"Do you call her 'Mom'?" Mercy asked, then quickly wished she hadn't. Reagan's scowl told her she was creeping into sensitive territory.

He surprised her by leaning down to press his cheek against hers. "No, I don't call her mom. I only have one mom, and that's you." He kissed her forehead, and tears welled in Mercy's eyes.

When they stepped out of the terminal, the blast of icy wind took both of them by surprise. Mercy's slicker wasn't insulated nearly enough for this kind of weather. Reagan, wearing only an Atlanta Braves hoodie, visibly shuddered.

"Holy cow. Now this, I don't miss," he said.

Once they got Reagan's gear stowed in her trunk and had climbed into the car, Mercy pulled out her phone.

"While the car warms up, I've got to call Daniel. He's worried about us getting home in this weather. It was freezing rain an hour or so ago out there."

Reagan didn't appear to have heard her. He was busy on his own phone, probably texting his father. Mercy sighed.

This was her new world. Might as well accept it and move

forward.

When Daniel picked up the call, he was frantic.

"Mercy, please, listen to me. Leave the car parked at the airport. Call the Marriott or one of the other hotels that provide a shuttle from the terminal. I don't want you driving home in this. It's awful. They've already shut down the Mass Pike west of Springfield. I'm guessing you'll be off-routed before you make it to Corby."

Still drifting on her high from having her son back in her arms, Mercy had almost forgotten about the weather. "What's happening?"

"They're saying it's the worst ice storm in fifty years," he said. "Please, Merce, you've got to listen to me. I can't afford to lose . . ."

A stab of pity sliced Mercy's heart and she closed her eyes. "You're not going to lose me. Or Reagan. I'll call the hotels. If I can get a room, we'll stay. I promise."

Unfortunately, fifteen minutes later, Mercy discovered that everyone else in the vicinity of the airport had the same idea. There were no rooms to be had, anywhere.

Taking a deep breath, Mercy put the car into gear and started for the garage exit. She could do this. If it got too bad, she'd pull off and find something a little farther out of town.

The roads didn't seem bad. They were wet, and yes, it was sleet spitting onto her windshield. But it had been warm for several days. The ground was still warm. The roads couldn't possibly freeze.

Yet.

By the time Mercy cleared the last toll station in Newton, the highway was nearly deserted. An occasional flashing police cruiser sped past her going in the opposite direction, but few cars were headed west. When she saw a salt truck pull onto the highway at the intersection of Rte. 495, she breathed a sigh of relief. At least if she stayed behind this guy, she had a chance of making it home.

To her exit, anyway.

Daniel had called every fifteen minutes since she'd spoken to him, and she made Reagan answer the calls.

"Mom's driving, Daniel. No, the roads aren't bad. We're behind a salt truck." Reagan snickered. "Mom's going to need a new paint job when this is all over, but we're fine. We're gonna be fine."

There was a long pause, and Mercy could hear Daniel shouting even from where she was sitting.

Reagan shot her a worried glance. "We tried, Daniel. All the hotels were booked solid. We couldn't get a room. If it gets too bad, we'll pull off and see if we can find something. Mom promised."

DANIEL FELT like he was having a nervous breakdown. He ducked into the fridge and grabbed a beer, then shoved it back. This kind of emotional turmoil was not going to be extinguished with a Sam Adams. Reaching into the shelves under the china cabinet, he pulled out the bottle of Jameson he got for a Christmas gift from Conner last year. Whiskey doesn't go bad, right? He'd never even opened the bottle.

Tonight, he did, pouring two fingers worth over ice. He stood at the window, staring down his driveway. She was at least an hour out, he knew that, even if the conditions weren't nearly as bad as they were. But he couldn't help the need to stand watch. Waiting. Hoping. Praying.

The first sip burned all the way down, and his eyes watered. Was it the whiskey? Or was it worry? Was it wondering if he'd ever see his love—his new love—ever again?

Old memories rose like pungent steam into his mind. The waiting, the wondering, the secret knowing how the sad story was to end. He shook it off, pinching his nose between his fingers. Ouch, now that spot was still damned sore, where she'd clocked him with her head a few months ago. Her hard, stubborn, beautiful head.

Keelin had never broken his nose. He wondered now if she'd ever had a mind to.

CHAPTER 32

*A*s Mercy crept closer to the Corby exit, and farther away from the warmer air near the coast, the conditions worsened. The salt truck—thank Christ—had not pulled off. But when her exit came up, the damned, merciful, all-protecting-salt-truck-from-heaven kept on going.

From here on in, she was on her own.

Route 9 was a disaster scene. Flashing lights lit up the road every hundred or so feet. No matter how fast the trucks dumped the stuff on the road, it wasn't fast enough. The freezing rain kept falling. The salt washed away within minutes of hitting the pavement.

Reagan had been sitting perched on the edge of his seat, straining against the seat belt strap, since they'd exited the Pike. He kept glancing over at her, and Mercy did her best to keep it all together.

Breathe deep, she told herself. We'll get through this. We're almost there.

Just before the turnoff onto Rte. 30, Reagan turned to her and said, "I know we're close, Mom, but you know how Rte. 30 will be. There's a Red Rood Inn—"

"We're fine, Reagan. We're going to make it in just fine."

Stubborn, had Daniel called her? Yeah, well, maybe.

Daniel had called no less than twenty times since they left the airport. His concern didn't have a chance to warm Mercy's heart under the conditions she was driving. The only relinquishment she'd bristled at was when Reagan conveyed—which he didn't have to, Mercy had heard Daniel loud and clear through the phone's earpiece —that they come to his house instead of hers.

"It's three miles closer," he'd barked. "Come. Directly. Here." His demand allowed no rebuke.

"No," Mercy snapped. "Tell him we're fine. If we can make it to his house, I can surely make it to my own."

It was the last turn on crooked, poorly maintained Rte. 30 that did her in. Proved her wrong. The final bend in the road before her cute rental hadn't been treated with anything—no sand, no salt, nothing. It was a veritable sheet of ice.

As Mercy turned her wheel to navigate the last hundred feet before her driveway, her car refused to respond. Knowing better than to step on the brake, Mercy's right arm flew sideways to knock her son's body back against the seat.

"Hang on," she shouted. "We're going down."

It all happened so fast it barely took up the space of a heartbeat. Yet in Mercy's mind, the moment was thirty minutes long. Instead of navigating the bend in the road, the car continued on its merry way, sideways. With her house in full view, only a hundred feet ahead, they slid. As the wheels left the pavement, Mercy made sure her arm was pressed tight against her son's chest. With her other, she shielded her face from impact.

The initial contact jolted them the most. A pole stood between them and the narrow patch of woods beyond. The car's left fender hit the pole, grazing it. They were both thrown sideways then as the car spun, the rear swinging counterclockwise until the vehicle was parallel with the railway.

Still, the vehicle didn't slow. The ice was thick on the roadside grass. With no salt to dampen its effect, the car continued to slide, sideways, down the embankment. Mercy screamed and dove to cover Reagan's body with her own as the car plummeted, bouncing and jerking over rocks and ruts until it slammed to a stop.

Their landing spot was perilous at best. Both wheels on the passenger side of the vehicle were jammed up against the iron beams of the commuter railway. For several seconds, time stopped.

Mercy, breathing hard, sat up, examining her son's face.

"Are you alright? Okay?" she gasped.

Reagan's face was white, all color drained away. She spotted a trickle of blood on his temple, but it didn't look life threatening. Eyes round, he nodded, but he said nothing. They simply flashed to the scene outside the car windows.

"Mom," he said, "We're sitting on the rail lines. What if—"

His words were cut short when something began pummeling the roof of the car. Thump, thwack. Then buzzing, hissing—sounds Mercy knew all too well.

They watched as huge, black tentacles hit the ground around them. Engulfing them. Entrapping them.

Electricity. Live wires. Untamed.

What they'd hit was a power pole, she realized. Although the impact hadn't been all that hard, the lines above them were heavy under their icy mantles. The jolt must have been just enough for them to break free.

She and her son now sat within a car draped with electrical power lines. Live ones. The only thing saving them from frying to death were the rubber tires grounding them.

They were trapped. If they opened a door and placed a foot on the ground, they'd be electrocuted, instantly.

CHAPTER 33

*D*aniel was near hysteria when the call finally came in. He'd thought better of the Jameson after the first swallow. He needed to stay sharp, alert. He needed to be fully-functional and available if Mercy needed his help.

It was Reagan who called him, hysterical, his words almost incoherent.

"We're trapped, Daniel. Almost home. I can see our house, for Christ's sake. But, the power lines . . . they fell. They're lying on top of the car. We can't get out."

Daniel's heart splintered into a thousand pieces. "Where? Where are you?"

"The tracks. We slid off the road, and mom's car is sitting right up against the tracks. If a train comes, Daniel . . ."

Reagan's voice dissolved into sobs.

He heard a fumbling of sorts, and then Mercy's voice sliced through his brain. She sounded strong, confident, unafraid.

This was one strong, stubborn bitch. A real survivor. At least, he hoped so.

"Daniel, I've already called 911. I've alerted the railway system but who knows if they'll get the message in time. I need you to call again. Then call the power company. We're a literal electrocution in the making. We're trapped." Then, her voice broke too. "We can't get out, Daniel. If we try to get out, we'll fry like bugs on a zapper."

"Don't fucking move," Daniel ordered. Like they could, he thought. What choice did they have? They were like the damsel strapped to the railroad tracks in the old silent picture shows, helplessly waiting to be splattered when the train came rumbling by.

And the wires, down. Draped over her car like the tentacles of a giant octopus. Only this octopus packed an even more deadly punch than an eel.

Electricity. A natural wonder. A modern necessity. A powerful killer.

"I'm making the calls now, and I'll be there in ten minutes." His voice broke around the last words. This couldn't be happening. Not again. Why hadn't she just pulled off the road and gotten a hotel like he'd asked her?

After a curt conversation with a 911 operator, then a call in to Mass Power, Daniel threw on a jacket and a pair of leather gloves. His tool belt was in the bed of his truck. He had what he needed to cut the wires loose, but . . . what if the cables were still live? He would remain helpless. He would be unable to do anything until the electric company assured him the power was off at the main.

Power's shut off at the main.

Conner's words echoed in his memory from that first day on the job in Gravely Hall. The day Mercy almost got fried because there had been an alternate power source none of them knew about.

His heart twisted around itself, and his breath came in short, panicked bursts as he fumbled with the key in the door. He dropped the keys twice, finally throwing up his hands. Screw it. Who was going to come by and steal anything on a night like this anyway? What did he even have worth stealing?

Deep in his gut, Daniel knew. What he had worth stealing wasn't safe inside his house. It was, at this moment, trapped in a vehicle sitting up against a commuter rail line, draped with hot wires. Everything—his entire world—anything worth stealing, was a prisoner to the very commodity defining his life.

Icy roads be damned. He'd inch his way along Rte. 30 until he found them, got them out, and got them safe.

AFTER DANIEL DISCONNECTED THE CALL, Mercy looked over at her son, who was pale and trembling. She grabbed his ice-cold hand and squeezed.

"It's going to be okay. Daniel is making the same calls I did. Somebody will get the message. In just a few minutes, the electric company will be here and . . ."

Mercy trailed off when she spotted movement in the dark, in the woods on the other side of the tracks. People, a small group of them, emerged from trees now bent to the ground with the weight of their icy overcoats. Strange-looking people.

They were oddly dressed. The men wore drab work clothes, and the women were in old-fashioned housedresses. They wore no overcoats or other protection from the weather. Seemingly unaffected by the slippery footing beneath them, they made their way down to the train tracks, then stepped over and across the rails, with nary a foot displaced.

"Who are they, Mom? What the hell?" Reagan sounded like a little boy again, standing at her bedside after a particularly frightening nightmare. Mercy huddled closer to her son.

"I'm not sure, Reagan. Hopefully, they don't mean us any harm." She hesitated, noticing that in the complete blackness of the night, their bodies emanated an almost imperceptible, otherworldly glow. She sucked in a breath. "I hope they're here to help us."

Six men and two women approached Mercy's car. Their faces were devoid of emotion, and they did not make eye contact. At the last moment, when Mercy realized their intention, she lurched forward and started waving her hands.

"Don't!" she screamed. "Don't touch the wires. You'll be electrocuted."

Ignoring her pleas, the group marched up to her car and reached for the power lines. Mercy cringed and covered her eyes, afraid of the jarring, convulsive, sparking result she was sure she would see. But a moment later, when she dared to look, she saw the strange group grabbing the wires with their bare hands. Working doggedly as a team, they dragged them well clear of her vehicle and away from the train tracks. The cables, still live with high voltage, jittered and sparked as they fell onto the ice-encrusted hillside.

Yet these people showed no reaction at all. They remained unaffected. Unharmed.

These can't be live people.

"Mom," Reagan's voice trembled, "who are they? *What* are they?"

"I'm not sure, Reagan. But my guess is, this whole campus, at one time, was their home."

After pulling all the wires yards away from her car, one of the men caught her eye. He was the first—the only—to acknowledge hers and Reagan's presence at all. He signaled an all-clear with his hands, then stood there, staring at her.

In that instant, Mercy realized all the other people she'd seen were gone. Vanished, as though they'd never been there.

"Wait here," she cautioned Reagan who, obviously in shock, sat staring blindly through the window.

She opened her car door and, checking to see no wires lay anywhere nearby, stepped out, holding onto its frame to avoid sliding underneath the vehicle on the frozen grass. Mercy stood and faced the lone remaining rescuer.

"Thank you," she said. "I don't know how or why you're here, but I believe you saved our lives."

At that moment, a train whistle sounded in the distance. Way too close. The man's head snapped in the direction of the whistle, then back to Mercy. He waved his arms frantically toward Reagan.

Get him out! she heard.

Did she hear it? Or did it echo inside her head?

Adrenaline kicked in and Mercy didn't stop to think. She simply acted.

"Reagan, get out," she screamed. "Climb up here, away from the tracks. Reagan!"

It took a moment for the dazed boy to obey her command, but he did, slipping and sliding on the frozen grass beside her until they were both twenty feet up the hill toward the road. They huddled there, Mercy's arm wrapped around Reagan's waist.

The oddly dressed man with luminescent eyes stared at them both. Then he smiled.

"You turned out a right pretty lass, you did," he said. "Your mom, she'd a been right proud."

Then, he was gone.

A shudder racked Mercy's body, not only from the cold. Not only from the fate she and Reagan had narrowly escaped. An eerie chill coursed through her veins.

The train whistle sounded again, and Mercy sprang to action, dragging Reagan farther up the slope. How could the 911 operator not have gotten the message to the conductor in time? If she and Reagan were still in the car . . . if the wires were still lying in the path of the oncoming train . . .

Seconds later the commuter train rumbled through, seemingly oblivious to their existence. Upon impact with the front bumper of Mercy's car, its brakes squealed, along with the screech of metal against metal, even as the engine dragged the vehicle fifty feet or more along the rails. Finally, the vehicle tumbled free, landing on its roof beside the tracks.

Her car was destroyed. But as she sat in the icy grass rocking her shivering son, Mercy thanked God they were alive.

. . .

THE RAIN HAD STOPPED, giving the salt and sand trucks a chance to get ahead of the ice. It only took Daniel only about ten minutes to reach the scene of the accident. At the last bend before Mercy's house, the narrow roadway was lined with emergency vehicles. Splashes of red and yellow sprayed across the ice-laden trees, producing an almost blinding light show. When Daniel saw the ambulance, the bottom dropped out of his stomach.

Had they gotten out? Were they still alive?

He parked alongside the road and clambered out, jogging along the now-melting pavement toward the ambulance. The back doors were thrown open wide. His heart swelled with relief when he saw Mercy sitting on the bench inside, a blanket wrapped around her shoulders. Reagan sat on the gurney, and a medic was blotting a wound on the boy's temple with gauze.

They were alive. They got out. But how?

Mercy looked up and saw him, then scrambled down from the ambulance to wrap herself around him.

"How?" he croaked, burying his face in her hair.

"A miracle," was all she said.

ercy's house would have no power for at least the next several hours, and although the freezing rain had ceased, the wind was sharp and bitterly cold. Daniel took one look at the pale, shivering boy they helped out of the ambulance and made a decision. Discretion and propriety be damned.

"We're going back to my house. It's warm, and I have power." His eyes shifted toward Reagan, then to Mercy. "Reagan can take the guest bedroom. I'll sleep on the couch."

Nodding weakly, Mercy took Reagan's arm and followed Daniel to his truck.

An hour later, after he'd bundled them into warm and dry clothes that fit neither of them very well, Daniel cleaned up the dishes from the soup he'd fed them. From the kitchen, he watched them over the island. Mercy sat on the couch, her hands wrapped around a cup of hot cocoa. Reagan sat beside her, staring off into space.

"You sure you're okay, Reagan?" she asked quietly.

He nodded, then swiped his hands down his face. "Numb. Mentally, physically . . . I know you're a native New Englander, Mom, but the weather up here sucks. I'll take Atlanta's hot and humid any day."

Both she and Daniel laughed as he came to them, holding his own mug of tea. Tea with a little boost of Jameson. Now, he thought, I can indulge. They're here. They're safe.

"Why don't you both go on to bed. Mercy, you take my room. I'll be perfectly fine here on the sofa," he said, stroking her hair.

Mercy nodded and stood, leaning down to kiss her son on the cheek. "You need to rest, too, Reagan. It's been one hell of a night."

"I will. Soon."

After the bedroom door clicked shut, Reagan looked over at Daniel, who had settled into the recliner with his cup.

"You really care about her, don't you?" It was a statement, not a question.

"Damn straight I do. You may be uncomfortable hearing this, Reagan, but I'm in love with your mom." He took a sip from his cup. "Not just maybe. Damn sure."

Reagan nodded, and Daniel was surprised—and pleased—to see a small smile light up the boy's face.

"I'm glad. She's a great person. She deserves to be loved."

Daniel took another swig of his doctored tea, then a deep breath. No better time than the present, he thought.

"Reagan, being as you're the man in Mercy's life, I guess you're the one I need to ask. I was planning on asking your mother to marry me. I bought her a ring for Christmas."

The boy looked up and locked eyes with Daniel. After a long, tense moment, he asked, "You promise me you won't do her like my dad did? I mean, I love my dad, but what he did to her was dead wrong. I don't think she could handle going through that again."

Daniel considered his answer carefully before speaking. This was touchy ground. He wanted to say, *I'm not that kind of man.* But he had to be careful. It wouldn't be right to say anything to put down

Reagan's dad. Finally, he leaned forward, elbows on his knees, and held Reagan's gaze.

"I will love her and be faithful to her for the rest of my life. I promise you that. She'll be stuck with me until she decides she doesn't want me anymore." He drained his cup. "I just hope and pray that day never comes to pass."

Reagan shook his head. "It never will. My mom is the forever kind."

Daniel whooshed out a breath and stood. "Now, my man, it's time to get some shut-eye. I'm going to need that couch you're sitting on."

Reagan snorted. "I'm an adult, and I'm not stupid, Daniel. Mom's had a hell of a day. I'm sure she'd really appreciate the warmth and security of your strong arms around her."

When Daniel woke the next morning, he squinted against brilliant sunshine streaming through his bedroom window. He reached for Mercy, but the bed was empty.

He found her standing in the living room, her hands wrapped around a cup. His Bruins jersey fit her like a caftan, hanging almost to her knees. Her long, dark hair covered her shoulders in a tangled blanket. Daniel's heart swelled until he feared it would burst.

He never thought he'd get this lucky again.

"Good morning," he said, moving up beside her. She smiled and rose to her toes to kiss him softly on the lips.

"Look out there." She tipped her chin toward the window. "Isn't it absolutely beautiful?"

It was. Breathtaking. Ice covered every branch, every bush, every-thing—even his red truck looked like a candy apple. The sun sparkled on every surface, glinting, turning the world into a twinkling fairy land.

The white birch trees lining Daniel's property looked reverent. Bowed nearly to the ground, it was as though they were worshipping the beauty around them.

"Your birches look like they're praying," Mercy said, echoing his thoughts. "Too bad they may never resume their original stature."

Daniel turned Mercy to face him and cupped her face in his hands. "They're just like me. I will worship you until the day I die, Mercy May. No matter how much bending I have to do, I'll always be yours."

He kissed her, long and slow and sweet. They both jumped when Reagan's voice sliced through the moment.

"Hey Daniel, you got any food in this place? I'm starving."

THREE MONTHS LATER – Hillcrest Cemetery

"I can't believe you even got them to do this much, Daniel. You must have bugged the hell out of them," Mercy said.

Daniel stood with his arms crossed, tugging at his beard. It was warm for a March day, and sunshine reflected off the shiny surface of the marble marker. It was huge, but then again, it had to be. Into its surface had been carved 1041 names. Those who died and were buried nameless were nameless no longer.

"I did what I could. Are you still going to have a headstone made for your dad's grave?" he asked.

Mercy hooked her arm in his and laid her head against him. "I've already ordered it. But I'm going to wait until Reagan comes up for the wedding in May to have them set it. He wants to be here." She looked up at him. "For the memorial service, and for the wedding."

Daniel nodded. "Does Reagan realize that it was his grandfather he saw that night?"

Mercy lifted a shoulder. "Not sure. He struggles with it. But I know it was him. He recognized me. Called me a pretty lass." She smiled at the memory. "Said my mama would be real proud of me."

"It's *paranormal*, no doubt about it." Daniel put air quotes around the word. "But it makes perfect sense. Your father was one of the eight patients who died in 1973, right before the hospital closed. There were eight of them who saved you that night. Remember what Cierce said? Spirits can't manifest without an energy source. There sure was plenty of energy around that night."

"Electricity," Mercy said. She stepped around to face him and laced her fingers around his neck. "Just like the spark between you and me."

Her kiss was demanding, exploring his mouth with her tongue, and Daniel's body reacted.

He broke for air first, his breath coming fast. "Come on. I think we need to go home and fan that spark into a full-blown fire. Again." A mischievous grin split his scruffy beard. "And again, and again, and again."

A NOTE FROM THE AUTHOR

Thank you for joining Mercy and Daniel on their journey. I hope you enjoyed reading their story as much as I enjoyed writing it.

This is Book 5 in the Haunted Voices series. To find out about the first 4, please visit my Amazon Author page.

Please, take a few moments to leave an honest review on Amazon and Goodreads. Reviews are incredibly important to authors—it's how our stories reach more readers like you.

Members of my Author-Reader group are the first to know when the next Haunted Voices romance comes out, so please consider signing up at my website.

Also, visit me on Goodreads, Facebook, and Twitter. I always love connecting with my readers!

Made in United States
North Haven, CT
06 April 2022

17969666R00171